Finding Lisa

Sigrid Macdonald

TotalRecall Publications, Inc.
1103 Middlecreek
Friendswood, Texas 77546
281-992-3131 281-482-5390 Fax
www.totalrecallpress.com

ISBN: 978-1-59095-251-1
UPC: 6-43977-42510-2

Printed in the United States of America with simultaneous printings in Australia, Canada, and United Kingdom.

FIRST EDITION
1   2   3   4   5   6   7   8   9   10

This book is dedicated to my incredible family:
to Brooke, Kristin, and Alicia
for always being there.

ABOUT THE AUTHOR

Originally from New Jersey, Sigrid Macdonald lived for almost thirty years in Ottawa, Ontario and currently resides in Weston, Florida. She has been a freelance writer for years. Her works have appeared in *The Globe and Mail* newspaper; the *Women's Freedom Network Newsletter*; the American magazine, *Justice Denied*; *The Toastmaster*; and the *Anxiety Disorders Association of Ontario Newsletter*. Her first book, *Getting Hip: Recovery from a Total Hip Replacement*, was published in 2004. Her second book, *Be Your Own Editor*, followed in 2010. Although *Finding Lisa* is written in first person, Macdonald only resembles her character in the sense that she once had a neurotic fixation on her hair, and she has always been called by the wrong name; instead of being called Sigrid, people call her Susan, Sharon, Astrid, Ingrid and, her personal favorite, Siri.

Macdonald is a social activist who has spent decades working on the seemingly disparate issues of women's rights and wrongful convictions; she has worked at the Women's Center at Ramapo College of New Jersey and Carleton University in Ottawa, Ontario, and for many years, she was a member of AIDWYC, The Association in Defense of the Wrongly Convicted. She owns an editing company called Book Magic. She is a public speaker and a member of Mothers against Drunk Driving, Ottawa Independent Writers, the American Association of University Women, and the Editors' Association of Canada. Visit her website at http://bookmagic.ca/ or friend her on Facebook: https://www.facebook.com/sigridmac.

ACKNOWLEDGMENTS

I am grateful to Detective Sergeant Bob Pulfer, Detective John Savage, and Detective Mike Lamothe from the Mental Health and Adult Missing Persons' Department of the Ottawa Police force, for giving generously of their time to answer my many questions about police procedure. I would also like to thank Marie Parent, a private investigator from Quebec, currently living in Scotland, for providing me with a wealth of information about a local case that she helped to solve, and Tania Doucet, a mental health crisis counselor from the Royal Ottawa Hospital, for offering critical information about addictions and addiction services.

Emna Dhahak, Senior Bilingual Media Liaison Officer from the Communications Branch of the Ministry of Transportation, kindly replied to several inquiries about traffic laws: Rick Lavigne of the Ottawa Police did the same.

My dear friend, Joyce Milgaard, directed my legal questions to Joanne McLean, who promptly provided me with essential details about criminal law.

Tim Pattyson, Manager of Communications for the Ottawa Senators, helped me to navigate the team's website for me to get my hockey facts straight.

Reid's Taekwon-Do explained the martial art to me. My closest friend, Cathie Soubliere, acted as my French translator and drove me to Quebec so that I could record my impressions of the towns of Hull and Aylmer.

I sincerely appreciated all the practical help that I received from Gwen and Laura at Le Skratch billiard hall. They taught me the basics of playing pool, which was no easy task!

Two readers provided constructive criticism on my manuscript. They include Blair Roger, who has been a friend and confidant since we were teenagers, and Suzanne Pepin, a newer but equally treasured addition to my life. Special thanks to Suzanne for hours of meticulous editing.

I am grateful to my grammar consultants, starting with my beloved late mother, Muriel, and my brother, Brooke; Tracy and Pierre Gagnon also helped me with this onerous task on several occasions. The Ottawa Toastmasters offered invaluable lessons about organizing my thoughts verbally and manually. Brian Sutton from Toastmasters was particularly encouraging.

As always, I would like to thank my family for putting up with me and for supporting me throughout this project, starting with my phenomenal late mother, Muriel, my devoted sister, Kristin, my wonderful brother, Brooke, his wife, Alicia, and their boys, Oliver and Christopher. Although he passed away in 1996, the influence of, and my adoration for, my precious father, Hugh, will never die.

Many people on the Internet assisted me with this endeavor starting with my inspirational friend, actress Barbara Niven, and the fantastic contributors to her message board. Francine Silverman, author of *Catskills Alive,* and editor of the excellent *Book Promotion Newsletter,* has been a constant source of information and support over the last several years.

Craig Garber, copywriter extraordinaire, has provided innovative tips in his weekly marketing newsletter. And writer Dotsie Bregel manages a fabulous website called *Boomer Women Speak.* Dotsie and the members of her site have encouraged me and given me practical advice.

I am forever indebted to Steve O'Brien, Don Campbell, Tinhorn, and the late Gregory Banks for sharing their expertise about formatting, writing, and publishing in a timely, patient, and courteous manner.

Many heartfelt thanks to my friend Bruce Moran, the owner of TotalRecall Publishing Inc. and to his team. I am so grateful that you were willing to work with me on this book.

Last, but surely not least, I would like to thank Brunito, my brother and his wife's schnauzer, who brings endless joy into my life and on whom Tara's dog, Monday, is based.

CHAPTER ONE
April 2004
Ottawa, Ontario

"Imagine discovering that your husband is a bigamist," I exclaimed, as Lisa and I donned our jackets to leave the ByTowne Theatre.

"I'd kill him," Lisa retorted, as she put on her headband to brace the frigid wind.

"You'd have to stand in line!" I replied, as we forced our way through the large crowd that was waiting for the second feature.

The ByTowne was an old theatre with a widescreen, plush red velvet curtains, and hard, uncomfortable seats, which were so low that I felt that I was leaning back in a 1980s Corvette, waiting for takeoff. But the movie house specialized in foreign films. As a result, it attracted a faithful cult audience.

We had just seen *My Architect*, a docudrama produced by Nathaniel Kahn, son of the late Louis I. Kahn. The senior Kahn was a well-renowned architect from Philadelphia. He designed a number of impressive buildings including the town center in Bangladesh and the beautiful Salk Institute for Biological Studies in La Jolla, California. The movie depicted the son's search for the father that he had never known.

At his funeral, colleagues were shocked to learn that Louis Kahn had not one but three wives simultaneously. He had fathered three children with different women and only saw young Nathaniel when he could sneak away from his official family. Nathaniel's longing for his father was captured perfectly in one breathtaking scene where he rollerbladed through the vast and empty courtyard of one of his father's buildings overlooking the Pacific.

An older woman with long unkempt hair was standing in front of the movie house. She looked weathered and carried a tin cup.

"And you call yourselves Canadians!" the woman shouted when people passed by without giving her money. I dropped a coin in her cup, and she gave me a weary, toothless grin.

Lisa stopped to light a cigarette in front of a store called All Books. She leaned on a table. It was overflowing with used books with campy titles like *Soul Centred Astrology* and *Killing Rage*.

Lisa's match kept going out, thanks to the steady stream of snow that was falling. It was early April. This was probably the last snowfall of the season. Two men ahead of us were discussing the film.

"I really liked the play on words," the younger man said. "I mean, I. Kahn. Icon! Do you think that his fate was sealed by his name?"

"Oh, absolutely," his friend replied. "Look at all the children named Jesus in Venezuela. See the way they're prospering?"

"Maybe they'll get their reward in the next life," the first speaker declared.

Lisa and I laughed. "Want to go to Nate's?" I asked. We invariably went to Nate's Deli for a snack after our monthly excursions at the ByTowne. It was hard to say which we enjoyed more, the food at Nate's or analyzing the movies.

Occasionally, we'd vary our routine and walk down to

Tucker's Marketplace, a restaurant in the ByWard Market, which had an immense buffet. But tonight, the roads were slick with freezing rain, and the wind was gusting at thirty kilometers an hour, so I didn't feel much like hiking all the way down to Mother Tucker's.

Lisa nodded in agreement. "Follow me," she instructed, as she grabbed my arm and ran across the busy avenue.

"Lisa!" I screamed, to no avail. She was an incorrigible jaywalker whereas I always dutifully crossed at the corner.

Rideau Street was dark except for the flashing lights above the theatre. About one kilometer west of the ByTowne, Rideau became Wellington Street, which housed the Supreme Court, the elegant Fairmont Château Laurier Hotel, and the Parliament buildings.

The center block of the Houses of Parliament was destroyed in a fire in 1916. All the Houses had been rebuilt using a Civil Gothic design except for the library. The buildings were warm and ornate with gargoyles, stained-glass windows, and an ornamental fence. Parliament Hill stood on the south bank of the Rideau River just below the swirling waters that explorer Samuel de Champlain had called La Chaudière, meaning "The Cauldron."

The Hill and Confederation Square were impressive and were often displayed on postcards for tourists. This end of the road was old and run-down in comparison.

Lisa and I opened the door to 316 Rideau Street and walked up the short ramp. The smell of fresh bagels and cheese blintzes was tantalizing.

Nate's Deli was famous for its smoked meat sandwiches. The atmosphere was homey and somewhat schizophrenic. Clearly, the store had been an old-fashioned delicatessen years ago, but a modern annex had been added to convert the deli into a restaurant.

We passed mouth-watering displays of candy, juice, gourmet salads, and cooked meat. A waitress with honey-colored hair, tied up in a bun, seated us at the back in a booth. One wall of the restaurant was covered in glass mirrors. Next to it was a large poster that said, "You don't have to be Jewish," which made me smile.

We took off our coats, and I brushed the wet snow from my forehead. Lisa's dark brown hair gleamed under the yellow lights. She was wearing a tight pink sweater, which showed off her cleavage, snug Guess jeans, and a delicate gold cross. I felt dowdy in my sweatshirt and baggy Mom jeans.

Although we had been best friends since our late teens, I was always struck by Lisa's stark and simple beauty. She was everything that I was not: tall, angular, and shamefully thin with a spontaneous, impulsive, and charismatic personality. Her life was full of drama, even though she'd been sober for five years, and worked full time as a drug and alcohol counselor at a small agency downtown called "Straight and Narrow."

I, on the other hand, was imminently predictable. I worked as a nurse in the short-term rehabilitation unit of a local hospital. I'd been married to Mark, a professor of cultural anthropology, for fifteen years, which barely legitimized our fourteen-year-old son Devon.

The words that were most often used to describe me were dependable, loyal, and hard-working—polite euphemisms for boring. In the past, I had taken pride in those descriptions, but recently, I'd been feeling dull and disenchanted with my life. I was approaching forty. Just thinking those words sent a shiver down my spine.

Turning forty sounded as appealing as being a prisoner in Abu Ghraib. *Dead Woman Walking*, I mused to myself. I was already sprouting gray hairs and had been making frequent trips to my hairdresser, Chan Juan, to have her color my hair darker. My hair was an odd shade of henna at the moment, but I couldn't change it since I had colored it four times in the last two months. It now had the texture of a Brillo pad, and toxic metals were probably seeping into my already imbalanced system.

I had heard the argument that forty was the new thirty, but I suspected that the phrase had been invented by someone in her fifties. If I were lucky enough to live until eighty that would mean I was already halfway through my life. What had I done with it? Where was I headed? I could be hit by a bus or develop breast cancer, like my mother, who died when I was ten.

Every day at work, I saw people whose lives had been derailed by accidents and illness. Maybe I only had ten or twenty years left. What was I going to do with them? The faster I approached the big 4-0, the more I envied Lisa her relative freedom.

Lisa had never gotten married. She'd had a succession of boyfriends. "Cereal" monogamy, she joked. "They stay for breakfast. Then I kick them out in the morning." Her tone was flippant, but I knew that Lisa wanted stability in a relationship as much as anyone else.

When she was doing cocaine, that was impossible. She was involved with one loser after another including men who ended up in jail, disappeared for days at a time, and stole money from her. One even slept with her cousin.

After she began her recovery, Lisa went through a long period of voluntary celibacy to reflect on the qualities she wanted in a mate.

Eighteen months ago, she met Ryan at a meeting of Alcoholics Anonymous. He seemed like a bad bet to me. At thirty-six, Ryan had been clean for three years and attended meetings regularly.

According to Lisa, some people go to AA but don't actually work the steps, which involve taking one's own inventory and making amends to those one has wronged. Consequently, the half-hearted members don't have good sobriety.

Ryan was different. He devoted himself to the program, completing one step after another and volunteering to help other tortured souls who were still drinking. However, he had a history of physical abuse. Ryan's last girlfriend left him after calling the police several times during their domestic disputes.

I had cautioned Lisa about Ryan's propensity for violence, but she believed in him. Her whole life revolved around addiction and the program. To have doubted Ryan would have been tantamount to questioning her entire career, as well as her own recovery.

She was like a televangelist since she'd joined AA. Of course, I'd never say that to her face. Obviously, I preferred her clean and sober to drinking and snorting white powder, but I didn't understand her need for AA after all these years.

We were both partyers back in our university days, but for some inexplicable reason, Lisa crossed a line in her drinking. Alcohol became something that she had to have, and it changed her personality. Her grades went down the drain, and she was often evicted from bars for being too boisterous, but the next day she'd have no recollection of what she had done.

After Lisa realized that she had a problem, she went to the Addiction Research Centre in Toronto. She received outpatient counseling at ARC, and they encouraged her to go to daily meetings.

One night, Lisa brought home a quiz and waved it in my face. "Look!" she said. "Here's one test I passed with flying colors. It says I'm in stage two alcoholism. Scary! Stage three means I'm ready for the asylum. People lose jobs, marriages, and become institutionalized at that point."

I grabbed the quiz and studied it with interest. I decided to take it myself. Lisa had no objections, but she was surprised when I scored high enough to qualify for stage one alcoholism.

"Oh my God, Tara. You need to get into the program!"

I had no intention of joining the Bible thumpers and no real worries about my drinking either.

"We'll save a seat for you," Lisa had said at the time, but it never proved necessary. I got pregnant with Devon when I was twenty-four. It was easy for me to quit drinking during the pregnancy. Afterward, my alcohol consumption dropped drastically. Who can take care of an infant and continue swinging from the chandelier at the same time?

On the one hand, I knew that alcoholism was a disease, but I couldn't help wondering why Lisa couldn't cut back her consumption by herself, the way I had, by using more discipline and self-control. Sometimes, I wanted to scream when she talked endlessly about her meetings and used those little clichés: easy does it, one day at a time, live and let live.

Shut the hell up! I wanted to say. It seemed so self-indulgent that Lisa spent twenty-four hours a day dealing with addiction. It was bad enough when she had an ordinary job as an assistant at Nortel and went to meetings every night. Now that she was a bona fide alcohol and drug counselor, she was addicted to addiction—a full-time naval gazer.

And I was a disloyal bitch of a friend to think those things about her. I knew that. Tara—loyal, dependable, and resentful as hell.

Lisa was aware of my disapproval. She sensed that I wasn't thrilled with her job, and she was disappointed that I never gave the thumbs-up to Ryan, although I understood her attraction to him perfectly well.

Tall and lanky with dirty blonde hair and athletic good looks, Ryan had always been a ladies' man. He worked as a landscaper in the summer and plowed driveways in the winter, when he worked, which was not that often.

I suspected that he was a lazy bastard, who preferred to live off Lisa. They'd been living together for about six months, and I wasn't eager to hear the latest details about their relationship.

We opened the menus, which said "Nate's—where famous people come to eat." I'd never seen anyone famous in the restaurant, but I kept one eye open for Matthew Perry, Dan Aykroyd, and Kiefer Sutherland to stroll in. Apparently, Kiefer had gone to a Catholic boarding school in Ottawa as a teenager.

I ordered roast beef on rye with coleslaw, fries, and a dill pickle. Lisa religiously followed the Atkins diet. She requested the "Quick Burger Platter," which consisted of a cheeseburger with bacon. She wanted the coleslaw but asked the waitress to hold the potatoes. We both ordered decaffeinated coffee.

Decaf: a public announcement that we were too old to drink caffeine after dinner. We may as well have requested Maalox or Metamucil. Next, it would be the senior citizen discount. I sighed.

"Still persecuting yourself with the American Heart Association diet?" I asked Lisa, feeling the heavy weight of my thighs as I shifted my legs under the table. No wonder she was so fantastically thin, but I could never give up carbohydrates. Even if men stared at me open-mouthed, I refused to part with my rocky road ice cream.

"Works for me," Lisa retorted.

"I don't know how you can stand to live without bread and your mother's pasta. That's not to mention what that diet is doing to your arteries and your kidneys," I said.

"It's great, the food plan. Who else would let you eat an unlimited amount of cheese, steak, and bacon?" Lisa asked. "Atkins used to have a dessert of macadamia nut butter that he mixed together with whole cream."

"That probably killed him." I shook my head. "Eat up. It's your funeral."

We had this conversation routinely, and I could tell by Lisa's expression that she was tired of my ongoing lectures. Years of being a nurse and a mother had made me a nag, constantly worrying about other people's health, and righteously telling them what to do to improve it. I also had fifteen pounds to lose. Obviously, my jealousy of Lisa's appearance had reared its ugly head. I apologized hastily and changed the topic.

"Getting back to the flick," I said, "wasn't that a great line when one of Kahn's colleagues said that we all have some sort of secret to hide? Mark and I just rented a movie called *Normal*, which dealt with a different theme, but it was kind of similar. A couple had been happily married for twenty-five years. Then one day, the man announced that he'd been born in the wrong body. He wanted a sex change, but he didn't want to leave the marriage. It was really well-written and starred Jessica Lange, but I can't remember who played the guy."

I thought about how attractive Lange had looked in the movie. She was old. I now defined "old" as anyone older than me. Lange had to be at least fifty or fifty-five, and she was still gorgeous. That buoyed my spirits until I remembered that I didn't remotely resemble Jessica Lange, who had undoubtedly been a knockout in her thirties.

"Kind of like *Boys Don't Cry*, except with a happy ending," I continued, "because eventually: the family came to accept his desire to transition. It was hard to imagine how the couple could stay together—although, of course, he was still the same person after he became a she—but it was better than watching the protagonist being gunned down like Hilary Swank."

"And what does that have to do with bigamy?" Lisa asked, as she bit into her cheeseburger.

"Both men were hiding something. Kahn deliberately deceived his wives and children—he *wouldn't* tell them about each other—and Lange's husband *couldn't* tell her his real feelings. They each had different motives, but the result was the same. The partners in their lives never really knew them.

"Are most of us like that? Does everyone have some deep, dark secret?" I waved my arms, so Lisa would know that I was including the other patrons in the restaurant.

"I've lived my whole life as an open book. What you see is what you get, or it used to be." *Except for my deep-seated resentments,* I thought grimly. "But with my birthday looming in the distance, suddenly, I don't know who I am anymore or what I want. I don't even know *who* I want, but I can't see myself growing old with Mark."

I bit a hangnail and glanced around the room. Two guys in their twenties had just sat down at the table across from us. The Asian woman with them was talking about Tibet, the Dalai Lama's upcoming visit to Ottawa, and whether Prime Minister Paul Martin would agree to meet with him. His Holiness, the Dalai Lama, was as popular culturally as a rock star. The trio was arguing over how the Dalai Lama could refer to himself as solely a spiritual leader, without any political affiliations, when he had spent his entire life in exile, working for the independence of Tibet.

"It's an outrage. Almost 1.2 million Tibetans have died from starvation, imprisonment, or murder since the Chinese took over. Surely, that constitutes genocide: but the United States, the world's self-appointed policeman, does nothing to stop the slaughter," the woman declared.

"The States turns the other cheek so that they can maintain their billion-dollar trading relationship with China," her companion replied. He was wearing a yellow baseball cap on backward, a dark blue, short-sleeved shirt, and large baggy pants with balloon figures on them.

The background music by Alanis Morissette suddenly stopped. Melanie Doane was now crooning, "You leave a lot to be desired."

"Speaking of Mark, this song could have been written for him," I said, returning my attention to Lisa.

"Could've been written for any man," Lisa said. "Don't be crazy, Tara! You're still an open book. You're as transparent as pantyhose: the same today as you were in university. You're just having a midlife crisis. And what's this big secret of yours? Your huge crush on the clerk at the grocery store?"

Lisa laughed. "My God, even Devon knows about that! He says you're always weirding out before you go into the grocery store, stopping to put on lipstick in the car or to comb your hair."

"Devon said that?" I felt embarrassed. I thought I had been discreet. How could I tell Lisa that it was so much more than a crush? This boy had taken over my thoughts. My brain had turned to mush. It was as though there were a hole in my head that had always been there, just waiting to be filled with thoughts of Alain.

I fantasized about him day and night, wondering what it would feel like to run my hands through his crisp black hair. At least Alain had hair. Mark's favorite expression was "hair today, gone tomorrow." His hairline had been receding for years, and he had started growing a beard to compensate. Mark had tried Rogaine, acupuncture, and brewer's yeast in a vain attempt to restore his lost locks. He lived in baseball caps; fortunately, he was not the type to shave his head.

Alain's hair was alive with little spikes. He had a brush cut, and I often pictured him applying gel to his hair in the morning after his shower. My thoughts would immediately degenerate to images of Alain naked and embracing me: on top of me, inside me, all over me. Graphic images of devouring the supermarket boy left me feeling giddy and young again and prevented me from concentrating on my work at the hospital.

When I was giving out medications, I was imagining how much hair Alain had on his chest. Did he have hair on his back, as well? That didn't appeal to me. Or would he have a smooth, muscular, and relatively hairless chest? Could he keep it up for hours, the way young boys do? Was he a cuddler, or did he like to roll over and fall asleep after sex?

These were the pure and professional thoughts that preoccupied me as I dispensed Cipro to my 101-year-old patient, who was recovering from pneumonia. It was a miracle that I hadn't poisoned him by giving him one of my female patient's hormone replacement pills.

The intensity of my desire for Alain shocked me. It had been so long since I'd had any sexual interest in Mark. We'd never had a passionate relationship. Our connection was based more on affection and compatibility than lust. After years of marriage, our sex life was about as exciting as doing community service. I knew exactly when and where Mark would touch me, and how many minutes he would allot to lovemaking.

Moreover, Mark had a strange habit of talking throughout sex. He would talk about everything from current events to work to telling me jokes.

Mark and I had been so young when we got married. I remembered watching Lisa suffer heartbreaks with her "bad boys." She seemed fatally attracted to the wrong men. I swore that I wouldn't make that mistake. Mark was decent. He was faithful, brilliant, and kind-hearted. I could count on him, and that was important to me.

We had much in common in our youth. Our parents had been classic left liberals, who had ardently supported the far-left New Democratic Party. Both Mark and I were active members of the NDP, and we used to love the same authors like Stephen King and John Grisham.

Now he likes Michael Ondaatje, and you can't pay me to read his works. Like Elaine on Seinfeld, I almost fell asleep during the movie *The English Patient*. Nor can Mark tolerate my favorites like Carol Shields, Amy Tan, or Philip Roth, who he thinks is "too

American."

American. He says the word in the same disparaging tone that one would use to refer to the kitty litter box in the kitchen.

"What about King and Grisham? They're American," I protested.

"Yes, but I'm over them now. I'm only reading Canadian fiction and listening to Canadian music."

"That should leave you lots of free time," I snapped, when Mark had first made that idiotic announcement.

Lisa was American. Mark often said to her, "I won't hold that against you," but his joke fell flat with me since I knew the depth of his antipathy toward the States.

Lisa grew up in New Jersey with her first-generation Italian family. When she was eighteen, her father decided to join his brother in the restaurant business in Ottawa. The family moved here and set up a fabulous restaurant called Enzo's on Preston Street. Although she's lived in Canada for two decades, Lisa has retained her Jersey accent and still views herself as American, whereas Mark prefers to see her as an Italian immigrant, which is a step up in his mind.

It's hard to pinpoint a particular time when my relationship with Mark began to sour. It may have started when he began to spend more time sitting on committees and working on his research. His area of interest is comparative religion, and he's studied aboriginal people in Manitoba and Quebec. His current fascination involves the role of religion in organ transplantation. Mark hopes to publish a book on the topic. Thus, he's been spending countless hours behind closed doors working on his research.

We had also begun to argue over the right way to raise Devon, who had become an avid rapper, with an attitude that was almost as big as the ring in his nose. Recently, Devon came home with a tattoo on his arm that said, "Rot in Pieces." He claimed that he was only copying Eminem.

What kind of a role model is Eminem? I've been a feminist all of my life. I've taught my only son to respect women, yet he idolizes and emulates a punk with bleached hair, who sings songs to his daughter about how nice it would be to cut up her mother and put her in the trunk of the car. How am I supposed to react to that?

Mark said, "Just relax, Tara. Dev's going through a phase, and it'll pass more quickly if we don't make a big deal about it. If we get upset, he may become increasingly attached to Eminem and Fifty Cents, or whatever the hell his name is."

I suggested taking Devon with me to a meeting of WAR, Women Against Rape, a small group that I belong to, which has educational and political components. We give lectures in high schools to raise awareness about sexual assault. Although some of the members of WAR have become a bit too radical for me, essentially, I'm proud of the work that we do.

Mark thought that the group was hostile. He didn't like the name of the organization, but I believed that we needed a dramatic acronym to get people's attention. Mark was opposed to me taking Devon to a meeting. He thought that WAR was full of man-haters.

Women haters were okay. Devon spent hours every day listening to records that referred to women as "bitches" and "ho's." I wanted to temper that with some reality. Let him hear real girls talk about what it was like to be sexually or physically assaulted.

TV Ontario has an excellent show on Sunday nights called "Renegadepress.com." It's all about issues that teens deal with, from meeting strangers on the Internet to bullying to racist attitudes toward Native American kids. I tried to get Devon to watch with me, but it was a losing battle.

"He's a kid, for God's sake. Why would he want to sit at home and watch public television with his mum?" Mark asked in an exasperated tone. He believes that Devon's fascination with violence on TV and in music is normal for young boys and won't provoke him to act dangerously or irresponsibly. I disagree, and now I have two problems: one with Devon and the other with Mark.

Not only do Mark and I argue most of the time, but he's also constantly irritating me. For example, he has a habit of repeating a story a dozen times, always prefacing it with, "I don't know if I told you this..." And I want to die laughing at his pronunciation of the name Zdeno Chara, defenseman for the Ottawa Senators. Mark invariably places emphasis on the wrong syllable.

Worse, he acts as though he knows Chara and drops his name in conversation regularly because he stood behind him once in line at Home Depot and got him to autograph a piece of paper for Devon. Since that fateful day, Mark has acted as though he and Zdeno Chara are best friends. He rambles endlessly about how tall the hockey player is—six foot, nine inches standing and seven feet even in skates—as though this information is not common knowledge to any viewer who doesn't need a magnifying glass to see the screen. Mark also has an annoying habit of being absolutely charming and joking with bank tellers and gas station attendants, then turning right back to me and reverting to his serious self.

But it can't really be these trivial things that bother me about my husband. I suppose my irritation stems from the fact that our love for each other has died, but neither one of us is ready to face that fact, rife as it is with unpleasant consequences for our lives.

"Alain is not a grocery clerk," I said indignantly to Lisa, defending my lust object. "He's the assistant manager of the meat department."

"Oh, excuse me," Lisa replied, grinning. "Now who's the snob?" she asked, referring to my lack of enthusiasm about Ryan's landscaping job. "At least Ryan is old enough to vote."

Alain was twenty-four. Lisa knew that perfectly well. She was just goading me.

"But I assume your fantasy man has his high school degree," she added and winked. I looked blank, not catching her reference.

"You remember the B&E kid? She was one of my clients. Had a long procession of asshole boyfriends. Then one day, she met someone new. Kept bragging about him. Said this one was a keeper because he had his high school diploma and didn't have a criminal record." Lisa paused, noticing my lack of response. "She set a low bar, she did." I remained silent.

Lisa had spoiled the mood, comparing Alain to the paramours of the B&E kid. I had wanted to tell her that Alain was rapidly becoming an obsession. I had increased my trips to the grocery store and doubled our meat order, much to Mark's chagrin, claiming that I was entertaining. Alain must think that we have an inordinate number of barbecues.

I was conscious of my clothes now when I went to the supermarket and tried not to go shopping after work when I knew that he wasn't on duty.

Sometimes, I called his house just to hear the sound of his

voice on the machine. I was careful to call from a pay phone or to use the *67 function to disable his call display and block my call. I had become Stalker Mom, and it scared me.

Not only had I memorized Alain's work schedule, but also I was forcing myself to listen to a double album by Pearl Jam because Alain loved the band. Listening to Pearl Jam was about as much fun as studying for a physics exam. I found them bleak, maudlin even. Their CD was called *Lost Dogs* and had one cheerful title after another like "Sad," "Down," "Alone," and "Fatal." These boys made Pink Floyd look like Dale Carnegie. Then suddenly, almost at the end of their second CD, the band let loose with their rocking hit of the cover song by The Cavaliers, "Last Kiss."

Thank God for that song, so I had something positive to say to Alain about his music. I couldn't bear the idea of him thinking I was ancient, matronly, or clueless. I barely knew the boy, but having him like me was so crucial to my self-esteem that I was studiously analyzing his likes and dislikes so that we would have more in common. What was next for me? Midriff tops, hip hugger jeans, and liposuction?

I had become Jack Nicholson. For years, I had admired Nicholson's talent. From *Five Easy Pieces* to *The Crossing Guard*, he was an amazing and versatile actor. But once I heard him on a talk show, and he sounded like a dirty old man—a buffoon, really—going on about young girls and his new wife, who was in her thirties. WAR had no respect for middle-aged men who traded in their older wives for newer models, although this was a time-honored tradition.

Women who went in search of men twenty years their junior would look even more shallow and pathetic. The only older women who took young lovers and didn't look ridiculous were the rich and famous like Demi Moore. Dazzling Demi could have anyone she wanted, but that didn't prevent Jay Leno from having a field day mocking her relationship with Ashton Kutcher.

I was a carnal being. My needs were not being satisfied at home. I was just going through the motions with Mark when we had sex, and the only way that I could get excited was to think about Alain. Lisa was wrong in assuming that I might not act on my fantasies, but she seemed uptight tonight, and I had lost interest in confiding in her.

"Come on, Mary Kay Letourneau. Give me the dirt about the grocery boy," Lisa said.

"Mary Kay who?"

"Letourneau! You know, the teacher from Washington State who had sex with her thirteen-year-old student. They had two babies together, and now they're getting married. So there's hope for you and the meat man."

"Goddamn it," I snapped. "You should think about ordering fries next time around. You have all the sensitivity of cement."

"It's not the diet," Lisa sighed. "I'm a drag. I know. It's just that, um, I don't know how to explain this." Her voice trailed off. Lisa fumbled in her purse for her cigarettes.

"Shit," she lamented, remembering that she couldn't light up in the restaurant. She flagged down the waitress and ordered another decaf. "This is just between us. I don't want you telling Mark."

"Lisa Campana, you're not listening to me! I can barely talk to Mark about the movie we just saw let alone anything intimate."

"Oh, Tara, I'm sorry. I'm spaced out tonight. My period is late. I haven't had it for almost ten weeks. I took one of those, you know, tests from the drugstore, and it said that I'm …"

Lisa couldn't finish her sentence. She brushed away her bangs. It was a nervous habit that she had adopted when she was unable to smoke. "The doctor confirmed it yesterday."

"Lise!" I took her hand across the table. "I don't understand. I thought you and Ryan were trying to get pregnant."

"There's more," Lisa said, removing my hand from hers, as she began playing with the silverware. "Remember my slip?"

"Yeah," I said slowly.

Lisa was just about to celebrate her fifth anniversary of sobriety when she fell off the wagon and got plastered in January. She'd had a difficult time getting through the Christmas holidays, which had involved extra parties and temptations. One day, she was feeling down about Ryan's unwillingness to get married. He claimed to be committed to her and wanted to have children, but he had an aversion to the institution of marriage.

Lisa had been listening to an old song by the Pet Shop Boys, which reminded her of her party days. It was that simple. The memory provoked a craving for cocaine, and her depression made her vulnerable to its calling.

"Well, I don't really know what I did that night. I blacked out and was in the mood for Indian food. I do get tired of Atkins! Especially, I miss food with sauce and rice. And I was crashing big time from the Coke, so I was ravenous. Anyway, I was in some bar on Merivale, but I must've left there because the next thing I knew, I was in an Indian restaurant stuffing myself with tandoori chicken. A guy at the table next to me got to talking. Then it's a blur. All I remember is being in his apartment, putting my clothes back on, and him asking if I was okay to drive." Lisa's voice was barely audible.

"You went home with a complete stranger?" I was incredulous.

"You might want to say that a little louder," Lisa replied coldly. "I think the guys at the back table missed it. Oh, and you should have said *black stranger*."

"Black? I thought he was Indian."

"He was, but he referred to himself as a black man. And if this is his baby, it'll be black, too! You think 'Mr. I Don't Want to Get Married' will be happy about that?"

My head was spinning. Lisa hadn't wanted children in her twenties, but when she'd hit thirty-five, her maternal drive erupted like a volcano. She had often said that even if she didn't have a partner, she wanted a baby. Now that she was sober, the slip notwithstanding, she was capable of raising one by herself. She would want this child, but there was no telling how Ryan would react to the news that it may not be his. What if the baby was born white? If she told Ryan, would Lisa ruin her relationship with him for nothing?

Worse. She had kept this from me. She hadn't trusted me enough ten weeks ago to have told me about the encounter with the stranger when it occurred. Not that I could have done anything about it, but I assumed Lisa and I told each other everything. I thought she viewed me as her closest confidant, yet she had been worrying and feeling alone all this time: all because of my judgmental attitude.

"I don't know what to say. I feel so bad for you! You have some tough decisions to make. Are you going to keep the baby? Will you tell Ryan? What about the Indian guy? Pregnancy should be a happy time, especially at our age. I mean, it's not like we're teenagers, desperately trying to avoid an unwanted pregnancy." I paused.

"I also feel terrible that you hid this from me. We're best

friends. You can tell me anything. I didn't mean to be so critical about Ryan or your relationship. I've been a real idiot, but it's only 'cause I want the best for you."

"Stop apologizing, already! I lead a crazy life compared to you. You're an old married lady. You don't understand the singles' life, let alone the complications of the life of an addict. We've always been different that way, but it hasn't affected our closeness. Yeah, I admit I didn't want to hear your moralizing, which is why I never told you about the guy—whose name I don't know, so I could never find him—but also I didn't tell you because I didn't want to make it real.

"I didn't want to say it out loud. I didn't even tell my sponsor. Pregnancy was the last thing on my mind! Ryan and I've been trying for so long, with so little success, that I never wear my diaphragm anymore. That leads me to believe this isn't Ryan's baby since the timing is just right for my slip." Lisa took a large gulp of her coffee, which had become cold.

We stared at each other. Finally, she suggested that we get the check. I'd wanted to order the cherry cheesecake with coconut, but I always felt like a glutton eating desserts in front of Lisa. Moreover, I had lost my appetite listening to her story, and it was apparent that she was keen to leave.

I asked if she wanted to come back to my house to talk in private. She shook her head. She wanted to go home. It was after ten p.m., and we both had to get up early in the morning. We walked out of Nate's on a somber note. Our light-hearted evening had turned serious.

Lisa had parked in the underground lot at Loblaws whereas I'd been lucky enough to find street parking. We hugged goodbye, and I told her to call me the next night.

"You can always count on me, Lise. I may be a smug married, but I still love you. And I think you'll make a great mother. Just send the kid out for adoption when it reaches puberty." I smiled weakly. She returned my embrace, but her green eyes were vacant when I looked up into them. Lisa lit a smoke, opened her cell phone to check for messages, and walked off in the opposite direction.

CHAPTER TWO

The road was slick. I was careful about walking on the ice since I spent the better part of my days attending to people with broken hips, knees, and ankles. Concentrating on the slippery sidewalk helped to take my mind off Lisa's dilemma.

I located my car, which was sandwiched in between two vehicles with Ottawa Senators flags. I had forgotten that the playoffs were on, and I was wearing my University of Toronto sweatshirt.

I removed the thin layer of snow from my windshield and got into the car, flipping on the radio automatically. Magic 100 was issuing a warning about several fender benders on the Queensway, our local highway, which was the route that I had taken downtown to the theatre. I decided to take the back roads home.

The trip to my house in Country Place seemed to take forever, partly due to the weather, but mainly because of my worries about Lisa's pregnancy. How beautiful that baby would be, mixed with Lisa's olive skin and dark brown hair, and how it would destroy her life.

As I approached my neighborhood, I was careful to drive toward the center of the white line. Going southbound on Merivale, there were deep ditches on the side of the road, which were easy to miss.

One night when Lisa and I were teenagers, we drove across the bridge to Quebec to a nightclub where my favorite band, Powerhouse, was playing. I had the hots for the drummer, who didn't know I was alive.

Lisa and I had fun dancing, drinking, and rocking to the band, but I wasn't paying attention to how much she'd had to drink. At that time, I didn't understand that she had a problem. She drove me home, and just before we reached Country Place, her car veered off onto the shoulder of the road. It was a real shock to find ourselves lying sideways in a ditch. Luckily, we weren't injured and managed to crawl out of the car.

We had to call my father to bail us out. We would never have considered calling her parents since they were much stricter than mine. Without complaint, my father got up at 2 a.m. on a work night and called a friend, who came out to tow Lisa's mother's big blue Chrysler out of the gully.

God, were we embarrassed. Now there were sidewalks on the right-hand side of Merivale, but the ditches were still visible on the left-hand side of the road.

There was a small mall in front of our neighborhood that wasn't there when our home was erected. It housed Inuit artists, a group of architects, an archival imaging technology firm, and a communication systems division.

Finally, I arrived home. I pulled my Saab 9000 into the driveway and brought the garbage can in from the curb. I stopped briefly to admire our house and to worry about my magnolia tree. The tree didn't flower last year although it did produce a number of buds. I'd read that magnolias preferred an acid-rich soil, so I was planning to add something to lower the pH balance, such as peat moss or aluminum sulfate from the garden center.

Otherwise, our hedge was intact, and I had lots of time before I had to weed the garden beds, which I usually planted with geraniums, dahlias, ginkgoes, and orchids, although they were extremely delicate.

Our house had been custom built in the early 1970s, and we'd moved in when I was seven years old. My father was an engineer. He had never recovered from the helplessness and frustration of watching his wife die from cancer. Before my mother got sick, our house had been a happy and festive place with friends and relatives coming and going at all hours.

After we lost her, my father became a virtual recluse. He went to work but forfeited all social activity. He stopped golfing and playing tennis with his friends. My younger sister, Denise, and I were the only things that kept him going.

A few years after my mother passed on, my dad met and married Marie, a thirty-eight-year-old fashion designer. Recently, they moved to Kingston. He's retired now but takes the occasional consulting job.

Denise is a high-powered businesswoman, who lives with her boyfriend in Calgary. We keep in touch on email, but we don't talk much on the phone.

Mark and I bought the house from Dad and Marie. It was unnerving living in my childhood home at first, but eventually, I got used to it. In many ways, it felt comforting and nostalgic. The house was a virtual museum of memories. I'd always felt that part of my mother lived on here, and Mark and I loved the neighborhood.

The house was silent, but soon I was greeted by our dog Monday, an excitable little schnauzer who always looked angry or sad, depending on the way his mustache turned down. Monday barked with enthusiasm when he saw me and spun around in circles three times.

"Yes, baby, Mommy missed you, too," I said soothingly, as I stroked his little gray and white head. I went into the pantry, grabbed a dog chew for Monday, and came face to face with a package of Reese's peanut butter cups. *What the hell?* I thought, as I popped two of the tasty morsels into my mouth. Who would have believed that chocolate and peanut butter would have made such a heavenly combination?

Even though I hadn't worked today, I was happy to be surrounded by bold colors in the house after the bleak institutional walls at the hospital. Mark had never been interested in decorating and had allowed me to redo the whole house myself when my father and Marie moved out.

I chose a deep lilac background for the downstairs, which offset our black leather furniture and prints: *I and the Village* by Chagall, Degas's *Ballerinas,* and the *Lovers* by Gustav Klimt. Mark insisted that I include one painting by the Group of Seven; I wasn't big on wilderness landscapes, although I didn't mind Tom Thomson, who inspired them.

The walls were also lined with photos of Mark, Devon, and me, as well as Lisa, my dad and Marie, Denise and her boyfriend, and three or four precious shots of my mom.

I made my way into our big spacious kitchen, which had funky, yellow flowered wallpaper. The large windows and southern exposure made it bright and sunny during the daytime. An electric fireplace in the family room kept us cozy and warm during the winter.

I made coffee for the morning and defrosted chicken for dinner tomorrow night. With dread, I climbed the stairs, hoping that both my men were asleep by now.

Although Devon doesn't actually have a "Do Not Enter" sign on his bedroom door, he may as well have one. His door was closed, and I deliberated about whether to knock. It was after

10:30 p.m., but Devon was a night owl, and I could hear the sounds of television.

Sure enough, he was lying on his bed watching *Finding Nemo*, probably for the nineteenth time. I didn't understand how kids could watch programs over and over again. I rarely watched movies twice, but I did find it comforting that Devon, who acted like such a tough guy, still took pleasure in Disney movies.

Nemo was a heartwarming story, but the plot was too simple to hold my interest. However, I did enjoy the lush background of the coral reefs, and Lisa had clapped during the 12-step meeting for sharks when the head shark repeated, "Fish are our friends, not food!"

Devon was fascinated by animation, especially Disney/Pixar productions. He loved everything technical from computers to cars to math. Often, I found him watching Discovery or the History Channel just for fun. He was his father's son in that respect, except that he hated English and French, which both Mark and I had adored.

Devon's room was surprisingly neat and orderly. He had posters of rock stars and hockey players on the back wall, and the trophies that he'd won in sports were lined up on his bookcase. Devon played hockey and soccer and was an ardent fan of the martial arts. He'd been taking Taekwon-Do for years and had his blue belt, which was just two steps away from a black belt.

Mark and I encouraged him in his pursuit because we both admired the principles of Taekwon-Do: "courtesy, integrity, perseverance, self-control, and indomitable spirit." Except for perseverance, these were all qualities my kid seemed to lack at the moment. Devon had taken a break from training this semester because it required him to practice three times a week, and that conflicted with his hockey schedule.

My son was wearing a T-shirt that said, "Just Tie It, Domi." The head of Toronto Maple Leafs' notorious Tie Domi was superimposed on the body of a pit bull. I didn't really understand the meaning of the shirt. Was it a play on words like, "Just Do It, Dummy?" Or was "tie it" the equivalent of "stuff it?" Who knew? I was just glad it wasn't profane like Devon's music collection.

"Hi, Dev," I said, hesitating. "How was school?"

"The usual," he remarked, looking bored to see me and turning his attention back to the screen.

"It's getting pretty late."

"But Dory is just about to find Nemo!"

"Honey, you've seen that movie a dozen times. Why don't you call it a night? Dory will find Nemo again in the morning. He'll be fine in that fishbowl until then."

"In a minute, Mum," he said, sounding exasperated. I noticed that the movie was about to end. I glanced at the poster of fallen soccer god, Diego Maradona, on Dev's wall, conceded defeat, and walked down the hallway in search of my other disinterested partner.

Mark was already in his pajamas. He was crouched over the computer, reading glasses perched on his sharp nose, and typing furiously. The television was on. No doubt, he was waiting for the eleven o'clock CTV news, which we both watched before bed.

"How was your day?" I asked, feigning enthusiasm.

"Piled higher and deeper in paperwork," he replied. Mark often uttered this complaint, but I knew that he thoroughly enjoyed his job teaching undergrads about ritual, religion, sorcery, and magic.

"Working on the book?"

"Nope. Just finishing up an ethno scenario. Won't take long."

Ethnography was the study of symbols. Mark usually used one or two ethno quizzes for his students. The first one involved them pretending that they were accompanying Gulliver, of *Gulliver's Travels,* to the flying island of Laputa. No one there spoke English, so the students had to choose five objects to bring with them that would tell the inhabitants of Laputa something about them.

The other scenario that Mark employed involved space travelers who had been sent to Earth to carefully study the population. They'd landed in a McDonald's restaurant and had to carefully observe and analyze the furniture, the food, the division of labor, and the structure of the family in order to draw conclusions about Canada to send to the mother ship.

"Why not have them land in the middle of the Corel Centre at the beginning of the playoffs? Judging by the number of players who smash into each other and the flags that say, 'Go, Sens, Go,' the aliens would probably conclude that the Senators were a warrior race," I said.

Mark was not amused. He never appreciated my sarcasm about hockey. The thrill of watching grown men bashing into each other, dislocating their shoulders, losing their teeth, and crushing their fragile brain cells was lost on me.

We didn't even have a homegrown hockey team anymore. Most of the players had been imported: another sign that the almighty dollar ruled over hometown spirit.

We made small talk as I got undressed. Mark inquired about the movie, and I told him that it was about polygamy.

"Bigamy," he said, "not polygamy." Mark took great pleasure in correcting me.

"How do you know what it was about?"

"I read the review in the *ByTowne Guide*. Polygamy is a marriage where a spouse has more than one partner at a time. Bigamy is the act of entering into a marriage with one person while still legally married to another. Polygamy dates back to biblical days. In the book of Genesis…"

"Isn't polygamy legal in Utah?" I interjected.

"Not really. Bigamy is illegal in most countries. However, some places still tolerate polygamy because it's practiced mainly for religious reasons. Colorado and Utah have the greatest number of polygamists, but the Mormon Church no longer condones non-monogamous relationships. They'll excommunicate practitioners, but that doesn't stop some of the more radical sects.

"Understandably, the practice offends many people because some polygamists marry underage girls. One could argue that polygamy is nothing more than a sanctioned form of statutory rape since many girls who're taken as plural wives are only fourteen or fifteen years old."

Mark sounded as though he were preaching at the podium and had a remarkable talent for turning the conversation back to himself. Somehow the movie, *My Architect*, got lost as he expounded on religious law. As usual, Mark had missed the emotional component of the problem—the betrayal felt by the "unofficial" wives and the feelings of shame and abandonment experienced by the "illegitimate" children.

Shut the hell up! I thought to myself. Maybe I should get a button that said STHU. I could wear it on my lapel, and it would send out paralyzing vibrations that forced people to stop talking—sort of like a stun gun. When people asked what it meant, I would say, "Support the Halifax Underground."

I was reluctant to disrupt Mark's monologue because I didn't want him to ask about Lisa. I was so alarmed about her predicament that I was afraid my fear would be evident in my voice. And I was angry and felt hurt that she hadn't confided in me. I switched the topic to Devon.

"Oh, can you take Dev to the dentist after school tomorrow? I'm working seven to seven."

Mark nodded.

The news came on. We saw pictures of dead American soldiers being dragged through the streets of Iraq and desecrated. I shuddered.

Mark and I agreed that it had been wrong of the Americans to have gone into Iraq unilaterally. But Mark believed that they should stay there now to establish an interim government, whereas I thought they had worn out their welcome and Canada had been smart not to get involved.

I flicked the TV off right after a segment on a series of fires in a neighborhood that was close to Devon's best friend's house and went into the bathroom to take off my makeup. Frowning, I noticed the fine wrinkles under my eyes, along with the pallor of my winter white skin.

Mark was already in bed when I returned. He was lying on his back looking like a beached whale. Mark had gained at least forty pounds in the last year, which didn't make him particularly attractive.

I crawled into bed and gave him a perfunctory peck on the cheek. He turned toward me and gave me a big wet kiss, which tasted like cauliflower. He pulled me closer to him.

I protested, claiming that I had to get up early for work. It was the modern-day equivalent of saying, "Not tonight, honey. I have a headache and am lusting for the meat man."

Usually, when I wasn't in the mood, I would wear my cold cream to bed. Mark called this my "anti-erection routine." But I'd been too tired to remember my heavy moisturizer tonight.

Mark seemed disappointed by my rebuttal but didn't press the issue. I rolled over on my side to check the clock, turned off the light, and tried not to think about Lisa and her mystery baby.

CHAPTER THREE

I was kissing Alain, his hungry wet tongue probing mine, his rock-hard body pressed up against me, his right hand caressing my erect nipple when we were rudely interrupted by the alarm clock. Yawning, I stretched my arms, rubbed the sleep out of my eyes, and rolled out of bed. I am definitely not a morning person. In fact, I stumble through the early hours in a semi-coma until I've had at least two cups of coffee. A hot shower helped to revive me. I skimmed the newspaper and inhaled a bowl of bran flakes and a banana. Then I was off to the office.

The drive to the hospital was pleasant. Last night's snow had melted. I took Prince of Wales Drive, which had a scenic view of the stunning Rideau Canal. One hundred and twenty-three miles long, the canal formed the world's longest skating rink. The waterway was built after the War of 1812 when Canada defeated the imperialistic Americans. The goal was to provide a secure supply route from Montreal to Kingston. Construction began in 1826, about the same time that Ottawa was settled under the name "By Town." Lieutenant Colonel John By supervised the daunting and dangerous project.

Thousands of laborers trudged through the bush, swamp, and rocky terrain. The bush was so hard to penetrate that much of the work on the canal had to be done during the winter when traveling on the frozen river was more manageable. The men cleared the forest, excavated the rocks, and designed the magnificent stonemasonry for the locks. It was hard to believe that all the work was done by hand. Skilled labor was performed mainly by French Canadians, who had experience on other lock projects, and British stonemasons.

Irish immigrants and French Canadians comprised the unskilled labor. Most of the Irish workers were new immigrants, who were desperately in search of wage work. These brave men were accompanied by their families, who lived under harsh conditions in small shanties infested with disease.

About 2,000 men a year worked for seven years to build the canal. Almost half died of malaria, starvation, and worksite accidents. That didn't include the women and children who emigrated with their Irish husbands and succumbed to the fatal bite of the mosquito, dysentery, or smallpox. Memorials to these unsung heroes, who lay in unmarked graves, had been erected in Kingston and Ottawa.

Now, Ottawa embraced the Americans—our third-largest industry is tourism—and encouraged them to take boat rides down the Rideau River in the summer or to enjoy Winterlude, our wonderful winter festival. From downtown to Dow's Lake, about eight kilometers of the canal were maintained as a skating rink.

Mark, Devon, and I had spent many happy Sunday afternoons skating until our faces turned bright red, and our toes were frozen. We were always eager to view the ice and snow sculptures and to buy a Beaver Tail at one of the kiosks on the ice. Beaver Tails were pastries in the shape of a beaver. The cinnamon ones were the best.

Ottawa had become a thriving little city: one of Canada's best-kept secrets. Lisa often joked about how misinformed her American friends were about Canada. She said that when she told people in New Jersey that she was moving to Ottawa, even some of the most well-educated had responded with bizarre comments like, "That's great. You'll love living in the country!" Or "Ottawa, huh? That's in Alberta, isn't it?"

Lisa excused this appalling ignorance because she suffered from it herself before she moved here. The last time she studied Canada in school was in grade five when she learned about the Hudson Bay Mining Company and the fur traders. Some of Lisa's friends still envisioned Canada as a place where people traversed the land by kayak and skied in July: a barren wasteland marked by one or two major cities like Toronto or Vancouver. Others didn't think about Canada at all. Their time was taken up with more important foreign countries like Iran, Afghanistan, and the Middle East.

Musing about the development of the canal made the drive pass quickly. Before I knew it, I had arrived at work. Central Hospital was an old building made out of decaying red brick. There was construction going on because we were doubling the size of the emergency room. Some of the corridors had nothing but plaster on the walls, and the carpets were torn.

Like most hospitals, it had a musty smell that was somewhat disguised by disinfectants. There were bright green tiles on the floor and several shops downstairs including a pharmacy, a gift shop, and Timothy's coffee shop.

Catching an unexpected glimpse of myself in the wall-to-wall mirrors under the bright fluorescent light, I winced at the sight of my pear shape. I decided to forgo the Chocolate Lovers' Latte since I would be seeing Alain in a few days. Instead, I opted for a large, black Columbian.

It was a long walk through the main floor of the hospital up to the rehab unit. I got off the elevator and cleaned my hands with the Purell sanitizing liquid that was now placed throughout the building since the SARS scare. The linoleum floors were slippery, and yellow cones on the floor indicated that caution was warranted. One of the cones didn't have a top, and I spotted a small hole in the wall on the corridor outside of the Day Surgery department.

Did this hospital ever need a facelift. There was even paint chipping off the walls. Scenic waterways, first-class musical acts, and busy outdoor cafes were clearly a priority in this town; new hospitals were not.

Several years ago, two of our hospitals closed down. The burden was such that the health care system never recovered. Now, people frequently wait six to eight hours in the emergency room and months for a consultation with a specialist.

Good luck if you need an outpatient psychiatrist. It can take eight or nine months for a depressed patient to get in to see a shrink: kind of like the old joke where a person calls a crisis center and someone answers the line and says, "Suicide hotline. Please hold." Elective surgery is even worse. Some people wait for more than a year or two for joint replacements and MRIs.

Jean-Claude was the first of my colleagues to greet me when I reached the station. He was four years younger than I, and he was a nurse. Patients were always confusing him with the doctor, asking why he hadn't studied medicine or assuming that he was gay. But Jean-Claude didn't mind because, unlike me, he loved the job.

I had been nursing too long. I was so far beyond burnout; I was cremated. I had been energetic and optimistic about helping patients when I first became a rehab nurse. I knew that it was my role to motivate them, to teach them, to advise, and to help them come to terms with their multiple losses. I was the cheerleader who would be there to remind them of what they could still do rather than to focus on what they could never do again.

But I'd seen too many patients who created or contributed to their own illnesses by refusing to implement lifestyle changes. Patients who wouldn't adhere to their diet for diabetes or wondered why their knee replacement gave out prematurely when they refused to lose weight or exercise after surgery. Coronary cases and people with chronic bronchitis or emphysema who kept smoking. People who could have helped themselves but didn't.

Then there were the tragedies. The young boys with skiing accidents, who had been healthy as an ox one day and quadriplegic the next. The girls with cervical cancer, who would never be able to have children after their hysterectomies. Sturdy middle-aged men and women who suddenly had a heart attack or stroke and failed to recover their strength or ability to speak.

We were in the twenty-first century. We could send probes to Jupiter, Mars, and Mercury, yet modern medicine could not cure cancer, heart disease, or diabetes. Neither could we control chronic pain without medications that ate holes in people's stomachs or increased their risk of stroke. And we had yet to develop the decency to let the terminally ill die in peace.

I'd felt so idealistic and powerful when I started nursing. I was convinced that I could make a difference in people's lives, but I felt useless and unsure of myself now. Who was I to assure the man who would never walk again that his life was still full of promise and possibility? What sage advice did I have for the woman whose rheumatoid arthritis was destroying her joints so that she lived every day in agony? I could no longer stand my inability to alleviate the suffering of my patients and to make their illnesses disappear.

Soon I would have to think about a new profession. Like my relationship with Mark, I couldn't face it. What would I do? Go back to school, at my age? What would I study? Cradle robbing? How to free myself from twenty-five years of disappointment? I couldn't think about a career change at the moment. It was overwhelming.

Jean-Claude and I chatted for a while until Allison, the charge nurse, arrived with a large cup of tea in her Big Hug Mug. The three of us took our beverages into the morning meeting. Once a week we had a multidisciplinary meeting of the whole team. It usually consisted of the nurses, the family doctor, the physiatrist (a specialist in physical medicine), two physical therapists, a social worker, the home care coordinator, and an occupational therapist. We had a small unit, which was only equipped to handle twelve patients.

Oliver Rathwell began the meeting by announcing that it was too hot in the room. Although the weather was still brisk outside, the heating system in the hospital was antiquated and nearly annihilated us with blasts of hot, stuffy air. One of the physios jumped up to open a window for the well-respected doctor.

Rathwell was distinguished looking with his white hair, tan complexion, and smashing suits, but sometimes his proper demeanor intimidated the staff. Rumor had it that he was warm and approachable to the patients but tough and demanding on the staff. He cleared his throat and started the roll call for the patients.

"Three new admissions today," Rathwell announced. "Julie Appleton, Caucasian female, twenty-nine years old. Fibromyalgia and agoraphobia. Hasn't left her apartment in seven years.

Tripped over her cat and smashed her foot. Neighbor heard her screaming. Called 911. Compound fracture of the left ankle. Non-weight bearing on crutches and lives in a third-floor walk-up, so she can't go home. Tylenol for pain. Refuses psychotropic meds even though she's been informed that low-dose tricyclics may relieve muscle pain from the fibro. Won't leave her room and was hysterical on orthopedics."

"Psych consult?" Allison inquired.

"She's been seeing Deschamps but isn't keen on him. Had to be given Xanax against her will last night and was quite upset about it."

Andre Deschamps. Talented guy but no bedside manner. He would have been better off in research, I thought.

"Would you like me to try to talk to her?" Joanna, the social worker, asked.

"It's worth a try," Rathwell replied. "I'm not optimistic about talk therapy, but physio won't get anywhere with her in this shape. I'm going to ring Deschamps to discuss her objections to medication."

Evan Steinberg, the rehab medicine specialist, said, "I'll check for swelling in that ankle." He turned to Tron, the physiotherapist. "Assess the joint, and have her exercise in her room until we get a better handle on her psych problem."

"Next," Rathwell said. "Justin Drake. Caucasian male, age fifty-two. Legally blind from retinitis pigmentosa. Won't use a cane. Cut his hand making supper. Sliced into the flexor tendon, couldn't move his index finger, required surgery. Needs physio and extensive OT since it's his dominant hand. Recently divorced. Lives alone. We're holding him for two weeks to help him regain functionality. After that, we'll release him to one of the retirement homes until he can manage on his own."

Tron agreed to visit Justin, and Joanna offered to call the retirement homes to see who had vacancies. Rehab has changed a lot in the last twenty years. Hospital stays have become much shorter. On the one hand, patients no longer have the luxury of spending months adjusting to their new disability, nor do they have as many resources as they had in the past. On the other hand, shorter stays mean that patients are much more likely to go home or into an appropriate care facility as soon as possible.

"Last lucky lady, Lily Yokomoto. Asian female, age sixty-seven. Revision arthroplasty. Had her first hip replaced three years ago. Developed an infection, and had to have it redone. Married. Husband had back surgery last year and can't cope with her at home."

Rathwell stopped to remove his suit jacket. Most of the doctors don't wear suits anymore; Rathwell was old school. He reached across the table for his glass of ice water.

"Takes Lipitor, twenty milligrams a day, Synthroid, 100 micrograms, and Oxycocet, ten milligrams PRN for pain. Jennifer, take her for physio. and Catherine, I'd like you to see her for OT."

Rathwell continued his update on the other patients on the floor. A young woman with chronic lymphocytic leukemia had just received a bone marrow transplant. My feisty 101-year-old was recovering from pneumonia. A diabetic had lost three toes on his right foot to gangrene. And we had one stroke victim, an amputee, a woman with MS, and a total of two hips and one knee replacements.

One by one, the team reviewed the patients' individual needs to determine who would require speech therapy, physical therapy, grief counseling, additional medical and psychiatric consults, and assessments by social work or home care. I was assigned to the cancer case, the old man, the diabetic, one hip, one knee, and—to my dismay—the unwieldy agoraphobic.

As Rathwell cited the various injuries and illnesses of our new clientele, I tried to feel for these poor unfortunates. But I lacked empathy. My well of compassion ran dry long ago and was replaced by a brusque clinical manner. Once when I was leaving the room of an outspoken patient, I heard her call me "Nurse Ratched." That hurt, but I couldn't afford to over-identify with the patients anymore. In the past, I had tried too hard to help. I took the patients' problems home with me. On occasion, I had even given them my home phone number.

Now I was always on guard against losing myself emotionally in the quicksand of their illnesses. Sometimes, this manifested itself as coldness toward the patients, which was not what I felt. What I felt was much more conflicted and complicated. I did care about them, and I did want them to recover. I just doubted my own ability and that of modern medicine to put them back on their feet.

I decided to do the most unpleasant task first. Thus, I made my way through the cluttered corridor to see Julie Appleton. I didn't know how the patients managed to walk at all in the hallway. There were carts full of fresh sheets and towels, laundry baskets, empty wheelchairs, medication carts, blood-pressure machines, and stretchers lining the corridor. The rooms were a bland, cream color, but the bedspreads were a screaming yellow, red, or robin's blue.

Julie hadn't left her third-floor apartment since the onset of the new millennium. She was a small, thin girl with long, stringy brown hair, a sallow complexion, and wire-rimmed glasses. Already awake—she probably hadn't slept all night—Julie was huddled in a chair in the corner of the room, peering out the window. She was wearing two hospital gowns, one that tied in the front and the other that tied in the back. It was customary for patients to wear hospital gowns in other wards, but we preferred our patients to dress in their street garb on the rehab unit.

I wondered if Julie had been able to get her clothes from home. She was single and had been imprisoned in her house for years. How did she buy clothes that fit? What would her social life be like? Did she have any family in town? How could an agoraphobic keep up her friendships?

I didn't understand panic disorder. I wasn't the nervous type. When I felt pressured, I overate, and that calmed me down. But according to what I'd read, panic attacks could be debilitating. Some practitioners believed that the feelings of terror were caused by severe trauma like a car accident, war, or sexual assault. Others argued that certain people were biologically predisposed to panic. Some had attacks without any provocation, and others felt fine until a stressful life event or hormonal imbalance triggered the condition. My understanding was that panic and agoraphobia were treatable with drugs and behavior therapy, but the sufferer had to agree to the treatment. In addition, Julie's symptoms would be compounded by her chronic fatigue syndrome.

Julie's roommate was my hip replacement case. She was a strong-willed woman in her mid-seventies, who had been on the ward for ten days, which was ten days too long for me. Eleanor was a chronic complainer. She moaned about everything from the pain in her leg to her defective TV set and was distressed by the slow response of the nursing staff when she repeatedly pushed her call bell.

I forced myself to smile at Eleanor and said, "Good Morning."

"What's so good about it?" Eleanor grumbled.

I ignored her comment and tried to summon sympathy for this widow, who had been in excellent health until a man knocked into her in a shopping mall and fractured her hip. I helped Eleanor to bathe and dress before physio arrived. She cursed the anti-embolism stockings that she was forced to wear for her poor swollen leg.

My mind drifted off to Alain. I envisioned him breaking his leg and lying helplessly in a hospital bed. I would take care of him and nurse him back to health. I would caress his good leg to get the circulation moving, and he would beam at me with gratitude. Alain would fall in love with me. I would leave Mark and fly off with Alain to Montreal, a more cosmopolitan city.

"What's making you so happy today?" Eleanor asked. "I don't know what you're on, but I want some!"

"Just, uh, planning my summer holiday," I said lamely, finishing with Eleanor as Tron arrived to take her to the gym for physical therapy. Now I could concentrate on Julie.

I approached Julie and introduced myself. She was shivering, sitting rigidly with her arms clasped to her chest, and barely responded to me. Was she also reacting to Eleanor's negativity? I made a mental note to discuss a possible room change with Allison.

Gingerly, I sat down on the bed across from Julie, careful not to knock into her crutches, which were propped up against the empty beige wall. I offered to help her bathe.

Julie looked unsteady when she got up on the crutches. She

towered over me by at least four inches. I went to put my hands on her waist to ensure that she didn't fall, but she shouted at me, so I backed off. With caution, Julie made her way from the chair to the bed while I prepared a basin for her. She seemed angry when I asked how she was feeling.

"How do you think I'm feeling?" Julie snarled. "I've had panic attacks ever since 1995. Tried everything from meds to behavior therapy to psychic healing. I've seen homeopaths, chiropractors, psychiatrists, psychologists, and nutritionists. I've had ozone therapy and gone off gluten and dairy. Read all the books on panic and chronic fatigue syndrome. God, I could write one myself! But nothing's worked for me.

"The panic and exhaustion keep getting more intense, although it's weird because sometimes I have bursts of energy that come out of nowhere, but they disappear just as fast as they arrive, and I feel worse afterward. Anyway, eventually, I started resting more and stopped going out, and the attacks eased up. Now, this happened, and I was forced to come here."

"I know how frustrating that must be for you," I said, hoping that some kind words might calm her ire.

"No, you don't! Have you ever been trapped in your house? Unable to walk to the corner store to get a video? Can't go out with your friends week after week, month after month, until finally, people stop asking? Had to let your driver's license expire because you couldn't get to the DMV to have your photo taken?" Julie stopped talking while I washed her back and the area around her ankle cast.

"I'm sorry. You're right. I've never been through anything even remotely similar. I was only trying to let you know how bad I feel for you." My words sounded hollow. Clichés and platitudes: that's all I had left to offer the patients now.

"I don't want your pity," Julie stated. "I just want this to go away. Everyone keeps pushing Xanax on me. The other day I had a horrible anxiety attack in orthopedics, and the shrink made me take 5 mg of Xanax. Xanax doubles my anxiety. It shouldn't, but it does. It makes me really jumpy. I'm already half out of my mind just being here. I'm so goddamn tired, and I'm in pain! My ankle hurts like hell. I'm not seeing that man again. I don't care what you say. You can't make me see him."

I asked Julie if she wanted some Percocet; she declined, explaining that pain meds gave her headaches. I reminded her that she should be elevating her leg and went off to get an ice pack and some extra pillows so that she could prop her leg up. On my way out of the room, I noticed several chocolate bar wrappers next to her night table and wondered how she had managed to get them. Maybe one of the orderlies or volunteers had brought them in for her.

When I returned, I broached the subject of the psychiatrist. It was critical for her to work with Deschamps. She needed to walk the long hospital corridors and get to the gym for physical therapy to maintain the muscle strength in her legs. Surely Xanax wasn't the only medication for panic disorder. I asked if she'd tried antidepressants, and Julie rolled off a long list for me, properly pronouncing the names and dosages of all of them.

It was evident that this intelligent woman had done her homework and knew far more than I did about panic and agoraphobia. Normally, I would simply have discussed her dislike of Deschamps with Rathwell. But something about Julie's predicament moved me. She was young, smart, and driven. She wanted to get well. Unlike Eleanor, Julie could be resurrected.

She could have a second chance, but she needed someone to throw her a lifeline.

Ugh. I didn't have the energy to get involved in one of my patient's dramas. Rathwell was going to love the fact that already I was trying to change her psychiatrist and her roommate.

Luckily, the cleaning staff came in right after I finished my conversation with Julie. I don't think she would have been as candid with me if another staff member had been in the room. I nodded at Fowsia, the cleaning woman. She was from Somalia and had been a radiologist there, but those credentials were of no use to her in Canada. It was shocking to discover how many of the blue-collar workers at the hospital had degrees from other countries. Talk about underutilizing talent.

The day passed uneventfully. I made small talk with the RP patient, who turned out to be a photographer. Justin Drake was no victim. Even though he could barely see any of his pictures, he continued to take photos for other people to enjoy. Sometimes his photos were disembodied: a glimpse of a doorjamb, part of someone's body missing the head, the bottom of the refrigerator. Justin captured bits and pieces of life the way he "saw" it.

Retinitis pigmentosa is a degenerative disease of the retina, which causes a steady loss of peripheral and depth vision. The afflicted can't see in the dark and often become color blind. They see life through a tunnel that gets smaller every year. Instead of being bitter about this, Justin was philosophical. He told me that most of us have a sense of entitlement about our health. We expect to be able to see, believing that it's our right.

"You have been told that life is darkness, and in your weariness, you echo what was said by the weary," Justin declared.

"Who said that?" I asked. "Gandhi?"

"Kahil Gibran," Justin replied. "We all face different types of darkness, and we're all blind about life in some respects. I can't see well literally, but I see in my heart.

"Walking, talking, seeing. They're all gifts. None of them is our birthright. Life gives and sometimes, ah, sadly, life takes away. I'm grateful just to be in one piece, after nearly cutting off my hand."

There were bruises all over Justin's legs that I noticed when I helped him to wash. He told me that people with RP were continually banging into things.

"Tables, large chairs, even small children. Especially small children! I'm always knocking them over. It's an occupational hazard for someone with RP," he said. "I have an appointment to see that OT. What's her name? Crystal?"

"Catherine."

"Yeah, Catherine. My roommate said that she's fabulous. She took him to a simulated kitchen and bathroom here in the hospital."

"You'd be amazed at how many things you can do in that miniature kitchen. I've watched Catherine whip up an entire lunch that looks more appetizing than the food in the cafeteria downstairs," I reflected, as I checked his hand for signs of infection and reminded Justin not to move his afflicted finger. "But it may be a while before you can fix yourself a snack, let alone a full meal."

"I have all the time in the world, Tara. I'm a very patient man. Ha ha!" He laughed at his own pun about being a patient, and I couldn't help but admire his spirit.

My job definitely helped to keep my life in perspective when

I felt discouraged. Without exception, every person in my ward was in worse shape than I was.

I asked Justin why he refused to use a white cane, and he replied that often, people with RP didn't need a cane. Although they were legally blind, many retained partial vision. Justin didn't think of himself as a blind man; he viewed himself as someone who was partially sighted. And he preferred to maintain his dignity by passing as a fully sighted person whenever possible. I considered this to be dangerous, but I respected his courage and tenacity.

As I left his room, I heard Justin fumble for the radio, and the sweet sound of Mozart filled the room. What a cultured and refined man he was. I felt small in comparison and embarrassed that I rarely listened to the CBC radio, much preferring the mind-numbing effects of lightweight music.

At noon, I helped to serve the patients in our small cafeteria. We had a poster on the door that said, "Hard Rock Café." What a joke. It would have taken a wild stretch of the imagination to envision anyone on our floor, including the staff, rocking in anything except a hammock or wicker chair.

All the patients managed to get to the lunch room except for Julie and Erwin, the diabetic who was having trouble with his insulin levels. The kitchen delivered the meals with some mushy looking chicken tetrazzini. I passed out trays, filled a large pitcher with water, and asked who wanted Coke, juice, or diet soda.

All the while, I was wondering where Alain was and if he had finished his lunch. Was he standing outside the supermarket, smoking and looking over at the students on the lawn of Merivale High School? Did any of the sexy co-eds appeal to him? Girls today wore so little clothes. I couldn't imagine how the boys could get any work done with so much supple, young flesh exposed around them.

After lunch, I returned to the nursing station to catch up on my paperwork. The station was covered with charts, flowers, a big bulletin board with names of the patients on it, a fan, fax machine, figurines, and some droopy looking plants. I made phone calls to doctors and followed-up on various tests that were scheduled for my patients. I had two reports due by tomorrow, so I scribbled out my notes about patients' progress toward their goals and commented on any problems they were having.

I spent my afternoon doing paperwork, making the beds that I had missed in the morning, organizing consultations, and arranging the room change for Julie. Allison and I decided to put Eleanor in with another older woman who was hard of hearing. We moved Rebecca West, the eighteen-year-old bone marrow transplant patient, in with Julie.

I grabbed a quick dinner downstairs—mostly starch—and dropped two sugars into my coffee to survive the rest of my shift. Then I went to check on my 101-year-old. Alfred Erickson was quite a character. He was in the early stages of Alzheimer's. Sometimes he was lucid, but other times, he was delusional. Hopefully, at his age, he wouldn't live long enough to suffer the full ravages of that merciless disease.

Alfred was in the rehab unit because he was recovering from pneumonia. The last time I saw him, he thought that I was Mary Walsh, a comedian from *This Hour Has 22 Minutes*. Walsh also conducts an open book discussion group, which Alfred enjoys watching, although he's never read any of the books that the group analyzes. Tonight, Alfred didn't remember me at all.

"What do you want?" Alfred asked. He was propped up in

bed watching *National Geographic*. His hearing aid sat on the table next to him, so it was unlikely that he was able to follow any of the program.

"Hello, Mr. Erickson. I wanted to check in on you again before I left for the night. How are you feeling?"

"You're too tall!"

"I'm the same height that I was this morning," I said, feeling as though I should apologize.

"No, I had a shorter nurse this morning. Bring me back the shorter nurse," he said, flicking the channel. Up close, his skin looked like fine wrinkled parchment paper. Pieces of the chicken tetrazzini that he'd eaten for lunch had landed on his pajama top.

"Sorry, everyone on duty is over six feet tonight. It's the NBA league."

"What's that?"

"We'll be changing shifts soon. Now, I want you to take this pill before I go," I implored, as I looked over at Alfred's roommate, who was sleeping on his side with his underwear in full view. I wondered if Alain wore boxers or briefs.

"I don't want any vitamins. I get all the vitamins I need in my three squares. Take your goddamn vitamins and stick them where the sun don't shine!" He turned back to the television.

"Mr. Erickson."

"Sssh. Can't you see that I'm busy now? I'm going to be on the six o'clock news. I've won the Nobel Peace Prize for my work with Jimmy Carter. They're going to be announcing it any time now."

"I need you to take this medication for your pneumonia."

"I don't have pneumonia anymore. God took my pneumonia away. Isn't that wonderful? Yes, He took it from me and gave it to the boy down the hall."

"Well." I hated to lie to the patients even when it was absolutely necessary. "God gave me a message for you. He said that there was one essential vitamin missing from the hospital menu."

"God said that, eh?"

"Yes, He did."

"Are you sure that it was God? You didn't confuse Him with somebody else?"

"Absolutely certain."

"Well, okay then," Alfred agreed. "But skedaddle now, so that I don't miss my award."

CHAPTER FOUR

Not much changed during the first week that Julie and Justin arrived on the rehab floor. Julie got along much better with Rebecca than she did with Eleanor, but she refused to see the psychiatrist again or to leave her room. This was a serious problem for Tron, the physical therapist. Julie needed to walk every day in order to maintain her strength.

Prolonged bed rest could significantly weaken even a robust and healthy person. That was why we got patients up right away after surgery. Julie was up all right, but she spent most of her time sitting in a chair, and the farthest that she had walked so far—or crutched, to be more accurate—was from her bed to the bathroom.

Each time she attempted to leave her room, she had a panic attack and felt like fainting; the only things that made her feel better were chocolate bars and orange juice, not exactly what the dietitian had in mind. Given the nature of Julie's injury, we couldn't afford to have her passing out. She could seriously damage her ankle that way and might require additional surgery. It was a dilemma that stumped us all from Rathwell to Deschamps, as well as the physios and occupational therapists.

Sundays were slow at the hospital. Maintenance crews cleaned the floors with huge orange vacuum cleaners—an unenviable job. There were no physical therapies or structured programs on Sunday.

Some of the patients had visitors in their rooms, and occasionally, they'd take a day pass to go home for six hours. Many of my people slept the day away, lying in dark rooms where the shades hadn't been opened. One was working diligently on a puzzle in the lunch room, and two others were sitting up in their rooms watching the boob tube.

A few brave souls were trying to ambulate in the hallway on their own. One gentleman looked so unsteady on his walker that I thought he might plunge to the floor at any moment. I kept a close eye on him. He was talking to a female patient, who was wearing bright plaid pants, black-and-white sneakers, and a blue, oversized sleeveless top. No one would be winning any fashion contests on this floor. Most of the patients dressed comfortably in old clothes that looked as though they had been rifled from the Salvation Army bag.

On the last day of my thirty-six-hour run, Joanna, the social worker, announced that she had contacted the Anxiety Disorders Association of Ontario and discussed Julie with them. Joanna discovered that the ADAO ran a companion volunteer program where they sent out a trained volunteer to meet with the person who had panic attacks. The client and the volunteer devised a plan of action, which consisted of setting small but attainable goals.

In her mind, Julie had drawn a line between the end of her hospital room and the beginning of the hallway. She now felt relatively safe within the confines of her room but could not set foot into the corridor without shaking or having palpitations.

The anxiety volunteer would sit down with Julie and have her describe her fear of what may happen if she left the room. They would practice relaxation exercises where Julie would imagine stepping out into the hall without panicking. Or Julie would picture herself having a panic attack and talking herself out of it with positive and calming thoughts such as, "This will pass. I've felt this way hundreds of times before, and it's never killed me. I will not let this condition destroy my life."

The social worker and I were hopeful that Julie would get along with Don, her new volunteer. Julie had already called him, and he was planning to visit her tomorrow. I was sorry that I would miss hearing about the visit, but I knew Julie wasn't leaving us any time soon.

I suspected that because Julie had already tried behavior exposure therapy and it was unsuccessful, the severity of her panic disorder necessitated medication. She was scheduled to see another psychiatrist, Renee Blanc. It was hard for me to persuade Rathwell to do this, but he finally conceded that Julie wouldn't make any progress with a psychiatrist she despised. Also, I planned to do some sleuthing on my own on the Internet to see what other drugs were effective for her condition.

The Information Superhighway was a mystery to me. I was always getting lost and spending countless hours trying to accomplish tasks online. Devon was supposed to be teaching me how to surf, but he rarely gave me any time. Maybe Mark would help me.

I finished my paperwork and dictated my report on the status of the patients for the next nurse on duty. I grabbed my ski jacket and waved goodbye to Jean-Claude before I left the hospital. Now I could devote my attention to my impure thoughts about Alain.

Pictures of him had been protruding into my mind hourly, but I'd forced myself to disregard them while I'd been at work. Now I could indulge in my sweet fantasies once again. I turned the radio up loud in the car, rolled my window down a bit, and sang along to the music, picturing Alain's jet-black hair and angular jaw. How I yearned to run my hand along the side of his beautiful face, to slowly unbutton his shirt, and to touch his strong, muscular chest.

Passing the Dairy Queen gave me a sudden craving for a chocolate sundae with butterscotch sauce, but a vivid picture of Alain's girlfriend floated through my head. I'd never met her nor would I want to, but he spoke of her frequently and with pride. She was a certified accountant, he boasted. I envisioned her as petite with long blonde hair in a ponytail. She would be terminally cheerful and would wear a size two dress. No, maybe she was too young for dresses. Did twentysomethings wear dresses anymore? I thought that I had seen them in short skirts.

My imagined rival would be irresistible. She would be a constant source of moral support, sexual stimulation, and encouragement to Alain. She certainly would not be gorging herself on an enormous chocolate sundae on her way home from work. This graphic, albeit fantasy, image of Alain's partner horrified me but succeeded in giving me the willpower I needed to bypass the DQ.

I was exhausted when I got home. It was Sunday night, and I was looking forward to a relaxing evening. I'd put on my jogging suit, throw together a quick dinner, review Devon's homework with him, and watch the episode of *Nip/Tuck* that I'd rented on DVD.

Mark was playing basketball at the university gym with his friends. He didn't belong to a league. Instead, he played "pickup," meaning that he shot hoops with whomever showed up that night.

Devon was in the kitchen, talking to his best friend, Jess, on the portable phone.

"Mum?" Devon asked. "Can I go over to Jess's to watch *Family Guy*?" Jess was even less receptive to adults than Devon and didn't have much discipline at home. His father had died suddenly of liver disease two years ago, and Jess's mother, Lucinda, had been struggling to raise him with her new husband, a man Jess despised.

I didn't want him going over to Jess's because the two of them had been out late last night, and Mark had texted me saying that Devon had slept in all morning. I never knew what those kids were up to, and the neighborhood seemed dangerous now that people were setting fires, but it was futile to argue with Dev over something so banal.

"As long as you've finished studying for that geometry quiz," I said. Most kids Devon's age were taking algebra, but he was gifted in math, so the school had moved him up to geometry. Not that gifted, mind you, because if he'd really applied himself, he would be taking Algebra II.

"Take the dog for a walk first," I added, as Monday jumped up on me, his paws wet from the garden. Devon groaned but seemed anxious to escape from the house.

"Will you pick me up at Dr. Wong's tomorrow? I can take the bus there from school, but I'm, like, probably going to feel like crap afterward," Devon said.

"I thought you were just at the dentist."

"I was. He recommended an endodontist for a root canal."

"Root canal? Haven't you been flossing? How many times do I have to remind you?"

"Thanks for the support, Mum. Screw it. I'll take the bus home."

"I wasn't trying to be unsympathetic, Dev," I said, silently calculating how much our dental plan would pay toward a root canal and then a crown." It's just that you could avoid a lot of grief by brushing your teeth more often and chewing sugar-free gum."

"You're such a pain in the ass, Mum. You just can't see yourself."

"Don't you dare speak to me like that," I replied. "I'll be there on Thursday," I added, right before Devon slammed the door and left the house without taking the dog. Monday barked. I frowned. Communicating with the kid was impossible. I always said the wrong thing. Why couldn't I have just sympathized with his dental problems? Why did I have to criticize him every time he opened his mouth? He was only fourteen; I was supposed to be the adult in the relationship.

Now I was truly alone in the house. I took Monday for a short walk so that he could do his business. The argument with Devon had put me in a bad mood, but the prospect of time alone filled me with anticipation. Maybe I'd give myself a facial or color my hair since the henna was intolerable. Not a good idea. I had promised my hairdresser that I wouldn't touch my hair until I saw her again.

I could finish the mystery novel that had been sitting next to my bed for the last two months. Or I could start *The Bonesetter's Daughter* by Amy Tan, which I'd just bought on CD.

I made a tasty chicken stir-fry with mushrooms, green pepper, onion, and water chestnuts. I topped it off with some spicy garlic sauce, crispy chow mein noodles, and steamed rice. Pouring myself a large glass of Chianti, I felt uplifted again and was just about to eat when the phone rang. I had no interest in talking to anyone, but I checked the caller ID and saw that it was Lisa.

Automatically, I picked up the receiver, knowing that she was one of the few people in the world I could talk to with my mouth full or who would understand how much I looked forward to a degenerate evening of doing nothing. I couldn't wait to hear what she had decided to do about the pregnancy. Had she told Ryan?

I was also glad for the opportunity to apologize for my seeming righteousness. I still felt guilty about projecting such a judgmental attitude about sex that Lisa had been unable to confide in me about her liaison.

To my surprise, it was Ryan, not Lisa. "Have you heard from Lisa?" he asked in an abrupt tone. "I haven't seen her since Friday. She just took off. Didn't leave me a note or nothing. I thought maybe she was with you or had went up to the cottage." *Had went? Who spoke like that?*

"Me? No," I said, uncomfortable talking to Mensa Man. "We went to the movies on Thursday. She didn't mention going to the cottage. It's a little early in the season for that."

"I'm worried about her," Ryan said.

"Worried?" I was beginning to sound like a parrot. "Don't be silly, Ryan. Maybe she went to stay with her parents," I said, although I was dubious, given how distraught Lisa had been about the pregnancy.

Had she told Ryan about the baby? I couldn't violate her confidence by bringing it up, so I decided to play it safe and say nothing.

Our conversation was brief. Ryan and I rarely had much to say at the best of times.

"I'm gonna call the police and file a missing persons' report if she don't show up for work tomorrow morning," Ryan said. I was beginning to think that English was his second language. Maybe

Ryan had lied about finishing high school, and this was why Lisa found the B&E kid's love life so entertaining.

Why was he overreacting? Lisa might have spent the weekend with her parents, biding time before she told Ryan about the Indian guy. Her sponsor, Laura Anne, would know where she was. Lisa was more serious about her sobriety than anything else in her life. She called Laura Anne every morning like clockwork, especially since she had fallen off the wagon. Surely, the sponsor would have heard from her by now.

So much for my quiet relaxing evening at home. My dinner was cold, and I couldn't summon the energy to put it back in the microwave. I forced myself to eat a couple of bites, wrapped the rest up, and put it in the refrigerator while I poured myself another glass of wine. I tried not to picture Lisa drunk in a bar somewhere or scoring coke downtown. Maybe she'd decided not to tell Ryan and had gone away to make plans to abort the baby.

I checked my address book and quickly located Laura Anne's phone number. I called her, and she sounded alarmed. She hadn't heard from Lisa since Friday either. Lisa's failure to contact her sponsor was definitely suspicious. Perhaps Ryan had been right to be concerned.

On the other hand, maybe Lisa would appear at work on Monday and act as though nothing had happened. I didn't know what to do. It was 8:30 p.m. I couldn't decide if I should call the Campanas or wait until the morning. I didn't want to upset them. If Lisa showed up at the center tomorrow, I would have embarrassed her, and upset her parents for no reason.

After much deliberation, I decided not to take any action. I ran a hot bubble bath and soaked for a good half-hour, starting the talking book, *The Bonesetter's Daughter*.

It was the story of Ruth and her mother, LuLing. Amy Tan went back and forth between San Francisco and China in her multigenerational tale. I'd reached a critical point in the book where Ruth, a second-generation Chinese American, took her mother to the doctor because Ruth suspected that LuLing was suffering from depression.

My bathwater had cooled off, and I was freezing. I got out of the tub and looked at the CD player to find my place on the disc. It said that I was still on section one. I was confused since I'd been listening for almost forty minutes. I ejected the disc and inserted it once again; to my chagrin, there was only one section on the disc.

How could that be? The main reason I loved books on CD was that each disc was separated into six to twelve segments. I could listen to several segments in a row and manage to keep track of where I was in the book when I flipped the machine off. I rarely had one solid hour to sit and listen to a CD. Who did?

Feeling resigned, I decided that I would listen to *The Bonesetter's Daughter* in the car. That way, I could hear half the disc on the way to work and the other half on the way back. But I wasn't happy about the arrangement because I preferred to listen to music in the car.

After my bath, I dried my hair, applying a special conditioner that I'd bought to restore the luster to my over-processed, limp mane. I used an expensive exfoliant, followed by an astringent on my face, and went downstairs. After I reheated my dinner, I sat down on the worn, blue velvet couch in the family room and watched *Nip/Tuck*.

Sean's son, Matt, was attempting to circumcise himself because his doctor father refused to listen when Matt complained that being uncircumcised made him self-conscious and served as an impediment to his sex life. Matt hadn't been circumcised at birth because he'd been born prematurely.

I could hardly watch. The very thought of the boy taking a knife to the Crown Jewels filled me with pity and revulsion. What a great nurse I was! I felt much more compassion for characters on adult soap operas than I did for real live folks in the rehab center. Matt was bleeding profusely. It was obvious that he would have to call his parents for help when Devon and Mark walked in together.

They must have met up in the driveway because I heard their loud male voices in the garage. I asked Dev about his evening, and he gave me perfunctory replies. Devon doesn't provide many details about his personal life, but he did mention that a girl named Tabatha had been watching TV with them: someone that Jess met at the bowling alley. Devon wasn't dating anyone yet, which made me happy because it was one less thing I had to worry about in his tumultuous teen life.

Mark told me all about his basketball game, but I found it hard to concentrate. My mind kept wandering back to Ryan's phone call. I still didn't want to tell Mark anything about Lisa. It seemed like such a girl thing. She had trusted me, and I didn't want to betray her. Moreover, I didn't want him to judge Lisa for her infidelity or the possibility that she had slipped again when her life had been going so well.

We made small talk about his evening, and Mark went upstairs. I finished the end of *Nip/Tuck*. Matt's father and his plastic surgeon partner fixed him up. That didn't seem very realistic. How often did surgeons operate on their own kids? But basically, it had been an enjoyable episode.

Disturbed about Lisa, I went up to bed around 10:30. I was exhausted and wanted to go to sleep earlier, but I tried not to go to bed at the same time as Mark anymore. He knew I was avoiding him sexually, but he wasn't a very assertive guy. He couldn't talk about his feelings. It was much easier for Mark to make a physical move than it was for him to ask me what was wrong with our sex life. It was cold and selfish of me not to explain my disinterest to him, but I didn't know what to say. How could I tell him that he used to arouse me, but that time was long gone?

CHAPTER FIVE

I loved Mondays. That was why I named the dog after the first day of the week. I had a friend once who liked the word honey so much that she named her first child Honey Sue; at the dinner table, my friend called everybody honey, and the poor child was constantly raising her head wondering if her mom was talking to her.

If I weren't working, I'd go to aerobics and do a series of errands on the first day of the week. I'd return home for a late lunch and save the grocery shopping for last. That way I had time to fix my makeup or adjust my wardrobe before I saw Alain.

Sometimes, I changed clothes three or four times before I encountered the Boy Wonder. One sweater seemed too tight and made me look fat. Another was a bad color, emphasizing my pale complexion. He must have thought that I had an extensive wardrobe because I never wore the same outfit twice in a row. Although I had difficulty remembering what someone said to me thirty minutes ago, I could always recall precisely what I wore the last time I saw Alain.

I usually arrived at the store during Alain's afternoon break. We would talk for fifteen or twenty minutes outside while he smoked and devoured a large Pepsi. When his time was up, we would go back into the store, and I'd choose my meat.

For weeks, I'd been trying to get up the courage to ask Alain if he'd like to have lunch with me at Montana's, but I was afraid that he would turn me down because of his girlfriend. Moreover, once we left the confines of the grocery store, there would be no going back. We would no longer be constrained by the manager

/customer relationship. I'd be free to say and do whatever I pleased, and that scared me.

I had a feeling of dread rather than anticipation on this chilly Monday morning. First, I called Straight and Narrow to see if Lisa had shown up at work. She hadn't. Bad news. Lisa would never miss work.

My fear was mounting as I dialed Ryan's number. He confirmed that Lisa hadn't come home on Sunday night either, so he'd called the police to file a missing person's report this morning.

"They sent a cop out here. Asked a million questions like what was she wearing, did she have any medical problems, was she new to Ottawa?"

Ryan provided the officer with names of Lisa's friends, acquaintances, old boyfriends, colleagues, and family members. I asked if he had contacted the Campanas. Ryan said no. The Campanas had never been fond of him, and the police had promised to call Lisa's parents. I offered to go over to see them. They didn't leave for work until late in the afternoon on Mondays. Ryan declared how much he loved Lisa and that he couldn't function without her. I affirmed that we'd find her soon, and we hung up.

The Campanas lived in an old sixties type neighborhood off Meadowlands Drive. They had a modest, sprawling ranch with huge, barren trees in the backyard. Soon the birds would chirp, cherry trees would flower, and their little hedge would blossom. When the trees were in bloom, the majestic oaks and maples curved right over the road.

Lisa told me that some parts of New Jersey resembled a jungle. The trees were massive and bent, and the streets were so narrow and hilly that the trees met overhead on the road, forming a tunnel.

Lisa and I had always wanted to visit her old hometown in Jersey and to storm Manhattan. I'd never been to the Metropolitan Museum of Art, the Museum of Natural History, or the Cloisters. Lisa raved about the Staten Island Ferry and the scrumptious food in Chinatown. She insisted that we go to Mama Leone's, the Italian restaurant in the Billy Joel song, and to see a play on Broadway. We talked about our prospective adventure all the time but had never committed to a date.

Reluctantly, I rang the Campana's front doorbell. Lorenzo Campana opened the door. It's funny being almost forty. All my life, I've called Anna and Lorenzo "Mr." and "Mrs.," but recently, Mrs. Campana asked me to call her Anna. It was hard to break the lifelong habit of calling her Mrs. Campana, so now I called her Anna sometimes, and other times, I called her Mrs. Campana. Usually, I just mumbled something unintelligible when I saw her because I couldn't decide which term was more appropriate.

I would feel ridiculous calling Mr. Campana "Lorenzo" since he was a proper, old-world gentleman. Consequently, I always addressed him as "Mister." The issue of titles had become awkward, but first names versus surnames were the least of my worries on this cloudy April morning.

"Tara, my dear," Mr. Campana said with enthusiasm. "It's been too long since you came to see us. Come in, Tara!" He never missed an opportunity to call me by name, which he pronounced as "Tira." Sometimes he'd use my name fifteen or twenty times in a single conversation. I found this endearing, even if his pronunciation was slightly off the mark. I was accustomed to that. For some reason, people had trouble with my name. They called me Karen, Sarah, Tina, or my personal favorite, Sharon.

After a lifetime of continuously spelling my first name and my street address, I swore that I would give my child an ordinary Anglo-Saxon name like James or David. But naturally, I fell in love with the name Devon. Dev didn't like his name any more than I liked mine, and he hated being mistaken for the opposite gender. He received mail on a regular basis addressed to "Ms. Devon Richards."

It was clear from his sunny disposition that no one had spoken to Mr. Campana about Lisa. I swallowed several times to get rid of the lump in my throat. I didn't want to be the first one to tell him. Mr. Campana had had bypass surgery last year. He'd made a good recovery but wasn't as strong as he used to be. He didn't need any additional stress in his life.

As he ushered me into their cozy living room, Mrs. Campana rolled around the corner, carrying a newspaper and a cup of coffee. She was a heavyset woman with thick, furry eyebrows, black hair with streaks of gray, and a slight mustache. She usually wore an oversized housedress with sandals. In the winter, she wore her sandals with socks. At the restaurant, Anna dressed up in full-length black skirts with blousy tops and long strands of pearls.

Her husband was equally stout and well-fed. He had a square chin and a long receding hairline with white hair.

"Sweetheart!" Anna Campana said. "I knew I recognized that voice. I have fresh muffins in the oven. Since she went on that crazy diet, Lisa won't touch my baking, but you will eat with me."

The smell was heavenly and brought back memories of Sunday mornings long ago when Lisa and I sat around her kitchen table talking about everything from disappointing boyfriends to current events to the teachers we liked least in university. I wanted so badly to sit down and gorge myself on oatmeal raisin muffins and pretend that nothing was wrong, but I had to break the distressing news.

I said that I hadn't seen Lisa since Thursday night when we went to the ByTowne. I was really afraid now that I was withholding essential information. Surely, I would have to tell the police about Lisa's pregnancy but should I also relay this private news to her parents? Who was I to decide what was pertinent when someone had disappeared?

No matter how many years the Campanas had been in Ottawa, at heart, they were traditional, first-generation Italian Catholics. It had taken ages for them to come to terms with the fact that their daughter had an alcohol problem. Promiscuity was another matter altogether.

Mrs. Campana looked alarmed. "I knew something would happen to her, working with those homeless people and homosexuals!" She dropped her knife. This was not the time to remind Lisa's mom that there was no connection between homelessness and homosexuality.

"She's been drinking again, Tara?" Mr. Campana asked.

"It looks that way. She hasn't contacted anyone including her sponsor since Thursday. And you know Lisa. Never misses a day's work."

"Like her old man. She's a hard worker, my Lisa." Mr. Campana beamed with pride.

"We should never have moved to this country," Anna Campana declared. "So our children will be safe, we leave Nutley and now this. I never approved of her working with those street people. And she was starving herself. What do you call that?

Bulimia?"

Lorenzo put his arm around his wife and asked for more details. I told them about my conversations with Ryan, Laura Anne, and Straight and Narrow. We decided to go to the police station right away. I reassured Anna that everything would be all right, but I was silently cursing Lisa for causing her parents this anguish.

The three of us piled into my Saab. Driving along Meadowlands, Anna urged me to slow down.

"There are speed traps," she reminded me.

I was doing my usual ten kilometers over the speed limit. I can't drive thirty-five. It's not me; it's my car. It drives too fast. You'd think that I would have learned my lesson since I'd already gotten two tickets on this road, and one cost almost $100.

Acknowledging Anna's admonition, I put my foot on the brake and slowed down to go south on Woodroffe. I went west on Knoxdale, listening to the Campanas ruminate about Lisa's addiction and how different she was from her sister, Sandra. Sandra was "such a good girl." She "never got into any trouble."

That's probably because Sandra hadn't left the house since the Pierre Elliott Trudeau administration. She wasn't agoraphobic like Julie, but Lisa's sister had no interest whatsoever in socializing or dating. At thirty-seven, Sandra was content to live with her parents, working diligently at her quiet job in a flower shop. Lisa and I were convinced she was a virgin. We were willing to bet money on it.

Before I'd met the Campanas, Lisa had said to me, "Beware! My family is mental." But she'd said this with obvious affection. Anna was a little high strung, but she was warm, loving, and devoted. Both she and Lorenzo were fiercely intelligent and strong emotionally. Lisa was very close to her family, even though she and Sandra were polar opposites.

We pulled up to the Nepean division of the Ottawa Police station at 245 Greenbank Avenue. Nepean was a subdivision of Metro Ottawa. Technically, since the city amalgamated its boroughs, we all lived in Ottawa. However, because the area had been subdivided into Nepean, Kanata, Orleans, and Gloucester for so long, we were accustomed to using the names for the old locations. Each of the boroughs had their own police station. Since Lisa and Ryan lived in an area called Craig Henry, located in the west end of town, Ryan had called the Nepean police.

After several minutes of struggling, I located the visitors' parking lot, which was irrationally located before the entrance to the building. We walked over a broken curb and on to the cobblestone steps leading up to the front door. The station was an old brick building made out of concrete and glass. It looked dreary today because it had just started to rain.

There was an ominous sign on the front door stating, "PUBLIC NOTICE—if you have a suspicious envelope or parcel, do not enter this facility. Stay outside and use the phone on your left. Place the item in the yellow container and do not enter the building." I wondered how useful this information would be to prospective bombers delivering anthrax or firearms to our beloved agents of law enforcement.

The three of us entered the building looking as though we were preparing for a colonoscopy. We were nervous as hell. The waiting room was small but pleasant with comfortable chairs, and a large, empty pine table. To our left, there were a number of pamphlets about crime prevention and warnings against drinking and driving.

A picture of a deceased captain hung on the wall with a letter stating that the foyer had been dedicated to this man of distinction. There was a black artificial guide dog for the blind, which made me think about Justin Drake and his valiant struggle to navigate the world with tunnel vision.

I marched up to the counter and introduced myself to one of the two police officers on duty. He appeared to be in his late thirties with dark brown, curly hair, a slightly pudgy face, and sideburns that ran all the way down to his chin. Colin McCarthy was soft-spoken. He said that he was glad to see us since he had been planning to call Lisa's parents.

McCarthy offered us something to drink, which we politely declined, and led us into a small room in the back of the station. The conversation was a bit chaotic at first with me and the Campanas talking at the same time, and Anna having a separate conversation entirely with her hands.

Detective McCarthy took a step back and said, "Please, one at a time. There's no rush. I have all day." He spoke slowly and deliberately, and I began to feel a little more relaxed.

The Campanas started first, saying how worried they were about Lisa and how uncharacteristic it was of her not to have contacted anyone for three days. Even when Lisa was drinking, she called in sick to work. She never shrugged off her responsibilities.

Detective McCarthy asked me to describe my night out at the movies with Lisa and our snack at Nate's Deli. After much deliberation, I concluded that I had to tell the man about Lisa's pregnancy. If Lisa had started drinking again because she was afraid to tell Ryan that she was pregnant, the police needed to know.

McCarthy didn't blink when I told him about Lisa's liaison with the Indian man, but the Campanas gasped with horror. I felt guilty that I hadn't told them this salacious detail when we were alone. At least they would have been able to process it in privacy. I kept making one bad judgment call after another. First, I had criticized Devon about his dental care, and now I'd inadvertently hurt the Campanas by refusing to tell them about Lisa's fling earlier.

McCarthy made notes and asked a number of questions, including whether Lisa had any disgruntled clients and if anyone new had appeared in her life recently. We said no, but I reminded McCarthy that Ryan had a history of domestic violence. He assured me that the police were aware of this. He told us that he would be interviewing people at Lisa's office, the neighbors, Lisa's sponsor at AA, and anyone with whom she associated in the 12-step program.

The police would retrace Lisa's day on Friday to get a clear picture of what she had been doing. And they would check Lisa's credit cards and bank information to see if she'd used her ATM card or withdrawn any large sums of cash.

"Ninety to ninety-five percent of all missing people can be traced back through their banking transactions," McCarthy said. At the end of our interview, McCarthy stood up and shook our hands. His palm was warm and comforting, but his words held less promise.

"We'll talk to everyone who's been involved with Lisa. She's been gone now for three days. According to Ryan Whitman, she arrived home on Thursday evening at about 11 p.m., after she went to the movies with you, Karen. She went to work on Friday, so she must've disappeared sometime Friday night because she didn't make it home that night. We need to gather more data."

I wanted to tell him that my name wasn't Karen but thought it prudent to allow him to finish speaking.

"Meanwhile, details about Lisa will be entered into CPIC, the Canadian Police Information Center, which is a national computer system. If you know her AA sponsor or anyone from her former drinking life, you could speak to them. We'll be asking Ryan for Lisa's phone records, her bank statements, and a diary if she kept one." He put his mug down on the desk. "I assure you that I'll keep in touch and keep you in the loop."

"What about Ardeth Wood?" I asked. Ardeth Wood was a twenty-seven-year-old doctoral student at the University of Waterloo who came home to visit her parents in Ottawa last summer. One afternoon, she went out for a bike ride on the Aviation Parkway and was never seen again. Hundreds of people searched for the beautiful, brilliant philosophy student. Her body was found a few days later in a park, but her killer remained at large.

"That was completely different," McCarthy said. "Highly suspicious circumstances and a direct location. It was easy to get a search team assembled. But we have no reason to believe that your friend is in any immediate danger." McCarthy drew circles on the top of his legal pad. "Let us do our job. First things first, eh? We'll begin by meticulously retracing her steps. I'll be in touch," he said kindly, as he ushered us out of the office.

The ride home was tense. Anna and Lorenzo were mad at me for withholding information about Lisa's affair and the resulting pregnancy.

"What are you—trying to protect us? You think we live in the Dark Ages, Tara?" Anna asked me. "I don't care who my daughter sleeps with as long as she's alive!"

"Don't talk like that, Anna," Lorenzo reprimanded. "Of course, she's alive. She is simply in trouble with the alcohol and drugs again. We will find her, and she will come to her senses about Ryan. That she should have been so afraid of him not to have told him about the baby—that makes me angry."

We sat in the driveway a while, trying to decide what to do next. I volunteered to call Laura Anne to find out about Lisa's old watering holes. The Campanas deliberated over whether or not to call the newspaper. If Lisa had gone on a bender and booked a motel across the river, she would be humiliated beyond words to see her name all over the local papers. But that was so unlikely. Lisa had never left town before during a drinking binge, and she would not have missed work without calling in.

If she had come to some harm, and we refused to take action for fear of embarrassing her, we would never forgive ourselves. The Campanas concluded that they would contact the media.

I was glad to pull up in front of the Campana's house shortly after noon. We were all feeling volatile, and I knew that I had handled the situation badly. I said that I would call them every day until we heard from Lisa. Then I picked up a burger at McDonald's and was off to Canadian Tire, the video store to return *Finding Nemo* for Devon, and to the gas station to fill up my tank. Gas was more than $.90 a liter, which was shocking. I seemed to be receiving one surprise after another in my normally predictable life.

CHAPTER SIX

I had missed my aerobics class since I spent the morning with the Campanas and the police, so I forced myself to work out on the stationary bike at the YWCA. It was strange being alone because I enjoyed commiserating with the other reluctant gymnasts in my class, but the solitude allowed me to ponder the latest events. I thought about Devon while I peddled my sixteen kilometers and wondered why I had such difficulty talking to him. All he'd wanted was a little TLC for his tooth, but instead, I'd given him an obnoxious lecture.

Still, I couldn't win with Devon. If I had been kind or solicitous, he would have pushed me away because he's at that age where he needs to pretend that he doesn't need a mother. Unfortunately, my insensitive behavior had reinforced that very notion.

My mind shifted back and forth between Devon and Laura Anne. After I finished my cardio workout, I called Lisa's sponsor from my cell but only reached her voice mail.

Catching a glimpse of my bright henna hair in the mirror, I shuddered. I looked like I was on my way to a Halloween party.

I ran out of the exercise room down to the hairdressing parlor in the mall. Unfortunately, my regular hairdresser was on duty. I had been hoping to avoid her since she had chastised me last time for frying my hair. I babbled on about how hideous the color was, and Chan Juan took pity on me. She agreed to put in some blonde streaks.

"Not going to like it," Chan Juan declared. "Nobody want to put blonde in red hair. Better to dye hair brown. Much more natural looking. Make you look younger."

"I don't want brown! Brown is my original color. I want to look different," I emphasized, although I was instantly intrigued by her use of the term "younger" and tempted to try her suggestion.

"Going to look different all right," Chan Juan said. "Going to look like before picture on *Extreme Makeover*."

"Don't worry, Chan Juan. I don't have the emotional energy to sue you."

"Use heavy conditioner every night. Don't forget. Hair is stiff now and limp like rag doll," Chan Juan reprimanded.

I sat under the dryer thinking about Lisa. Where on earth could she be? Lisa didn't have much money. She had taken a tip from the movie *The Graduate*, which had correctly prophesied that plastic was the trend of the future. Lisa paid for everything on her credit cards. She owed about $12,000 on her VISA alone. Ryan's salary was meager since his work was seasonal, and he had a penchant for living off women. Lisa couldn't afford a motel.

She'd seemed so upset about her last slip. Sobriety was her whole life. I would have thought that after leaving me, she would've called Laura Anne, broken down and confessed that she had slept with the restaurant guy, discussed the pregnancy, and asked Laura Anne what to do.

Lisa also trusted her family doctor, a woman who was about our age. Why wouldn't she have approached the doctor and told her about her dilemma? She had eventually confided in me. The next step would have been to have called Laura Anne, unless she went home that night and told Ryan. Maybe he hadn't taken it well.

There was his battering history. What if Lisa had told Ryan

and he'd gotten mad, pushed her, shoved her, or hit her? Perhaps he'd abducted Lisa and hidden her in a trailer. He may have planned to keep her captive for the next six and a half months until she delivered the baby so that he could determine whether it was his. I'd seen a psycho-freak do that once on the British mystery series *Cracker*.

Detective McCarthy hadn't seemed much like Robby Coltrane, the slovenly but brainy, street smart, take-charge kind of guy who played the criminal psychologist in *Cracker* and solved the tough cases effortlessly. I'm not sure if we got through to McCarthy. He didn't seem that alarmed about Lisa's disappearance.

The bleach was starting to burn my scalp. It felt indulgent to be at the hairdresser's when my friend was in deep trouble. My stomach lurched, and suddenly, I wanted to get out of there. My heart pounded. I rang my bell for Chan Juan and tried positive self-talk. Bad things don't happen in Ottawa. They happen in Houston or Detroit, on *CSI* and *Law and Order*. Not here! What was I thinking? That Ryan had killed Lisa and buried her in the backyard with a shovel? Preposterous.

Chan Juan's prediction was on the money. My hair was hideous. I looked like Ozzy Osbourne on a bad day. My first impulse was to take the large pair of scissors on the counter and chop the whole thing off, but Chan Juan grabbed my hand as I reached for them.

"Told you," Chan Juan giggled. "No worries! Will look much better in week or two, especially with nightly conditioner. Don't forget!"

So much for giving myself a psychological boost in the midst of the crisis. By the time I checked my watch, I realized that

Alain's shift was over, and I wouldn't be able to see him. What a day this was turning out to be.

A group of Muslim girls was in front of me as I walked toward the car. They were wearing long scarves on their heads. How did they feel when they passed the Gap or the Levi store? Left out? Disenfranchised? I didn't question their religious beliefs, but I did feel sorry for kids who went to school in traditional garb when their classmates were wearing sexy tube tops and skin-tight jeans. The Muslim girls must die of the heat in the summer, too, but I could have used one of their hijabs today to cover the disastrous mess that I'd made out of my hair.

Those kids wouldn't have to worry about their hair at all. They could grow it down to their waist, crop it off with a razor, and forget about washing it for weeks at a time. Who would know except their parents? In some respects, it would be liberating not to be so preoccupied with appearance, but it was a bit late for me to convert to Islam.

When I returned home without any groceries, Devon was sitting in the family room, watching TV and looking like a chipmunk. His face was swollen and bruised, and he glared at me, refusing to speak. Oh, my God. His root canal! The appointment had slipped my mind. I'd been so preoccupied with Lisa that I had forgotten. *Lisa, Alain, and my hair*, I thought. I felt woefully negligent and didn't know how to make up for it.

We were out of food, and there was nothing soft in the house for Devon to eat. I asked if he wanted to go to the store, promising him the DVD of his choice, which ended up being *Kill Bill*—yet another gratuitously violent movie by Quentin Tarantino.

I didn't go to Loeb but rather to Loblaws where I bought four large strip steaks, potatoes, broccoli, an under-ripe avocado, romaine lettuce, and whole wheat bread. I picked up special soup for Devon at the deli, some ice cream, and two vanilla yogurts. Wishful thinking on my part. Devon hated yogurt although it was better for him than ice cream.

Laura Anne called when we were driving home. She was a character. A long-time member of Unity Church, Laura Anne was devoted to metaphysics, Reiki, and her Tarot cards. I could hardly hear her on her hands-free phone. It was a bad connection, and we spent several minutes talking about the static.

"Can you hear me?" I shouted.

"I can't hear you too well, Tara. What didja say?"

"I'm going to hang up and call you again."

"Sorry, I didn't catch that."

I called her back, and Laura Anne complained about the poor reception on her new toy.

"God, we have talking refrigerators that can tell us when we're out of freaking milk, but Bell Canada can't devise a car phone that doesn't make me sound like I'm calling from the Australian bush!"

I filled her in on my conversations with Ryan, the Campanas, and McCarthy. She gave me the names of a few bars where Lisa used to drink but reiterated that Lisa hadn't been a regular there for years. During her last slip, she drank at home while Ryan was at his weekly poker game. Later on, she had gone to O'Malley's for a nightcap and ended up at the fateful Indian restaurant.

I didn't know where that left me in terms of barhopping, but Laura Anne said that she'd ask people in AA if anyone knew where Lisa had bought her cocaine after Christmas.

We talked briefly about Ryan. Laura Anne had much more faith in him than I did. She praised him for his commitment to the program and doubted that he'd had anything to do with Lisa's disappearance.

"Ryan has really turned his life around. You can't judge him based on who he was before. It's not fair. It was the drugs that caused him to be abusive. He's like another person now.

"And remember, everything happens for a reason. I asked my Tarot about Lisa this morning and got the Hermit card."

"What does that mean?" I slammed on my brakes at the traffic light.

"The Hermit represents solitude and meditation, a time to get away for soul-searching and clearing the mind. Lisa may not be drinking, Tar. She may have gone up to Quebec for a couple of days to work things out quietly on her own. Decide what to do about the pregnancy and all."

"She would never let us worry like this. No way!"

"Well, whatever. Regardless of why she left, it'll be a happy problem when she returns."

I laughed. Lisa used to tell me that Laura Anne called everything a "happy problem," and had other funny sayings like referring to someone as "an unguided missile."

"Visualize her returning," Laura Anne said before she hung up. "Thoughts are things. We attract not what we want in life but what we're thinking about. If we think fearful thoughts, we can't expect a positive outcome."

I wondered what my patient, Rebecca West, would think about that simplistic philosophy. If she envisioned herself celebrating her thirtieth birthday, would that put her leukemia in remission?

Dev and I got home about six o'clock, just in time to greet Mark and to catch a broadcast about Lisa on the news. The anchor mentioned Lisa's pregnancy, which irked me. She was going to be really pissed off that her private dilemma had been divulged to the entire city.

The news team emphasized her drug addiction and Ryan's history of domestic violence. They made Lisa sound like a basket case when nothing could have been further from the truth. Aside from that one horrendous slip, my best friend had been stable and squeaky clean for ages.

Lisa looked beautiful in the photograph on TV. It had been taken at a Christmas party at her parent's restaurant. Ryan, the Campanas, Mark, Devon and I were all standing in the background. I remembered Lisa clapping her hands and holding up her bottle of Perrier to make a toast. How could things have disintegrated so rapidly since then?

Devon seemed disturbed by the broadcast. He began to fidget in the chair, and his face turned scarlet. He was clenching his jaw, so I gave him a cold compress for his aching cheek, and checked to see if it was time for him to take another Tylenol with codeine.

I tried to explain how precarious addictions were. How a person could be straight and working their program diligently for years, but then something beckoned them back to the world of drugs. It could be something exciting like preparing for a wedding or getting a new job. Anything that caused stress could act as a potential trigger.

Same with memories. Lisa might have seen an ad on TV for Molson Ex, which could have set off a craving for alcohol that was too tough to resist because of her predicament.

Dev didn't respond. His eyes darted around the room, and he began playing with the dog. Monday started barking and licking Devon's hand. I used to find it so endearing when Monday would lick my hand, my leg, or even my jeans, and I would stroke his little gray head and tell him what a good boy he was. Then one day I had to move quickly when the dog was licking my leg, and he promptly began to lick the couch. He never noticed the difference. I was so deflated.

Devon half-heartedly played with Monday, and it was obvious that he didn't want to talk to me anymore. He grabbed the ice pack and went up to his room.

My phone rang nonstop after the broadcast. I talked to several members of WAR, my Women against Rape group, all of whom immediately suspected Ryan.

"Once an abuser, always an abuser," JC declared.

JC, Jenna Callaghan, was the coordinator of our collective. She was two years younger than I, a lesbian, and a personal injury lawyer.

"Follow Ryan, and we'll find Lisa," she insisted. I was amazed at the way that WAR had jumped to the conclusion of probable foul play.

My father called, and I spoke to him and Marie. My dad was so supportive. He invariably managed to say just the right thing to make me feel better.

"She'll show up, honey," Dad reassured me. "She probably tied one on and is sleeping it off somewhere. Make sure to call me the minute you hear from her. And Denise sends her love. She's putting in fourteen-hour days lately, so she may not have time to call you, but she did send me an email, which I'll forward to you." I thought it was pretty cool that my sixty-six-year-old father was Internet savvy.

Marie asked all about the pregnancy and if Lisa had wanted children. I replied in the affirmative and said I would be shocked if Lisa had gone off to abort the baby just because it may not have been Ryan's. I also doubted that Lisa would have risked harming the fetus by going on a binge. Like my father, Marie told me not to worry, but unlike him, her tone of voice was not convincing.

Before I went to bed, I stopped in on Devon to apologize for forgetting about his dental appointment. He was groggy but still awake.

"I know how tough root canals are, Dev, and I wasn't very sympathetic about that yesterday, kiddo. It's been crazy since Lisa took off. I spent the whole day at the police station with her parents."

"It's okay," he mumbled, yawning and turning away from me.

"No, it's not okay," I retorted. "I haven't been myself lately, but I'll snap out of this once we find her. Can you wait that long for me?" I joked.

"Yeah," Devon said, as he closed his eyes. I pulled the duvet up to cover him and left the room.

It looked as though my son might have to wait a long time for me to get myself together. I was a wreck. I was still angry at Lisa yet terrified for her safety; irritated with myself for not telling the Campanas about her pregnancy earlier and ashamed for having forgotten about Devon's root canal on top of being unsympathetic in the first place.

It didn't help matters when Mark put his arms around me in bed. I pushed him away gently, and he whispered, "Come on, baby. Komodo dragons mate for half a day. I think we can sustain a half-hour."

"Mark, I'm not in the mood!"

"Christ, Tara. I thought you could use some comforting. Why do you jump like that when I touch you? You treat me like a leper.

How do you think that makes me feel?" he asked.

I couldn't answer. I stuttered, frantically trying to come up with a reasonable explanation for my behavior, but he had already rolled over. Soon, I'd have to decide what to do about our marriage, but I was in too much turmoil right now. I had to find Lisa. Then I would devote my time to Devon and make a decision about Mark.

CHAPTER SEVEN

All the carts were taken at the supermarket on Tuesday. I found one off to the side of the vegetable aisle. It had a defective wheel, which resulted in me almost overturning a display of cantaloupes. The cart was also enormous. No doubt this was a deliberate ploy on the part of the supermarket to encourage excess shopping.

"I feel as though I'm driving a school bus," I announced to the frail, pale orange-haired woman to my left, who was squeezing the small, unappetizing looking cantaloupes.

She smiled faintly and nodded. I wondered how she had the strength to push the heavy cart through the long aisles of the grocery store at her age.

For the first time in months, I hoped that Boy Toy, Alain Rivard, would not be on duty. I looked awful with dark circles under my eyes and my frightful hair, which I had unsuccessfully attempted to disguise under my "Central Hospital" baseball cap. But there he was, smiling as he saw me approach. Despite my exhaustion and anxiety about Lisa, I felt flustered at the sight of his classically handsome face.

Alain is on the short side, but he's about an inch taller than me. He's stocky with a strong, broad nose, sparkling brown eyes, and a perfect brush cut. His face has a hard angular look about it, which would make him ideal to sculpt.

Because he works in the food industry, Alain always wears a cap, which makes him look younger than his twenty-four years. He wears the same clothes every day: a long-sleeved shirt in white or cream, a belt, a pair of black pants and brown loafers.

"Hey, girl! How's my favorite customer?" Alain inquired.

"Not that great, I'm afraid," I said, as I explained Lisa's predicament.

"No!" Alain said with surprise. "I heard about that lady on the radio. She's your friend? Too bad! Whadda ya think happened to her?"

"I suspect that she may be drinking again. She was in trouble the last time I saw her." My eyes filled with tears at the thought of Lisa alone in a bar.

Alain noticed my distress and came out from behind the counter, his long apron stained with blood from carving beef. Without hesitation or any thought about the other customers, Alain hugged me and said in his firm, male voice, "Not to worry, Tara. We'll find her."

The touch of his warm, solid body was reassuring and alarmingly arousing, despite the inappropriate circumstances, and I held on to his embrace longer than I should have. I was also thrilled by his use of the word "we." Just a minute ago, I had been all alone. I had been "me," and he had been "him," but now suddenly, there was an "us!"

Alain proceeded to tell me that his father was a chronic alcoholic who had never been sober for more than a month at a time. Alain had become accustomed to going from bar to bar to find his father when he was younger. His mother had divorced the man years ago, but Alain still knew where to find him.

"We can go to her regular hotspots," he suggested. "Talk to people she used to drink with. Someone must know somethin' if she's still in town."

I told Alain that Lisa had been sober for years and rarely went to bars, but he said that it was worth a shot. I thanked him—much too effusively—and gave him my home phone number.

"I'll call ya as soon as I get off work," he said. How ironic. For months, I had pictured Alain calling me, but this was definitely not the scenario I'd had in mind.

"Oh, that's wonderful," I said, backing up as if to leave. I always had trouble leaving Alain, yearning for one last glance, one final comment that would cement our tie together. Being in his presence made me feel so electrified that I loathed parting with that feeling of exhilaration.

"You have no idea how grateful I am," I added. Now there's an understatement. How pitiful I would appear to sweet Alain if he realized how delirious I was at the prospect of spending time alone with him.

"Hey!" Alain shouted, as I walked away from the meat counter. "What's up with that hat?"

"Trying to drum up business for the hospital."

"Yeah, like they need your help. Try tripping a few people on the way out the front door." He grinned. I remembered my fantasy about nursing Alain with his broken leg. I felt that he could read my mind and see right through my idiotic smile and overly tight Tommy Hilfiger sweater.

Standing at the checkout counter, I read the tabloid headings. "Gay Aliens Found in UFO Wreck," and "The Fattest Stars," a stellar piece of journalism featuring unflattering shots of Martha Stewart and Rosie O'Donnell. I couldn't imagine how these rags stayed in business. It blew my mind to think of the people who actually subscribed to the *National Enquirer* or the *Star*.

On the other hand, the stories on network TV and in mainstream magazines were hardly any better than those in the trash mags. Like everyone else who needed to maintain their sanity, I had taught myself not to react to the news about people starving in the Sudan, suicide bombers in Palestine, or increased terror alerts in the States.

In fact, Lisa would often stop at the house on her way home from work, bringing fresh vegetables from the Parkdale Market. I'd barbecue a chicken, and she'd make a large salad. We'd eat with Devon and Mark, if he were home, and then we'd watch the news.

Lisa was a CNN junkie. I rarely watched American news unless we were in the midst of an international crisis, which was usually precipitated by the Americans anyway. But I was happy to sit with Lisa while she ate her sugar-free Jell-O and made profound commentaries about current events.

"Doesn't Paula Zahn's hair look fabulous darker? I wonder how old she is. I also like Nancy Grace's new style and color. Very flattering."

Mark and Dev were horrified by our chatter. They were actually listening to the newscasters roll off the daily death count in Iraq.

"Seven hundred American soldiers have died, and thousands have been wounded. God knows how many Iraqi service people and civilians have been slaughtered, and all you two can talk about is how much better you like Barbara Bush's white hair because she looks more authentic than Nancy Reagan? My God, that's pathetic," Mark once told us.

Lisa and I weren't airheads. We weren't ostriches either, but sometimes the news was so dismal that we had to tune it out. Call it a defense mechanism. Call it survival instinct. How many snipers, muggers, rapists, and shoe bombers did I need in my day?

Normally, I wasn't affected by the tabloids, but today, with Lisa missing, their headlines seemed crazier than ever. I would see what our local newspaper, the Ottawa *Citizen*, had to say about Lisa when I got home.

The cashier smiled at me as I gave her my debit card and she said, "Thank you, Ma'am." I hate it when people call me Ma'am. I don't like being called Miss either, or Sweetie, or Dear. Why is it that people feel that they have to call me something? Don't call me anything. A plain thank-you is sufficient. And please don't tell me to have a great day!

As soon as I left the store, I began to obsess about my date with Alain. I felt girlishly excited. At the same time, I was filled with despair. The conflicting emotions made me think of the good news/ bad news jokes that I used to hear in grade school.

Thoughts of black humor were prominent as I loaded my groceries into the car and pondered my newfound relationship with Alain. The good news—I would be able to spend hours alone with Fantasy Man outside the grocery store. The bad news—my best friend was missing and may be giving fetal alcohol syndrome to her unborn child.

Before I was able to enjoy any time with my lust object, I had to address reality in the form of one grumpy husband, who barely acknowledged me at the kitchen table. Mark had slept in and was having a late breakfast. His first class didn't start until one o'clock.

Devon was at school. Consequently, Mark and I were alone, face to face with the awkwardness that had resulted from me rejecting him last night.

I made Spanish omelets and served fresh melon with extra whole grain toast for Mark's voracious appetite. I brewed some

Brazilian coffee and thought of that line in the Springsteen song, *Tunnel of Love*: "Then the lights go out, and it's just the three of us. You, me, and all that stuff we're so scared of."

Mark," I said with hesitation. "I didn't mean to be so cold to you last night. I just, um, I just don't feel connected to you anymore. It's like I'm sort of going through the motions here."

"Can you be more specific?" Mark asked, scowling. "I don't have any idea what you're talking about." A small piece of fruit was sticking to the side of his mouth. It made me want to laugh, but I was afraid it would make him mad if I brought it to his attention.

I wanted to shout, "I feel trapped! I don't love you anymore. Our marriage is dead!" But I couldn't say those things.

Instead, I cleared my throat, crossed my legs, and began again. "I just can't explain it, but I feel angry all the time. I don't know why. Maybe it's because you're not the same man I married. You don't listen to me the way you used to. You criticize me. I can't remember the last time you complimented me or made me feel desirable, except when you reach for me in the dark."

As I was talking, I was aware that I was making attacking comments by starting my sentences with "you." How often had we been taught in nursing to make "I" statements such as, "I feel neglected?" Or "I feel that you're not interested in our conversations." But I was on a roll and couldn't stop myself from venting my suppressed rage.

"You're distracted, more enthusiastic about your teaching assistant's thesis or some stupid hockey game than about anything that goes on in my life."

"Oh, for Christ's sake! Is this about hockey again?"

"No! You're not listening!" I whined, feeling exasperated.

"Mark, this is serious. Our marriage is in trouble."

Mark looked puzzled and scratched his goatee. "Well, we'll go to counseling. Phil and his wife had trouble last year, and they saw an excellent therapist and straightened things out." Phil was Mark's best friend at Carleton University and was also on his basketball team.

"These things happen to couples in middle age. I don't know why they refer to it as the seven-year inch," he chuckled. "It's more like the seventeen-year itch, but whatever the hell it is, Tara, we'll work it out."

I resented him referring to us both as middle-aged when he was six years older than me. Perhaps his age had something to do with my declining interest. Once Marie had told me that the same qualities which often attract us to a man in the beginning are the ones that get on our nerves later on.

Initially, I was impressed by Mark's age because it seemed to make him more mature than the other boys I knew. Now, I felt that it made him boring, and being with an older man made me feel old, too.

Ditto for his steady personality, which I had perceived as an asset in my youth. Now I was dying for some spontaneity—any sign that he was a carbon-based life form.

I finished breakfast and poured myself a second cup of coffee, grateful that Mark had taken his serviette and wiped the remaining fruit from his face. He never asked me if there was someone else, which was a relief but rather insulting at the same time. Apparently, neither Mark nor Lisa thought of me as a sexual creature capable of attracting anyone else.

"I'll think about it," I remarked, regarding Mark's comment about counseling, but I knew that I didn't want to invest energy in rehashing our hurts and disappointments. The love was gone. My obsession with Alain had not caused the problem in our marriage. My infatuation was simply a blatant reminder of how little desire I had left for Mark.

I was leaning in the direction of a separation but couldn't think that far ahead. I just needed to forewarn Mark rather than continuing to push him away physically. It was only fair to verbalize my discontent instead of leaving him feeling wounded and perplexed.

"Don't forget that we have dinner at my parents next Tuesday night," Mark added gruffly.

I groaned. I'd never been fond of Mark's older brother, Peter, a redneck, card-carrying Alliance Party homophobe, with a penchant for black bear hunting. I searched my memory, fervently hoping that I would be working that night, but alas, I was free since I would be returning to work tomorrow.

I needed to say something about my plans with Alain because Mark would be home tonight, but I didn't know how to describe Alain to him. Should I call him a friend? The butcher? The wild stallion at the grocery store?

All the descriptions I came up with sounded ludicrous. I decided to refer to Alain as an acquaintance and told Mark that Alain and I would be searching for Lisa tonight.

"Tonight?" Mark said with disbelief. "The playoffs are on tonight. We finally have a chance this year! We beat them four to two in Game 1 of the Eastern Conference quarterfinals. Okay, we sucked on Friday, but we made an amazing comeback on Sunday with that brilliant goal by Fisher. And, that was an outstanding hit on Nieuwendyk by Chara in the third period! Now we've forced the Leafs into Game 7, and Alfredsson really thinks we can win this season." Mark's voice rose. "You won't find a red-blooded male within 100 kilometers who'll go out with you tonight after six p.m."

Despite the plethora of Senators flags on lawns and cars, I had forgotten entirely about the playoffs. I appeared to be living in a fog and figured that I should call Alain to defer our plans. Surely, he wouldn't want to go out tonight.

"We've lost every playoff in the last four years. Why should things change now?" I said, feeling irritable and snappy.

I felt depressed as I dialed Alain's home phone number, which I knew by heart because I'd called to listen to his voice on the answering machine so many times before. Hot Boy wasn't there. He must have been at work, so I got out the phone book and looked up the number for the grocery store.

Customer service paged Alain, who answered the phone at the meat counter. I was struck by the exuberance and energy in his young voice.

"No problem, Tara. I'm not a hockey fanatic. My game is pool. I even run a website on pool tutorials. If this was my pool night, I'd say, 'Not a chance!' But I don't care much about hockey, and besides, we're going to be at the bars. We'll be able to catch the score everywhere."

"Are you sure?" I asked.

"Absolutely!"

I was elated. A real live Ottawa man who was willing to miss the playoffs! I must have been dreaming.

The Campanas called right after I hung up with Alain. They sounded increasingly worried and bewildered. This was the fifth day that Lisa had been missing. She had never gone on such a bender before.

Every day, the Campanas went to mass to light a candle for her, and every night the church held a prayer vigil for Lisa.

The Campanas were also holding a daily press conference and complained about the way that Lisa had been portrayed in the newspaper as a chronic alcoholic with poor judgment in men. I'd been too preoccupied with my conversation with Mark to read the paper when I got home, but I skimmed it while I was talking to Anna.

The headline read, "Pregnant Cocaine Addict Missing since Thursday." Lisa would love that. I felt the Campana's anguish. There was nothing I could do to ease it except to promise that Alain and I would do everything humanly possible to find her.

I had a message on my voice mail from Ryan, so I called him while I was doing the dishes. Ryan's words sounded dramatic, but his tone was calm and dispassionate. Unlike the Campanas, Ryan didn't seem upset by the newspaper article. Nor did he sound alarmed about the pregnancy. I would have thought he'd have completely freaked out about the baby, but Ryan assured me Lisa had already told him that she was pregnant.

"Yeah, Lisa told me when she came home from the ByTowne. I couldn't believe it. We've been trying for such a long time. I thought it was hopeless, but now it's really happening. I'm gonna be a dad!

"I told Lisa she was crazy to think she'd get knocked up by one night with another guy. Geez, Lisa's a blackout drinker. She loses hours at a time when she's plastered. How does she know she even slept with that guy? I don't believe she did. She loves me! I'm her man, and I gotta find her to take care of her and the baby."

I was dubious about his explanation but didn't feel like being confrontational in the event that Ryan's explanation were true. I asked how he was coping, and Ryan said that his AA meetings had saved his sanity.

"I'm just turning it over, man. I mean, I'm as helpless about Lisa as I am about my own alcoholism and drug addiction. It's all a matter of acceptance. I can't control the media and the ugly things they say. That's not important. What's important is finding her, and I'm gonna do that if my life depends on it."

Ryan's role in the crisis was so confusing. I had no idea how I should react to him. If Ryan had nothing to do with Lisa's disappearance, then he was as much a victim as the Campanas, and he deserved my unconditional support. He was also a recovering addict, which put him in a vulnerable state emotionally. Lisa's absence could push him over the edge into using again or plunge him into a depressive funk. And he was right. He was going to be a father.

But if Ryan had harmed her, I'd be a fool to befriend him. From what Lisa had told me, Ryan sounded macho and possessive. He should have been irate at the possibility of the baby not being his. I shook my head. I would have to be extremely careful in my dealings with the enigmatic Ryan. I wanted to curl up with a good book, but my line kept ringing. Laura Anne called to say that she had spoken to a number of people at AA. No one had seen or heard from Lisa. I told her about my plans with Alain to visit Lisa's former bars. She urged me not to get my hopes up, reminding me that it wasn't likely that Lisa would return to her regular haunts if she were trying to avoid people.

Lisa could be holed up in some motel with a bottle of Jim Beam. Her photo had been on TV, and her story had been broadcast in two of the local newspapers. Lisa had probably left Ottawa last week if she didn't want anyone to find her, Laura Anne reminded me.

Feeling depressed, I realized that I could catch a step class at the Y after lunch if I got my ass in gear. I grabbed *The Bonesetter's Daughter* and set off for the gym, but when I put the CD in my player, I discovered that I had brought the second disc instead of the first.

I would return to the book later on in the day when I soaked in the tub in preparation for my first date with Alain. Of course, it wasn't really a date, but we would actually be alone together, the dozens of other patrons in the bar notwithstanding.

During the drive, I reviewed what Alain had said on the phone. I reflected on his vocabulary, his voice inflections, and the incredible fact that he was *not* hooked on hockey.

While we were marching up and down at the class and listening to Abba, I envisioned Alain's apartment. Was he neat and tidy, or sloppy and disorderly? Would I ever have the opportunity to see his abode?

I pictured him showering before our get-together. The thought of Alain naked made me almost physically ill. I wanted him more than I had ever wanted anyone in my life. God knows I never craved Mark that way, but I was desperately afraid that the feeling wasn't mutual.

Standing next to Alain in the store made me high, but imagining him making love to me was tormenting. My mounting desire was mixed with fear of his rejection and frustration that I couldn't have him. Even the thought of taking my clothes off in front of the Boy Wonder gave me conflicting emotions; I wanted him so badly, but I was terrified that if he saw my thirty-nine-year-old naked body, whatever erection he may have had in his fantasies would Peter out.

I half-heartedly hoped that Alain would do or say something juvenile that would turn me off tonight so that I could get over my ridiculous crush. Maybe my love sickness would be like a bad case of the flu. It would run its course and pass, leaving me sane but bereft in its wake.

Devon called to ask if he could have dinner at Jess's and watch the playoffs. I said all right. I asked if he had finished *To Kill a Mockingbird,* and he provided an incoherent reply. I said that he could forget about homework tonight, but I wanted to review his essay on the book by the weekend.

Both Mark and I had loved Harper Lee's classic about the trial of a black man who was accused of raping a white woman. But Dev had called it "a dumb story about a whack job who stayed inside his creepy house for, like, twenty-five years."

"You're missing the point! The main story is about…"

"Yeah, I know. It's about the black guy who rapes the girl."

"The guy who was *accused* of raping the girl."

"Whatever."

"No. There's a big difference between being accused of a crime and actually committing it. That concept is just as relevant today as it was in the 1930s when this story took place. So are the issues of class and culture. It takes place in Alabama, in the heart of the Deep South. Blacks are still viewed differently there than they are in the Northeast."

"Duh!"

"Dev, I thought you were interested in civil rights, the way you love Chris Rock and 60 Cents."

"50 Cent, Mum! Look, I gotta go. I'm gonna read the book. It's, like, too long and stupid the way it's told from the eight-year-old's perspective. What do I care what some little kid thinks? And what kind of name is Dill?"

"What kind of name is Devon? Maybe Dill would think that you have a weird name."

"Exactly! I've been saying that for years. When I'm eighteen, I'm going to legally change my name to Paul. Anyways, I'm gonna read it. Promise! But Jess is calling. Catch you later." Devon hung up.

Maybe if I sat down with him on the weekend and we discussed the book in detail, he'd get a better idea of what it was about. I wanted him to love it the way Mark and I had adored the book, but that was like asking someone who worshiped Oprah to switch to Bill Maher. I needed to work harder at accepting Devon for who he was.

CHAPTER EIGHT

At home, I made myself a Chef's salad, grabbed a Diet Coke, and got out a pad and a piece of paper to make notes. I wrote down all of the possible reasons Lisa could have gone underground for five days. She must have known that all of us would have been out of our minds at this point.

Maybe she'd gone hiking in the Gatineau. Lisa loved the outdoors and was very fit. She had run in three marathons. What if she'd gone cycling or walking on one of the trails and injured herself? There weren't many people in the foothills of Quebec in April.

Could she be lying on the side of a road somewhere with a broken leg? But she invariably carried her cell when she took those solitary trips. Ryan had tried calling her a number of times, but there was no answer.

My palms felt sweaty, and I wondered if WAR had been right about Ryan. I looked down at the notes that I had scrawled on the page. Left town? Injured? Worse? I couldn't begin to contemplate the "worse" category. That was unthinkable.

However, I was starting to question Ryan. Ryan was the one who told me that Lisa hadn't been at the cottage and wasn't answering her phone. What if he were lying? I dialed her cell phone again, and the mailbox was full. I pictured her phone ringing somewhere, way out of Lisa's grasp. Perhaps Alain and I would be better off driving up to the cottage rather than wasting our time in the bars.

It was time for my bath. I was feeling almost demented with lust for Alain, who was happily paired off with some size zero, twenty-three-old. I needed to take my mind off him and Lisa, so I located disc one of *The Bonesetter's Daughter* and let the CD play for twenty minutes before I entered the bathroom. I definitely did not want to hear the first half again. I lounged in the tub, luxuriating in the sensuous feel of the warm jets hitting my skin.

Again, I returned to San Francisco with Ruth describing an accident that occurred to her in the playground as a child, which had prompted her to stop talking. In order to communicate with her daughter, LuLing asked Ruth to write down what she wanted to say in the sand. Ruth did this for months until one day, LuLing began to believe that the ghost of her dead mother, whom she called Precious Auntie, was communicating through Ruth.

The Chinese belief in ghosts sounded silly, until I asked myself if it was any stranger that every Sunday morning at communion, millions of people worldwide symbolically drank the blood of a man who had been dead for more than 2,000 years. A man who walked on water and resurrected himself from a tomb.

I still hadn't finished disc one. I couldn't transfer the boom box from the bathroom to my bedroom because, in order to do so, I needed to turn the radio off. That would mean that I'd be starting the CD all over again from scratch. I cursed the mental midget who had neglected to partition off the talking book.

Ordinarily, I throw on the first clothes that I see in my closet as long as they're clean, match, and don't make me look fat. But now I was dressing for Alain. Everything in my closet was wrong and seemed to scream, "You are Devon's mother!" My man-tailored shirt looked matronly, and my yellow sweater made me look busty.

Just as some women think that one can never be too rich or

too thin, many believe that breasts can never be too large. But I'm a DD cup, and that's not all it's cracked up to be. First, it's nearly impossible to find attractive bras in that size. Second, if I wear a fitted shirt, men automatically think that I'm coming on to them. Last, bras made in DD have very little variety and are expensive.

Last week, before I dreamed that I would have any alone time with my love, Alain, I had thrown caution to the wind and ordered two pairs of matching bras and panties from none other than Victoria's Secret. Although I suspected that Victoria's true secret was that no one in the world looked like the models in the VS catalog, I was tired of my sensible Hanes Her Way underwear.

My first choice was the Victoria's Secret Miracle bra—nothing short of a miracle would help my drooping breasts—in embroidered satin. I had my heart set on the camellia pink demi bra until I realized that the largest size that it came in was a D cup.

Instead, I went with the classic Body by Victoria in teal and winced at its description as a "full coverage" bra, which made me sound ready for combat duty. I was happier with my second selection, the "Very Sexy" push-up bra, which I purchased in Promenade pink with matching fishnet V-string panties.

Ordering expensive lingerie from the States was an extravagance. Mark would hit the roof when he saw the bill, especially if he never got a preview of the underwear. The lingerie should be arriving any day now. I hoped that the parcel came on one of my days off so that Devon didn't tease me about it.

I selected a black-and-white pinstriped pullover, which was just snug enough but didn't make me look obscene. And I wore my good support bra by Warner's rather than my black lacy bra from the Bay, which was more attractive but made my boobs sag.

I felt like Bridget Jones when she was trying to decide whether or not to wear her huge panties, which would make her look better in jeans but would look ridiculous if the opportunity to disrobe arose. Bridget was lucky to have been caught in her funny undies on her first date. I knew for certain that Alain would not be seeing my lingerie tonight on our non-date.

I chose my black Liz Claiborne pants, which made me look thinner. Normally, I don't wear much makeup, but tonight I put on a thin coat of foundation, a touch of blush, my bold red lipstick, and a thin line of eyeliner. I carefully dried my tie-dyed hair and used the curling iron to get my limp locks to curl backward in that soft feminine, air blown look that was popularized by Meg Ryan. I gave my neck a squirt of White Shoulders cologne and looked in the mirror to admire myself.

I was a disaster. I looked like some sad, sorry, Volvo Driving Soccer Mom.

Back to the drawing board. I washed my face and managed to remove most of the harsh eyeliner. I doused my hair with water and blew it straight again. My hair was starting to feel like sandpaper. Then I removed the black pants in favor of my jeans and running shoes. Now I looked exactly the way I had looked an hour ago except that I smelled like a hooker. But I was running late and had to go. I wondered how Alain was preparing for our evening. At best, he probably brushed his teeth or changed out of his work shirt.

I felt nervous about spending time with my man/boy, which was an unusual feeling for me since I'm not used to having any drama or excitement in my life. I was also terrified that our efforts to locate Lisa would be in vain. I considered calling the

Campanas to ask their permission to visit the cottage. However, I didn't want them to think that I suspected Ryan of lying.

Lisa had given me a key to her cottage years ago. I had keys to her house, just as she had keys to mine, in the event of an emergency. After ten minutes of fumbling through kitchen drawers, I located the key to Lisa's cottage. Grabbing a light jacket, I was off to pick up Alain, a half hour late.

He was standing outside his apartment, looking adorable in a white T-shirt, a red-and-black flannel over-shirt, and off-white khaki pants. He grinned as I approached, and I felt my heart pound and my mouth go dry.

"Hey! Going my way?" Alain smiled, as he got into the car.

"Depends on what you have to offer," I replied, at a loss for anything clever to say.

"Just my scintillating company," Alain said. I apologized for being late, but he claimed that he hadn't been waiting long.

"Man, Christine was strung out today. Some problem at work. One of her co-workers is always doing emails, making personal calls on the job, and generally slacking off. Puts Christine in a bad position because she doesn't want to rat the girl out, you know?" He paused. "What did you do to your hair?"

"Oh, my hairdresser had some crazy idea about giving me highlights. They look kind of strange, but I don't pay much attention to my hair," I replied.

"They look fine," he lied right back at me.

I didn't want to talk about my hair, and I certainly didn't want to discuss his heartthrob, Christine. I switched the subject to Laura Anne, filling Alain in on what Lisa's sponsor had said about the unlikelihood of Lisa being in one of the local bars. I asked what he thought about going up to the cottage and said we would miss most of the playoffs if we went to Lisa's cottage in Dunrobin.

Alain reiterated what he'd said earlier. "I'm not much of a hockey fan, Tara. I don't care who wins. All I care about tonight is finding your friend."

My eyes began to water again. This was the second time I had cried in front of Alain, and I'm not a crybaby. I haven't cried since my father remarried because I was only a teenager at the time, and I missed my mother intensely. But something about Alain's easygoing manner made me feel as though I could be myself with him. I hadn't realized how lonely I was until Alain stepped into my private life.

Mark didn't listen, Devon saw me as the enemy, and WAR's politics were becoming too extreme for me. The people at the hospital were wonderful, but I didn't socialize with them. I viewed them more as colleagues than friends. Lisa was my best friend. *Is my best friend,* I reminded myself.

We drove along the back roads amicably. Alain turned on the radio and frowned when he heard *Magic 100*. He asked if he could change the channel to 106.9, *The Bear*. *The Bear* played hard rock, not my preference, but I wanted to make Alain happy, and that seemed like a small price to pay.

We talked about Lisa and discussed different scenarios that would explain her absence.

"The women from WAR think it's irresponsible to ignore Ryan's history of battering. What if he hurt her? What if it's like Laci Peterson?" I asked, referring to the pregnant Californian woman, who had been found dead one year ago in the Berkeley Marina. That was less than three miles from where her husband, Scott Peterson, told police that he was fishing on the day his wife disappeared. Scott had been arrested and charged with murdering Laci and their unborn child, Conner.

"Never heard of them," Alain said. "I follow Canadian news pretty closely—especially local politics because I want to know if someone's trying to screw me—and I listen to international news, but I'm not really interested in those missing ladies."

"Well, the Peterson story is big right now. Also, Chandra Levy came from Modesto, the same town in California as Laci Peterson. At first, everyone thought that U.S. Senator Gary Condit killed Levy because they were having an affair. Then it turned out that some thug had assaulted two joggers in the same park where Levy's remains were found. So she could've been murdered by that guy—he's in prison now—or by some serial killer," I said, feeling distressed to be talking about Laci and Chandra in the same breath as Lisa.

"Let's talk about something else," I suggested. Alain repeated that we were going to find Lisa, and he reverted to the conversation about Christine, confiding that they were having problems.

"She wants to get married, but I think we're too young. I wanna finish school and establish my own business before tying the knot. She wants kids right away, and I just don't want to go there. But I couldn't stand to lose her!"

I found him to be refreshingly candid, open and revealing. I turned my head to look at his perfect face with his long black eyelashes and dark bushy brows. The mere sight of him sitting so close to me nearly made me drive off the road. Sweet misery. Being with Alain made me feel joyful and alive. His optimism about Lisa gave me hope.

Secretly, I was thrilled to hear that he and Christine had their difficulties. Maybe they would split up. I could leave Mark and have an unabashed fling with the beautiful boy. But where would that leave Devon? And how long could I stand to listen to his music, which was simply one step up from Devon's favorite head-banging band, Metallica? I could already feel myself on the verge of tinnitus listening to whatever was playing on his hard rock station.

"Awesome," Alain exclaimed, tapping his foot to the noise on the radio. "Don't you just love Blink 182?" he said, referring to the song that was playing. "Wheatus are sweet, too." Sounded like screaming to me. Songs with choruses like "What's my age again?" or "I'm just a teenage dirtbag, baby" left something to be desired.

"How did you like Pearl Jam?"

"Not bad," I said, groping for an appropriate adjective.

"Who do you usually listen to?" Alain asked, sensing my disinterest in his music.

"Avril Lavigne, Christina Aguilera, Shakira," I said, feeling like such a girl. Alain would dismiss my favorites as "chick bands." "Matchbox Twenty, Evanescence, Sam Roberts," I added, trying to think of bands that might meet with his approval.

"Sam Roberts! Excellent! I love him. In fact, he's from Montreal, my hometown."

At last, Alain and I had found a shared musical interest. We talked about the Sam Roberts band and the songs we liked best during the forty-five-minute drive to Dunrobin. Dunrobin is a bucolic rural area, which runs along the river. There are farms, large estate lots, and small communities of former cottages. We passed through miles of countryside beyond Kanata and confusing road signs, some of which were lying on the street.

Finally, we arrived at a dirt road, and I could see the long winding laneway in front of Lisa's property. An old-fashioned post-box with the flag up was on the street, and the house was set back off the road so that no one could see it. It faced the river, and I could feel the brisk but pleasant breeze coming from the water when we got out of the Saab.

The small cottage was thoroughly modern with its cream-colored clapboard exterior, brand-new redwood deck, and Jacuzzi that Lisa and Ryan had built last year. Lisa could never have afforded the house on her salary. Her parents had given her a sizable amount of money, which had allowed her to purchase the old cottage and remodel it.

There was a stunning view of the lake with its still, cold looking water. I remembered the many barbecues that we had enjoyed here: grilling steaks, hamburgers, chicken, hot dogs, eating corn on the cob, and blueberry pie. We used to play croquet on the lawn and swim, boat, or kayak on the river. *We would do it again*, I resolved, as I inserted the key into the front door.

The cottage seemed abnormally quiet after the raucous noise from the car radio. We walked directly into the Great Room, a combination L-shaped living room and dining room. A big oval kitchen table stood adjacent to the large sliding glass doors, which led to the deck. Ashtrays filled with butts sat on the otherwise clear countertop. I was hopeful when I saw the ashtray until I took a closer look and realized that the butts were Ryan's. That meant that he'd been here to check on Lisa, just as he'd said.

There were no signs that Lisa had been in the cottage. Alain checked the refrigerator, which was bereft of food. No newspapers, no coffee cups, no mail. Alain found a can of Coke in the garbage, but Lisa never drank pop with sugar. We couldn't see anything out of the ordinary.

Feeling disheartened, Alain and I left Dunrobin. He suggested that we stop off at Le Skratch billiard hall for a game of pool. I teased him about just wanting to know the hockey score.

"So you have that Y chromosome after all?"

"Nah, pool is my game."

"Well, I have no idea how to play, and I don't think I'll be very good company."

"I'll teach you. It'll be good for you to take a break. We can't do anything more tonight. Let's shoot a few games and have some beers. Maybe that'll give us some ideas about what to do next."

Next! Alain had been sincere in his offer to locate Lisa. I was impressed but couldn't picture myself in a pool hall drinking with Alain. It seemed surreal, like I had walked through a portal into a parallel universe.

There were at least twenty concrete steps leading up to the billiard hall. It was dark when we walked into the huge bar, which smelled of fries and stale beer. I had expected it to be more crowded. I guessed that the diehard sports fans didn't go to a pool hall during the playoffs since pool required concentration. TV screens everywhere indicated that Toronto was in the lead.

Most of the patrons in Le Skratch were much younger than I. There were dozens of guys around Alain's age with spiky hair and baggy clothes. Some had pants that hung down three or four inches below their crotch. Devon's friend, Jess, dressed like that. I had a momentary twinge of guilt about Devon. What was wrong with him? He was so uncommunicative lately. Or was it just that I was a bad mother?

Most of the older men sat hunched over their bar stools, covering their potbellies with large dark T-shirts. The girls wore short tube tops and tight skirts, or bellbottom jeans in white, cream, or denim with wide belts. They sported lacy, black see-through tops with white bras, clogs, and shoes with wedges. I felt conspicuous carrying my purse since most of the twenty somethings wore backpacks.

"I play in a league," Alain informed me, as he put our balls down on the table. "Some of the players are so good they go to Vegas and make big bucks. I love to gamble!"

"Well, you won't be risking anything with me because you're sure to win," I said, not caring whatsoever who won as long as I could be with him. I had a momentary twinge of remorse and thought about calling Mark to tell him I'd be late but knew that he'd be annoyed if I interrupted his game.

I had played 8-Ball before years ago, but that was in my past life at university. Alain explained the rules. He chose a cue stick for me and said that it was important for me to check the tip.

"The stick has a tip, a shaft, and a butt," Alain said with a straight face.

"You're putting me on," I said.

"I promise!" Alain said. "I know it sounds lame, but that's really what it's called."

"Obviously, this is a man's game! Only a man would come up with those phallic names."

"Whatever!" he said and blushed.

The waitress approached, and we both ordered Heinekens. She asked if we wanted anything to eat, but I figured that a burger or Nachos would make my hands slippery and interfere with my game. There was the loud sound of cheering as the

Senators scored a goal. Even though hockey wasn't my favorite sport, I was enjoying the palpable excitement in the room.

In the background, Diana Ross and the Supremes were singing, "I'm going to make you love me." I wished!

The carpet was worn at the end of the pool table, and I was careful not to trip. Alain showed me how to hold the cue stick. He reviewed the basic rules for the game. The first person to pocket the ball had to shoot all their balls in stripes or solids, depending on which one they hit first. If you pocketed a ball, you got an extra turn. If you pocketed the cue ball, you forfeited your turn.

Carefully, I posed, concentrated, and aimed for a straight ball in the corner pocket. I pocketed the cue ball.

"Your grip is too tight, and you need to follow through," Alain said. "Stand with your left leg bent a little, and make sure you have your balance. Then bend over, and line up your shot. You'll need to cut your shot on an angle." I shook my head to indicate that it was too complicated, but Alain continued.

"Look, just draw a mental line from the ball to the pocket. Take your cue stick, and measure the line that your object ball has to travel to go into the pocket. Now, find the spot on the cue ball where you have to hit it, so it goes directly in that straight line."

Alain made it sound so easy. Then he walked toward me and took my cue stick. For a minute, I thought that he was going to put his arms around me to demonstrate the proper grip. But to my dismay, he just asked me to go to the end of the table to watch him shoot. Alain's arm was completely straight when he was shooting. That posture and a firm but gentle grip would result in a direct shot.

"Aim for the closest ball. And don't forget the chalk. I use a lot of chalk."

I couldn't take my eyes off his strong biceps. For once, I had a bona fide excuse to stare at his body. Good thing that I'm not male because my arousal would have been all too apparent.

Alain won the game effortlessly and made some fancy moves by bouncing the balls off the bank of the table. But I managed to pocket two balls and by accident, he sunk one of my balls.

"I think I'll take up ping pong," I said, just before there was a huge uproar from the crowd and some loud moans. Lalime had allowed another soft goal by Joe Nieuwendyk to slide past him. The Sens had lost! It was time for us to go home before the real crowds started pouring in.

Alain went to pay the bill while I watched a young couple sitting at the bar. She was wearing a multicolored shirt that matched my hair, with denim Capri pants. He was taller than she and stocky. The girl was leaning toward him, listening intently to him talk. She kept flipping her long hair backward and repeating words like "Really?" "Yeah?" "Right?" And "Wow!" Approval seeking words and body language.

He was reclining, looking relaxed, and making righteous statements such as, "People are stupid." "People are lazy." "They don't want to work out."

She pouted. "I always work out! You don't think of me that way, do you?"

She laughed at everything he said, even when it wasn't funny. When she told him how often she went to the gym, he said, "You'll gain weight that way. Muscle weighs more than fat."

The girl looked anxious and asked if he thought she was too fat.

"Of course not!" the guy retorted, but he'd already dug his grave. Men are in deep trouble no matter how they answer that trick question.

The pair talked back and forth easily, and they appeared to have a good rapport. But he wasn't really listening to her, and invariably, he turned the conversation back to his own life or to something that interested him like his car or his job.

So this was the dating jungle. I hoped that she wouldn't marry him because he would never understand her and would always be critical. I tried to picture myself dating other men if I left Mark. The thought was about as appealing as having Jeffrey Dahmer to dinner. I had been away from that scene for too long. I could never get back into it. The games, the facades, the deception. I would have to join a convent.

CHAPTER NINE

It was late, and I had to get up early for work tomorrow, but I was reluctant to leave Alain. He was very energetic compared to Mark, who was so detached and clinical that he could have been in a coma. Everything good in Alain's life was "awesome," and anything bad "sucked." Alain sprinkled his conversation with words like "for sure, absolutely, definitely, and whatever." He was so easy to talk to and to be with. He was such a girl!

Men had no idea what a compliment it was when one woman said to another, "Talking to him is just like talking to another woman." It was the ultimate praise although men generally didn't see it that way. All of the *Men Are from Mars* and *Women Are from Venus* bullshit disappeared, and talking to the guy was as easy as talking to a best friend. Although I'd only spent a few hours with Alain, I sensed that he was without pretense, strategies, and machinations. He hadn't been flirtatious with me, but clearly, he had enjoyed himself and my company.

We got back into the Saab, and Alain turned on the radio. I was shocked to hear a special news bulletin, stating that Lisa's car had been discovered on a small street off Aylmer Road across the river on the Quebec side. Her keys and purse were inside, but her cell phone was missing.

"The police are now suspecting foul play," the announcer declared. Talk about stating the obvious!

I started to shake. Lisa would never have taken off without her purse. Maybe she wasn't on a bender after all. And I'd been blaming her all this time. Horns were honking in the street, and it made me angry that the hockey fans were causing such a ruckus. Life in all its seasonal and celebratory glory was moving on. It was a happy time for the fans, but it was a dreadful time for Lisa, her family, and me.

"Hey! My friend might be dead," I wanted to shout, but somehow I managed to hold myself together and to drive Alain home.

We sat outside his apartment talking for an hour or more about the latest development. Alain reminded me that he ran a website for pool tutorials. He offered to start a site for Lisa and to link it to other missing person sites on the Web.

"I don't know much about missing people, Tara, but I know a lot about the Web, and it's the best way to get the word out to a lotta people. If anyone knows anything about Lisa, we'll be the first to find out about it."

God bless him. Alain was turning out to be a take-charge kind of guy like Fitz in *Cracker*. He hugged me good night, and I sensed my own neediness in my response. Alain was such a gem. I hoped that I didn't do anything stupid to scare him off because I really needed him right now.

"Give me a shout tomorrow." Alain winked, as he shut the car door.

It was late, but I reached Allison, the charge nurse, at home. She had missed the news bulletin because she'd been sleeping and was horrified to learn about the discovery of Lisa's car. I asked if I could have a few days off, but Allison refused apologetically. She said that Jean-Claude was out with the flu, and she couldn't spare me this week. If I could come in on Thursday, maybe she could find a replacement for me for Friday and Saturday.

At least I had tomorrow off. It was late, but I felt justified in calling the Campanas, who were frantic. Luckily, they had not learned about the abandonment of Lisa's Toyota Rav4 from TV. Detective McCarthy had called them earlier to break the news and to inform them that the case would be turned over to the Quebec Police. It was out of Ottawa's jurisdiction now, but the Ottawa Police would help out if the Quebec Police wanted their assistance.

Anna, Lorenzo, and Sandra were eager to work in conjunction with the police search team. They were planning to meet at 9 a.m. outside of the Hippodrome, a racetrack in Aylmer, Quebec. Since Lisa's car had been found close to the racino, the owner had kindly offered to allow the search party to use their large parking lot for several days. The Campanas expected dozens of people from their church to look for Lisa. I said that I would be contacting the members of WAR tomorrow, and I'd get as many as possible to join the search effort.

The laughs that I had enjoyed with Alain at Le Skratch came back to haunt me. I also felt bad for having doubted Lisa. I should have known that she would have called into work even if she had been drinking. It was obvious that she was in serious trouble.

****

I tossed and turned most of the night, picturing Lisa drowning like Laci Peterson, the woman from Modesto, California, who disappeared without a trace. Devon and Mark had gone to bed before the announcement about Lisa's car. They were both upset to hear the news at the breakfast table.

"This won't end well," Devon said.

"Don't be silly, sweetie," I responded, trying to believe my own words of comfort to my son.

"The police are doing everything in their power to find her, and we're going to help them." I told Devon about Alain's expertise on the Internet and my plans to contact WAR while I made him French toast.

"I don't know," he murmured, looking pale as he excused himself from the table. There was something going on with that boy. Was he really that upset about Lisa, or was there something else that I was missing?

Mark was reading the *Citizen*. The headline said, "Not Even Close." Both Mark and Dev were depressed about last night's game. Mark was also giving me the cold shoulder. He was concerned about Lisa but still angry at me and was not being particularly supportive.

I mentioned Alain's name in front of Mark for the first time, but he didn't exhibit any signs of jealousy or fear that I may have been interested in someone else. My infatuation with Alain now felt almost sacrilegious since I was paralyzed with fear about Lisa so it seemed inappropriate for me to be in love with a man half my age at the same time.

Before my men left the house, Mark informed me that he'd join the search team after lunch. He needed to meet with his doctoral student this morning and to conduct his 11 a.m. class. I was grateful that he didn't plan to take his anger toward me out on Lisa.

I took a shower, cleaned the kitchen, and grabbed a second cup of Colombian. I had planned to call JC to organize a collective meeting before I went up to the Gatineau, but the phone was already ringing.

"Kara? This is Elmore Stewart. I'm a reporter from the *Citizen*, and I'd like to ask some questions about your friendship with

Lisa Campana. Is this a good time for you?"

"Tara," I corrected him. "Yes, I have a few minutes, but I'm on my way to join the search team in Aylmer."

"I won't hold you up," Stewart replied and posed the same questions that the police had asked me about the night that Lisa and I spent at the ByTowne. He was kind and sympathetic. I felt that he really cared about Lisa's predicament until he started asking about her drug use. I insisted that Lisa had been clean for almost five years, but Elmore emphasized her recent slip. I was adamant that Lisa was a together person and it had been unfair of him to have depicted her as an irresponsible barfly in his earlier articles.

Elmore replied that there had been no reason to suspect foul play initially, but finding the abandoned vehicle had changed the situation. He assured me that he would be objective in his portrayal of Lisa and asked about Ryan.

"What do you think about the boyfriend? Do you believe he could be involved in some way?"

Elmore had touched a nerve. One reason WAR and I were having problems was that I had taken an interest in wrongful convictions in the '90s, and most of the people who are wrongly imprisoned are male. WAR thought that my sympathy and energies were misdirected because the "real" victims were the women or children who had been murdered in the first place. I couldn't convince them that both parties were victimized if the wrong person was put behind bars. Moreover, the families of the murder victims never had true closure if they thought that one person had killed their daughter when in fact it had been someone else. Last, and most important, that "someone else" was still out there if the wrong person was doing time.

"Innocent until proven otherwise," I declared with hesitation, expecting Elmore to argue with me the way that WAR did. "Nothing whatsoever links Ryan to Lisa's disappearance. Look at the publicity in recent years about wrongful convictions. There's David Milgaard, who spent twenty-three years in prison for the murder of that Saskatoon nursing aide; Guy Paul Morin, who was sentenced to life for killing nine-year-old Christine Jessop; and that American guy... What's his name? Rolando Cruz. He was on death row in Illinois. All of them were exonerated by DNA." I checked my watch. I had at least ten minutes to spare.

"Last year, I read a fascinating book by John and Patsy Ramsey from Denver, the parents of little JonBenet Ramsey, who was murdered inside her own house on Christmas Day. Her parents were the main suspects for years, but the police could never find enough evidence to charge them with a crime.

"The Ramseys appeared before a grand jury and were acquitted, but meanwhile their lives had been ruined. Two grief-stricken parents had to spend valuable time, energy, and money defending themselves against reprehensible accusations when what they really needed was to mourn the loss of their little girl. Since all that attention was focused on the Ramseys, other suspects were never investigated! Everyone believed it had to have been an inside job, but that was before Elizabeth Smart from Utah and little Cecilia Zhang of Toronto were abducted from their bedrooms.

"Look, I know Ryan has two strikes against him. First, he has a history of battering and drug abuse, and second, male partners are always suspected when women go missing. But Ryan's been sober and working his program for three years, and he's never touched, Lisa. She would've told me if he had ever hit her," I said, secretly wondering if that were true. Apparently, there were a lot of things Lisa never told me.

"So you're comfortable with Ryan Whitman being a part of the search team?" Elmore asked.

"Absolutely," I said, not at all comfortable about Ryan, but I would be damned if I would let a reporter know that at this point in the investigation. "Great talking to you, Elmore, but I have to go now if I want to get to Quebec by nine."

He wished me luck, and I looked forward to reading his piece tomorrow. I hoped that he could straighten out the misperception of Lisa as a drug addict and manage not to call me Kara at the same time.

When I got off the Champlain Bridge, I passed the Jehovah Witness Church. I was greeted by the familiar little colored flags of the provinces that lined the Alexandre-Taché Boulevard, which leads into the charming city of Hull, and the scenic town of Aylmer. I grimaced when I read the sign, "Je pense pietons," meaning "I think pedestrians," or less literally, "remember pedestrians." *Had anyone here remembered Lisa?* I wondered.

I went west, passing long sprawling properties, the scenic Château Cartier Golf Course, and a crowded parking lot where commuters left their cars to take the bus.

D'Amour Road was an innocuous-looking side street before Rivermead. What a cruel joke to have abandoned her car on the road of love. There were already dozens of people in the parking lot of the Hippodrome. Anna was in the middle of a small circle of people who seemed to be consoling her.

"They're searching the area around the car on D'Amour, the police," she said, her voice breaking. "Ryan and Lorenzo, they're going door to door. Members of the church are stopping cars, showing them posters of Lisa. They're asking drivers if they've seen her since Thursday.

"There's a new officer, Desormeaux. Head of Adult Missing Persons. Looks like a baby."

"I'm sure he's very capable," I said, as I put my arm around Mrs. Campana. I wanted to cry but had to be strong for her sake.

"Where's Sandra?" I asked, wondering if the notion of looking for her older sister was too gruesome for fragile little Sandra.

"At home making sandwiches for the searchers. She needed to go to Loblaws to buy cases of pop and bottled water. They'll bring food and drinks later, Sandra and Anthony. They're looking for flashlights, batteries, and first aid kits. We may even need umbrellas and rain gear," Anna said, looking up at the clear sky.

Well, I'll be! Sandra was not only as strong as the other family members, but she was also practical and resourceful. Bringing food and water had never occurred to me.

I asked Anna what I could do to help, and she said I could request volunteers from the community. One of the women at WAR had contacts at the radio station. I needed to call JC again. I had only reached her voice mail when I'd called earlier from the car.

I told Anna about my conversation with the reporter from the *Citizen*. She had also spoken to Elmore and had found him and the reporter from the *Sun* to be fair-minded. However, she hadn't appreciated the TV coverage from the major networks, which continued to depict Lisa as a promiscuous drug addict. We both hoped that would change now that Lisa's car had been found.

Anna surprised me by saying that Ryan told the police that

Lisa had planned to visit her ex-boyfriend, Rob Malveaux, at his house at Meech Lake. This was the first time Ryan had mentioned anything about Rob, and as a result, the police had begun to investigate Malveaux. They were using dogs to comb through the thick trees, dead limbs, and scrap lumber on Malveaux's property.

Before I could respond to this startling news, my cell phone rang. ESP. It was JC. She concurred that we needed an emergency meeting of the collective. She would notify all twelve members and see how many people she could assemble by nine o'clock this evening. She would also call her friend, Macy, a DJ who worked at the rock station *Chez 106 FM*. We would make public service announcements requesting volunteers to look for Lisa, the same way that people had come out en masse to search the fields for Ardeth Wood. Now we had a specific location. We knew that Lisa had been with her car in Aylmer.

JC offered to start a "fax tree," meaning that she would send a fax about Lisa to various women's groups in town. In turn, they would fax the description out to all the agencies that they worked with. It was important to get the word out nationally as well as locally.

JC would also contact Women's Day Bookstore to see if they would monitor a trust fund for Lisa. That would enable people who couldn't give their time to the search to donate money instead, which we could use to print flyers, posters, buy food for the volunteers, and for administrative tasks.

On the phone, JC and I composed a brief chronology of events and pertinent info about Lisa's disappearance. JC had an old photo of Lisa with the collective. She would enlarge it and crop Lisa's face out to have an image to place on her flyer. We'd put the phone number of the Ottawa Police at the bottom of the poster. I told JC that Ryan had printed out hundreds of flyers, and I'd bring some of them to the meeting tonight. She agreed to call me back with details of the meeting.

Returning to my conversation with Anna, I asked her to elaborate on Ryan's new allegation about Rob Malveaux.

"What a state he was in this morning, Ryan! The police weren't doing anything except interviewing him, he complained. They were 'barking up the wrong tree,' Ryan said, and that's when he brought up Rob. Did Lisa tell you she was planning to see Rob? I didn't think she spent time with him anymore."

"Never mentioned Rob to me except in a disparaging way. None of the men she dated before Ryan treated her well. I can't imagine why she would have made plans with Malveaux and not told me about it." But Lisa hadn't told me about the pregnancy. Apparently, there was much I didn't know about my closest friend.

"Oh, he became very chatty, Ryan, going on about Rob and what an unsavory character he was. He was pointing the finger at him, even accusing Rob of hitting my Lisa in the past! I don't know what to think."

Anna wrung her hands and took some Kleenex from her purse. She and Lorenzo didn't know whether Ryan was a friend or foe. They weren't sure if they could trust him, but they had no reason to doubt what he said. I told her that I was in the same boat.

Anna stopped speaking abruptly as Christopher and Isabella Santoro approached. They were a good-looking, older couple, who were part of the Campana's church congregation. The Santoros and I wanted to begin our search by flagging down cars, so we ambled along Aylmer Road. Like every other man in town except for Alain, Christopher was eager to discuss what had gone wrong in the playoffs last night.

"I don't blame Lalime for letting those soft goals slide by," Christopher said. "Think of the times that he carried the Sens in the past. Remember how he shut out the Flyers three nights running in 2002? He's a good boy and an excellent player. What's amazing is how much better the Sens play during the season than they do during the championship. They just don't stand up well to pressure even though the Leafs are moving past their prime. Johansson is—what? Thirty-seven now? He didn't even want to play hockey anymore until a few weeks ago, and Owen Nolan is out with a bad knee. Sundin has lower back problems, and Belfour just turned thirty-nine yesterday! Those guys are pretty old to be cremating us this way."

"Yeah, Patrick Lalime is a real pistol, but he was no match for Belfour last night," I remarked, thinking how sad it was that someone was considered to be an antique at thirty-nine.

Aylmer Road was long and wide and stretched for several kilometers in between stop signs. The team was covering the north side of the street, so we made our way back to Rivermead. We turned into an old neighborhood with stone houses, ditches, and a small elementary school. Many of the homes were empty since it was a workday. Sometimes, I sensed that there was someone at home, but it was probably a harried homemaker, who was too busy to answer the door: besieged by the endless demands of small children, no doubt.

One frail, older woman opened the door a crack and was delighted to talk about Lisa's disappearance. She had read about it in the paper and felt terrible about it. No, she hadn't seen Lisa or her car, but she would be happy to invite us in for tea and to meet her three cats: Novembre, Décembre, and Melynda. I was afraid to ask why Melynda hadn't been named after a month in case the lonely woman held us hostage any longer. We thanked her for her time and moved on.

Stopping motorists at the intersection wasn't much more productive. None of the drivers had seen Lisa.

"Peut-être qu'elle est partie pour les Barbades?" a young guy in an old, beat-up Honda Civic suggested.

"What did he say?" the Santoros asked.

"He asked if she could have taken off for Barbados! What a crazy idea," I muttered.

After hours of traversing the long boulevard, the Santoros and I became tired and hungry. We trudged back to our central meeting place at the Hippodrome. About forty searchers were gathered around the minivans, eating sandwiches that Sandra and Anthony had prepared. It was cold, but the hot coffee warmed me up.

Ryan appeared, looking glum. He accused the police of bungling the investigation by getting into territorial disputes over whose case this was—Ontario's or Quebec's. He claimed the police had searched Lisa's car without using gloves and pushed the seat back so far that no one would ever know if she'd been driving it.

"I think the car was planted there. She must've took off with someone she knew."

Lisa was too street smart to have voluntarily abandoned her car. If she'd gone with someone she'd known, surely she would have taken her purse and not just her cell phone. Ryan's explanation didn't sound plausible.

"Well, at least the police are taking the case seriously now," I said.

"The police aren't doing shit," Ryan replied. "They're only interested in nailing me. To them, I'm nothing but a felon. That's why I been busting my ass distributing flyers on the boulevard. And I'm gonna take my truck up north to Highway 5 and spend the rest of the day asking people around Malveaux's if they seen her. I'm not waiting for the police to pin this on me."

"What do you call this?" I shouted, as I pointed to the number of patrol cars. "Mrs. Campana told me they took bloodhounds up to Malveaux's. How can you say they aren't doing anything?"

My voice sounded shrill. I was flooded with rage. I didn't know who to blame, but Ryan seemed like a good target.

On the other hand, I felt sorry for him and worried about his sobriety. Lisa had just slipped after five full years, and Ryan only had three. Would he be able to handle the stress without drinking or drugging? I apologized for my outburst and wished him good luck with his queries.

I finished nibbling at my turkey sandwich in a pita wrap, which Sandra had covered generously with Ranch dressing. I was hungry, but the idea of Lisa injured and alone had killed my appetite. Grabbing my bottle of Dasani water, I went to say goodbye to Mrs. Campana.

I needed to stop at the pharmacy to get Devon's puffer for his asthma before I went off to meet WAR and Alain. I couldn't recall if I had any Gaviscon in the house. I would get an extra bottle, for my indigestion, at the pharmacy just in case.

JC had left a message on my voice mail saying that eight members out of twelve were available for our meeting, which was a high turnout for such short notice. We would meet at JC's house in Kanata at 6:30 p.m. I made a quick call to Alain, saying I'd be a little later than we had planned.

Anna gave me a big kiss when I left. I admonished her to take good care of herself and Lorenzo. He had continued plodding up and down the street long after Ryan had returned to the parking lot for lunch. It was futile of me to caution the Campanas against staying out too late. If Devon had gone missing, I would never have been able to leave the search site.

Mark was barbecuing pork chops in the garage when I got home and disguising them with an odd sauce to divert attention away from his pitiful culinary skills. He'd been unable to get away during the afternoon because his doctoral student, Maya, was having a "crisis" with her thesis. Obviously, Mark and I defined the word crisis differently. He promised that he would join the team tomorrow and presented me with fried onion rings and coleslaw to go with the pork. My plate looked like one huge sea of grease. I couldn't eat. I took a yogurt out of the refrigerator and sliced strawberries to put in it.

Devon was quiet during the meal. I noticed that he was wearing a silver chain around his neck which Lisa had given him. When I told Mark what Ryan said about Rob Malveaux, he shook his head.

"She hated that guy!" Mark observed. "Was Ryan the one who told you she planned to see Rob? What if he made it up?"

That had occurred to me, too, but it was just conjecture. I had nothing to base it on. Now that we were embroiled in the worry about Lisa, Mark was acting a little less frosty to me.

"Think I'll take the dog for a ride to Bruce Pit," Mark announced, as he loosened his belt buckle, and pushed himself away from the table.

I tried to imagine Alain stuffing himself like Elvis on all that heavy fried food, but I couldn't picture it.

Bruce Pit is a designated field for dog walkers. Technically, dog owners are prohibited from using certain entrances to get into the off-leash areas during the winter months. But some people use the entrances anyway and remove their dog's leash before they arrive at the public access points. These dogs run through people's yards urinating, defecating, and generally doing what dogs do.

"Great idea," I said. It was a beautiful day, albeit somewhat brisk, and Monday would enjoy his romp in the field even though he didn't really like other dogs, but I had been hoping that Mark would offer to go back to Aylmer. He still had another hour or two before it got dark.

"Make sure to keep her on the leash until you get into the Pit. We don't need any trouble with the police right now," I joked as I stroked Monday and told him what a good boy he was; he never seemed to tire of hearing it. Sometimes I would call him a very bad boy as well, and he would bark and crane his neck so far that it looked as though he was trying to kiss me. Not the smartest dog in the world, but out of all the boys in my house, he was my favorite by a long shot.

CHAPTER TEN

The Queensway was crowded, and the drive to JC's was slow, but I appreciated the congestion because it gave me time to think. I was sorry that I hadn't brought my book by Amy Tan and made a mental note to bring it with me in the car tomorrow.

JC was a junior partner in a law firm that specialized in sexual harassment cases. She would only take complaints from women. When a man claimed he was being harassed, JC called him "a lucky bastard" and closed his file. Not that she was a stereotypical, man-hating lesbian; far from it. She spent most of her free time with her adopted son, Matthew, and she volunteered to work with predominantly male teenage delinquents in a restorative justice project that brought young offenders together with the people they had victimized. The program offered restitution, reconciliation, and mediation, and tried to deal with petty crime and vandalism on a local level.

JC was tall with a military looking haircut, which seemed incongruent with her delicate, Nordic features. When she was off duty, she lived in sweatshirts, baggy khakis, corduroys, and Doc Martens.

Most of the members of WAR were in their thirties, although Sheila and her partner, Diane, were in their late fifties. Sheila had bipolar illness; she had difficulty stabilizing her condition with medication. She made a serious suicide attempt last year, but fortunately, Diane found her in time and rushed her to the hospital to have her stomach pumped. Diane had been incredibly supportive, and Sheila had made a good comeback; she joined

Toastmasters International to improve her public speaking skills and spoke to various civic groups about the importance of destigmatizing mental health issues. As aging hippies, they cruised around town in a pink-and-blue psychedelic van, which my dad nicknamed "the Partridge family bus."

The group was composed mainly of professionals. Their jobs ranged from computer programming to interpreting to alternative medicine.

Judith, a chiropractor, was obsessed with nutrition and never missed an opportunity to warn me about the danger of mercury poisoning in fresh shark and canned tuna. According to Judith, dairy products were harmful to the sinuses; foods with sugar or yeast encouraged the growth of candidiasis; gluten destroyed the digestive tract; and soy was toxic to the thyroid. I didn't know what kind of meal plan she advocated to avoid the plethora of herbicides, pesticides, dioxins, triglycerides, hormones, and carcinogenic agents that had poisoned the food chain. I sensed that Judith would have preferred to swallow food capsules instead of taking the risk on the real thing, which she believed to be irrevocably damaged. However, once I had seen her at Burger King wolfing down a double cheeseburger and fries. She had pretended not to know me.

Andrea was an active member of the women's underground. She hid women and children who were running from abusive mates. Andrea was short and skinny, with bright red hair, porcelain-looking skin, and the smallest wrists that I've ever seen: a case of osteoporosis just waiting to happen. She worked at the Rape Hotline and had a surprisingly ebullient personality, given the somber nature of her work. She was the first to crack a joke, could drink any man under the table, and was the proud owner of a Harley Davidson, which she referred to as her "antidepressant."

At sixty-nine, Donna was the oldest group member. She had retired from her job as Coordinator of the Women's Aboriginal Centre. Donna had white hair, which she tied in a bun on top of her head. She had a ruddy complexion and was quite lined from years as a sun worshiper. Invariably attired in mid-length skirts and flat shoes, Donna was fond of reminiscing about the good old days.

"I'm sorry that I missed the sexual revolution," Donna had said wistfully on several occasions. I tried not to laugh at this remark because first, I couldn't picture Donna having sex with anyone. Second, although I was thirty years younger than she was, I too missed the revolution since I had gotten married when I was Alain's age.

At the other end of the spectrum, we had Janie with fibromyalgia, who had been on disability for seventeen years. A survivor of incest, Janie had been celibate ever since I'd known her and wrote a column for the *Carleton University Womyn's Centre Newsletter* advocating celibacy as a viable lifestyle choice, as opposed to an aberration.   She yawned and sighed continuously throughout meetings, only opening her mouth to ask, "Could you repeat that, please?"

Janie was never animated unless we had an emergency. That got her adrenaline pumping. It almost seemed as though Janie was pleased to hear bad news. I suspected that was because of the chaos that she grew up with. She was so accustomed to melodrama in childhood that periods of calm now seemed dull and boring.

WAR members could be separated into those who were raped or sexually assaulted, and those who had never been abused.

Since the focus of the group was to educate the public about the horrors of sexual abuse, many of the members had been violated in this manner. We all agreed that rape and pedophilia were vicious and unspeakable crimes.

Incest was utterly beyond my comprehension. Although I had been a pacifist all my life and had opposed the death penalty under every conceivable circumstance, when I thought of fathers, uncles, school teachers or neighbors breaching the trust of children, I could only conclude that lethal injection was too good for them.

I was just as devoted and passionate about our cause as the next member but, at times, I felt alienated from the group because I was not a survivor of sexual assault. It almost made me understand the "bug chasers," the small but growing minority of HIV negative gay men who actively sought out the virus to feel that they were a part of the HIV positive community. I felt incredibly sorry for those poor saps, and I wouldn't trade places with a sexual assault survivor for all the money in the world. However, in some existential way, I wished that I could live inside the body of a rape victim just for one day, so I would have a better idea of how she or he really felt.

I was also the only woman who carried a purse and wore a gold chain and earrings. Like the young women at Le Skratch, everyone else at WAR used a backpack, a fanny pack, or a briefcase. WAR was preoccupied with the concept of dysfunctional families, which put me at a further disadvantage since my family of origin was great. My childhood trauma was the death of my mother, which destroyed me emotionally, but there was nothing toxic about my upbringing. The terrible sorrow that I endured losing my mom had brought me closer to my father, not farther apart. For many members of WAR, the villains in life were not cancer and illness, but rather male abusers.

In the movie *The Wild One,* Marlon Brando played a motorcycle gang leader. In one scene, he was asked what he was rebelling against, and he replied, "Whattaya got?" That's the way WAR approached social problems whereas my inner rebellious teenager never really developed because I felt as though I had to take care of my father. I became overly responsible at a young age. I was also terrified of losing him, so he was all the more precious to me after my mother passed on.

In many ways, I felt out of place in this group, especially since Lisa left. She was an advocate for survivors for years and was one of the founding members of WAR, but when the group's focus became increasingly narrow, Lisa opted out.

"I can't stand to hear one more word about the patriarchy!" she told me. "For God's sake, WAR never acknowledges the progress women have made over the last fifty years. Women are doctors, lawyers, and even Supreme Court justices. Do we still experience pay inequity, harassment, assault, inadequate day care, sexual double standards, discrimination against gays, and the need to live up to a ridiculous social beauty ideal? Damn, right we do. But not all men are selfish, psychopathic rapists, which is the feeling I get from WAR." Lisa made an appeal to the group to modify their stance, but she was voted down, and she left months ago.

I also believed that WAR had lost sight of the progress women had made, but I treasured the life-altering work the group did. And I was attached to them. Even if we weren't that close as friends, I admired them, trusted them, learned from them, and enjoyed the feeling of camaraderie that I had when I was with them. WAR had been a part of my life for so many years that I would have been lost without them. Moreover, I needed them urgently now to help me find Lisa.

JC brought the meeting to order and gave a brief update on Lisa's situation. JC was a nonstop talker, who talked in sentence fragments. Her mind raced all over the place, from one thought to another, and she had an irritating habit of interrupting other people.

"Okay. Down to business," JC began. "Most of you know that Lisa—living with that wife beater—hasn't been seen since Friday. Three things. One, get the word out. To as many people as possible. Two, organize a search party. To find her. Can't afford to rely solely on the police. Three, explore other resources. That may help locate her."

Macy, JC's DJ friend, had contacted the media. They were going to broadcast announcements about the need for volunteers to search the woods and fields where Lisa's car had been abandoned.

Janie would discuss Lisa's plight with her collective at the next Carleton University Womyn's Centre's meeting and see what they could do to assist us.

"She may have been afraid of Ryan if she told him about the pregnancy," Andrea said. She offered to look for Lisa in the women's underground in case she had gone into hiding.

I discussed my plans with Alain to distribute Ryan's flyer and to create a website about Lisa. I asked for a donation to pay for Alain's printing expenses and brought the group up to speed on my first day of the search. About eighty-five people had shown up. Approximately half of them were also attending the nightly prayer vigil for Lisa outside the Campana's church in Nepean.

"If you're going to disappear anywhere, do it in Utah," Sheila said. "One day, during the search for Elizabeth Smart, 8,000 people turned out to look for her."

"Helps if you have white skin and a pretty face," Amal retorted. "Hardly anyone's looking for Tamra Keepness, the five-year-old Native girl who disappeared in Regina."

"I don't think we can avoid discussing Ryan's role in this situation," Barb interjected. "A recent article in *JAMA, the Journal of the American Medical Association,* states that the leading cause of death among young pregnant women is homicide, usually committed by male partners. It's possible that some men may feel jealous of the prospective baby and the lack of attention that they'll receive when the woman gives birth. Or they don't feel emotionally prepared to become fathers."

"They should fry!" JC declared.

"Get real, Jenna," Barb said. "These deaths tend to be more violent than other murders. The women are strangled, suffocated, or stabbed. The men's actions are sudden and impulsive. The problem of pregnant women also raises the messy issue of the fetus. Is it a person? If so, killing a pregnant woman is considered to be aggravated murder, which warrants the death penalty in some American states. Utah is one of thirty-seven or thirty-eight states that view the fetus as a person. Fortunately, Canada has no such law."

"Hey!" I raised my voice. "Why is everyone obsessed with Utah? You're talking about Lisa like she's dead. Stop it! She's just missing. We don't know where she is."

"Of course, we can't jump to any conclusions at this point, Tara," Judith said quietly. "But you have to admit it doesn't look good. She's been gone for six days and has an abusive partner. Sometimes, Occam's razor applies."

"What's Occam's razor?"

"It's a principle from medieval philosophy that says the simplest solution is often the right one," Judith replied, as though she were talking to a small child.

"Too bad we're not in the States," Janie added, coming out of her usual slumber. "We could get on *Larry King Live* and get the message out to millions of people."

Shut the hell up! I wanted to scream, but instead, I felt my stomach lurch. The room began to spin, and I had a graphic image in my mind of the bloodhounds combing Malveaux's property, looking for Lisa. Lisa who had sat next to me at the movies, the same way she did every month: who had followed her rigid and oppressive diet the way she always did at Nate's. Lisa, who felt that she couldn't tell me her worries about the baby. I must have looked green because Diane got up and rushed over to my side, offering me ginger ale and asking if I needed Gravol, otherwise known as Dramamine, an antiemetic. I nodded, unable to speak.

Diane sat next to me, coddling me. She was adept at the caretaking role. I could see how Sheila had flourished with her loving care. Diane asked if I wanted to go outside for some fresh air, but I didn't want to leave the meeting. As sick as I felt, and as much as I feared the conversation that came next, I needed to be there to hear what they said.

All of the WAR members thought Ryan was our number one suspect. They wanted to know if he was going to be part of the search team. I said that he was a significant player. He'd already made up the flyers and had been pounding the pavement up and down Aylmer Road and the Alexandre-Taché Boulevard.

WAR didn't want to work with Ryan. They feared that he might deliberately lead us in the wrong direction. A lengthy argument ensued.

For those who have never had the pleasure of belonging to a collective, an argument of this sort had the potential to last for six to eight hours. Under normal circumstances, I would have been voted down, and the group would never have worked in conjunction with Ryan. But because Lisa was my best friend and I was the initiator of the search team, they gave considerable weight to my opinion. Also, I was the only one who knew Ryan personally.

"There is absolutely no evidence that Ryan was involved," I repeated wearily.

"Just the fact that he broke his first girlfriend's nose," JC offered.

"He was doing a lot of cocaine then. He's sober now. Doesn't that count for anything? Lisa never mentioned any..."

"Just because she didn't talk about it. Doesn't mean it didn't happen. Women are ashamed. It's not their fault. But they feel it is," JC said.

"I'm not participating if the wife beater is running the show," Amal stated.

I was furious. "Ryan is not a wife beater! He was never even married before. Until the police find some concrete proof linking him to Lisa's departure, we could all try the presumption of innocence. It may be archaic, but it's worked for hundreds of years!"

"Run him out of town. Picket his house. That'll show him he can't get away with it," someone declared.

"We can't do that. He may be the only one who knows where Lisa is," Ritu said.

It was unbelievable. I may as well have been talking to the wall. No one was listening to me because everyone had already assumed we were looking for a body and that Ryan had killed Lisa.

After much heated debate, we agreed that Ryan was going to be involved whether we liked it or not. Most of the women said they planned to avoid him except for me. I wasn't stupid, but I had to see some hard facts that linked Ryan to Lisa's disappearance before I cut him out of my life.

And, as much as I hated to admit it, Ritu may have been correct when she suggested that Ryan could have information that would be essential to the search. Nothing could be gained by antagonizing him now.

JC asked for a show of hands to indicate how many people would be available to look for Lisa tomorrow. Almost half the women volunteered. Like me, some did shift work. Two were full-time homemakers, one was retired, and another was on disability. That made six women who were free to start searching for Lisa in the morning.

Unfortunately, I wouldn't be one of them. But if I could find a replacement to cover me for Friday and Saturday, I'd be able to rejoin the team the following day.

As I was leaving, I was cornered by Judith, so I asked how she was doing since she had just started a new job with a pharmaceutical company; this clashed with her holistic approach, but she felt compelled to take the position for financial reasons. Judith seemed more concerned with the onset of pollen season than with her ethical dilemma.

Ottawa is gorgeous in the spring due to the proliferation of trees and flowers. But the city boasts one of the highest pollen counts in the country. As a result, thousands of people suffer the miserable symptoms of itchy eyes, runny noses, and sneezing attacks from April until the end of September, which are the most pleasant months of the year otherwise.

"Did you know that there are thirteen different types of maple trees and seven kinds of oak trees in Ottawa? That's not to mention the Largetooth Aspen, the Shagbark Hickory, and those beautiful, to-die-for magnolia trees. I should buy stock in Claritin or Reactine. They must make a fortune!" Judith said.

"Interesting."

"You know, the high pollen count may be the cause of Devon's asthma. I thought that was the problem with my daughter, Suzanne, but she was reacting to fungal spores. You should check that out."

"Thanks," I said, anxious to get away from her but feeling sad about her allergies. Judith had Multiple Chemical Sensitivities, and it was difficult for her to breathe properly. She had been talking about moving out to the country. Maybe she couldn't bear to part with her secret trips to Burger King just yet.

Barb was right behind me as I backed toward the door.

"Lisa belongs to all of us, Tar. I know you're upset that most of us have already concluded she's come to some harm. We're just trying to be realistic—to brace ourselves for the worst. Then we'll be pleasantly surprised in the event of a positive outcome. That's the way both you and I operate on the job. We're pragmatists."

"That's different!" I snapped. "There's no way I'm giving up hope for Lisa now. Not ever! Not until I see her lying in a black box. I won't give up on her, and I wish you wouldn't either."

As we were talking, JC's cat came up behind me and rubbed itself against my leg. I screamed and was shocked by my own overreaction. My nervous system was falling apart. It felt like I was plugged into a wall socket, but I appreciated Barb's attempt to console me after the meeting.

CHAPTER ELEVEN

Heading off to Alain's, I hoped that he wouldn't be as negative about Lisa as WAR had been. I called Devon from the car to make sure he had heated up the supper I'd cooked earlier, and to see if he'd made any progress with Harper Lee. He assured me that he was about one-third of the way through the book and that it was getting "a little better." He was now eager to find out if Boo Radley was ever going to leave the house. I was thrilled and said that I was looking forward to discussing it with him when he was done.

Alain's apartment building was old and run-down. Some of the windows were broken, and remnants of Venetian blinds were hanging from the balconies. I buzzed Alain from the outer lobby, and he opened the main door for me.

The elevator was small and cramped. It jumped nervously from floor to floor like a person with Parkinson's, and the elevator fan made a loud whirring noise. Ads for local bars and restaurants lined the wall to my right as well as a sign that said, "This proves that elevator advertising works!"

I wasn't so sure that was true because I couldn't recall what was underneath the sign. There was a notice about the Terry Fox Run for Cancer Research; Terry Fox was a national hero who had attempted to run across Canada on only one leg to raise money for cancer. He made it for almost 3,000 miles before he collapsed, went into remission, and eventually died when he was around Alain's age.

The back wall of the elevator was composed of a full-length mirror that allowed me to see way more of myself and my crazy looking hair than I could handle.

I stood next to a large man who appeared to be in his third trimester. His boobs were twice the size of mine. The man was friendly and complained about the lack of heat in the building. He was right. It was a bit chilly, and I wished I had worn something warmer, rather than opting for appearance over comfort.

The hallway smelled damp and musty, and the unpleasant aroma of fish floated through the air. The red printed carpets were faded, and the color scheme on the wall was garish. Peach walls greeted me on Alain's floor. The apartment doors had been painted a deep maroon with wide gray borders and a pine finish. I needed my sunglasses.

Bicycles, children's toys, and unread newspapers littered the hallway. Some of the overhead light bulbs had burned out, and the corridor was dim. Many of the apartments had double bolts on their doors, which made me imagine how I would feel spending the night, as though that were ever going to happen.

Alain gave me an enthusiastic welcome into his tiny studio apartment, which was the size of a postage stamp. It reminded me of Pee-Wee Herman's Playhouse. If I had been any taller, I would have had to bend over not to hit the ceiling. The walls were stark white without a single poster or painting, and he had parquet floors, which were dull and lifeless.

Alain's kitchen consisted of a sink and stove. A small wooden table sat in the corner of the room with two of Alain's accounting books on top. Several hard-wooden chairs were pushed up close to a mismatched kitchen table. There was an ancient coffee table, which was barren save for the *Ottawa Sun* newspaper. A small orange crate sat next to his large futon couch, and dishes were draining on a board next to the sink. I pictured Alain dutifully washing the dishes every night, and this domestic fantasy aroused me.

I searched in vain for a bookshelf, but all I found was Alain's large workstation. The only furniture that looked as though it belonged in this century was the large TV and the 480 gig processor with its Bubble Jet printer. I tried to think of something complimentary to say about his Spartan abode, but I was at a loss for words.

Alain seemed embarrassed about his apartment. He was saving money so that he could move to a better area because a neighbor of his had his car radio stolen right out of the parking garage.

"Those little slime buckets," Alain exclaimed. "I would've killed them if I'd caught them stealing my car."

Talking about the thieves got Alain excited. I could see the little gap between his teeth when he grinned, which made him suddenly look very boyish.

"What kind of car do you drive?"

"Well, I don't have a car yet. But I'll have one someday."

To his credit, the apartment was neat and orderly. I looked around for photos of the elusive Christine, but there were none, which was a blessing. Alain offered me a drink, and I said I'd love a glass of red wine. He looked sheepish and confessed that he only had beer. I replied that would be great, and he said, "Cool."

Although Alain was still wearing his white T-shirt, long-sleeved, black-and-red checked over-shirt, and torn blue jeans, he looked particularly handsome. Being alone with him and sitting close to him on the rickety couch was so distracting that I feared I would never be able to concentrate on Lisa.

The beer helped me to relax and allowed the horror of the day to wash away—that haunting picture of the searchers, the anguished look on Anna Campana's face, and the heartless way that WAR had talked about Lisa. I wanted to kick my shoes off, put my feet up on Alain's misshapen wooden table, listen to Sam Roberts, and hear all about his pool game.

Reluctantly, I began describing my day in Hull and Aylmer, and the meeting in Kanata. Alain didn't react the way WAR did. He didn't jump to conclusions about Ryan. All he wanted to do was to stay "goal focused."

"Look, we have no idea what happened to her. So it's pointless to speculate. Let's just make a plan and implement it."

Alain suggested that we take Ryan's flyer and create a version in French. We could scan both flyers and upload them to various websites. At the top of Ryan's flyer, the caption read, "MISSING since Friday, April 16, 2004. LISA CAMPANA." It described Lisa's age, height, weight, eye color, complexion, and hair. Sitting on a small computer chair next to Alain, I dictated the following for him to translate into French:

Lisa Campana left her home in Ottawa West on Friday morning, April 16th, 2004. She planned to go to Meech Lake, Quebec, to visit a friend. Her white Toyota RAV4 was abandoned on D'Amour Road in Aylmer and was first noticed at about 9 p.m. Tuesday. Her car was locked with her purse and belongings inside.

At the bottom of the flyer, there was a large photograph of Lisa, which Alain scanned onto his hard disk. We deliberated about whether to say that Lisa had been planning to meet with Malveaux at Meech Lake because that had not been substantiated. However, that was what Ryan had said on his flyers, and we wanted them all to have uniformity. We stated that any information about the disappearance or whereabouts of Lisa Campana should be called into the Ottawa Police at 613–236–1222.

Lastly, we added that a "private trust fund had been established to continue searching for Lisa Campana. Donations can be made to 'search for Lisa Campana trust fund' and sent in care of Women's Day Books, 279 Albert St., Ottawa, Ontario K1P 5G8."

True to his word, Alain turned out to be a real whiz on the Internet, even though he was one of the few people on the planet who was still on dial-up, and it took forever for his Web pages to load. He'd already created a blog, which he'd dedicated to Lisa. A blog was like a diary, he informed me. Alain could write in it every day and update it. Also, it was free. Alain uploaded Lisa's photo to the blog, which he had called *Find Lisa Campana*.

Alain carefully entered data from the flyer onto the website and asked me for pertinent details about the search team that he could post. "I want to request volunteers, too. We're gonna need a lot more than eighty-five people, for sure!" He also began searching for sites about missing people, so that we could tell them about Lisa.

"Hey," he stated. "Here's one called *Missing Persons' Cyber Center*. But wait a minute. It's all screwy. The links are wrong. I guess the site closed down a while ago, and the message board isn't active anymore. It's confusing because some people posted looking for friends from high school or university, but others posted urgent messages about their family and friends who disappeared." Alain took a long sip of his Labatt's Blue.

"There's a site called *Missing You*, which has a disclaimer. Listen to this! Oh, man. It says websites for missing persons are being used by scam merchants to send out emails with the subject title, *'Missing You.'* Can you fucking believe that?" he asked and quickly added, "Oh, sorry."

Was he apologizing for swearing? Oh, my God, he must have thought that I was a dinosaur. Did he think four letter words weren't part of my vocabulary? Actually, they weren't, but perhaps I should swear back at him, just to reassure him that I was not offended by his language. I could spew out a steady stream of expletives to sound younger and more hip. I tried to think of something really foul to say, but I drew a blank.

"No problem," I replied, worrying again that I was mimicking his vocabulary.

"Excellent," he said, turning his attention back to the websites, which were turning over more slowly than my geriatric patients recovering from hip surgery. His hands were calloused from cutting meat, and his fingernails were short.

"More dead-ends. This site called *Missing Persons* is really about a band. And this one, *CanadaFind*, looked promising, but it's, like, a business, eh, and it's gonna charge us money to find someone. The *National Missing Persons' Helpline* looks useful, but it's in the UK."

"Is it always this hard to find things on the Internet?" I asked. Most of my experiences surfing the Web had been negative. One day, I spent over two hours trying to book reservations from Ottawa to Winnipeg on the Air Canada website until it occurred to me that I could have completed my transaction in ten minutes if I had just picked up the phone.

"Depends," Alain replied. "Sometimes it's fast and easy." He snapped his fingers. "Other times, doing stuff on the Net is so inefficient that it'd be easier to go down to the place in person or just call them. But we don't have that option." He returned to the computer.

"Hey, we're in luck! Look at this one. It's called *Missing Persons' Links* and accepts info on both adults and children as long as they're genuinely missing." Alain looked pleased. "*The Missing Persons' Page* and *Missing Persons throughout the World* look awesome, too." He began to compose a form letter that we could individualize and send off to the sites on email, telling them about Lisa and asking if they would establish reciprocal links with our blog. Then he submitted several posts to various bulletin boards for missing persons.

"What's this?" I asked. "It says it'll send free traffic to our site. Should we sign up?"

"Nah. Most of those things are scams. They're full of adware, spyware, and browser hijackers."

"Spyware? Who would want to spy on our website?" I felt ignorant, as I often did when Mark or Devon were using Internet lingo that I didn't understand. It was all geek to me.

"They don't spy on the site. They collect personal data on you like where you surf or shop, your name, address, and credit card number—stuff like that. I can give you a shareware program that'll help remove adware from your machine," Alain offered.

"Thanks," I said, knowing full well I'd never understand how to run his program but wanting to take anything that belonged to Alain as a reminder that I had actually spent time alone with him.

While Alain was typing, I stared at the digital images of missing children with their smiling, well-groomed faces. A seven-year-old boy was last seen in Missouri in 1997. A twelve-year-old girl, wearing braces and a party hat, left her grammar school in New Jersey in 1999 and hadn't been seen since.

I was gripped by an overwhelming feeling of heartbreak. I could hardly look at them. They had been gone for years. Where were they now? Had they been abducted by psychotic, postpartum mothers whose infants had died? Had they been forced into a life of pornography and child prostitution? Were they taken by estranged spouses, the best case scenario? Or were they all a pile of ashes and dust, leaving their friends and families devastated by the loss and further destroyed by the lack of answers and closure?

The roll call continued: five-year-old Jessica Koopmans went missing from Lethbridge, Alberta in May of 2001 and was found murdered one week later. A family "friend," Tony Gallup, was convicted of killing her and given a life sentence. Little Cecilia Zhang was kidnapped from her home in Toronto while her parents slept in October of 2003. Her body wasn't discovered until March of 2004.

At least the parents of the deceased found out what had happened to their kids. It was a small consolation, but they were not left endlessly waiting and hoping, trapped in some state of tortured limbo, praying for news about their children. Waiting for Godot.

Los Desaparecidos. That's what the people were called in Chile when they went missing in droves under the Pinochet regime: the disappeared. In Argentina, mothers of missing soldiers formed a protest group that dressed all in black, waiting in a public square for their sons and husbands to come home.

They were known as Las Madres de la Plaza de Mayo. Was it any comfort to those families to discover that they had lost their children or spouses to war rather than to the evil deeds of men that lacked military sanction?

JC would be foaming at the mouth, ranting about the patriarchy if she could see this roster of missing kids. It was as though a huge Bermuda triangle was just waiting to swallow up women and children.

I was sickened to think that Lisa had joined the ranks of these unfortunates and that her photo was being circulated over the Internet along with their pictures.

In order to see the faces of the children on the screen, I had to sit so close to Alain that I could see his five o'clock shadow. He was talking, but I couldn't process what he was saying because I was thinking about the lost kids.

And I'm ashamed to admit that I was aroused by Alain's masculinity and his nearness. I hated myself for wanting him while we were viewing such tragic images, and yet the conflicting emotions of desire and revulsion seemed closely attuned. It was life versus death, and all I wanted was for Alain to take me in his arms again, the way he had in the store, to affirm the fact that we were alive and safe even if Lisa and the children were not.

When my mother died, I was ten, and my sister, Denise, was only six. We shared a bedroom, not because we didn't have the space to have our own rooms, but because we liked to be together. Night after night, I would lie in bed listening to Denise cry.

One night, we had a thunderstorm, and Denise couldn't stop sobbing, and calling "Mommy, Mommy!" I went over to her twin bed and got in beside her, cradling her in my arms, and stroking her hair. I kept repeating, "It'll be all right, you'll see. Everything will be okay again."

It was hard for me to express my own grief because I needed to be strong for Denise. In many ways, I grew up too fast, trying to be a surrogate mother to Denise before Marie arrived and looking out for my dad. Now I wanted someone to mother me. I was tired of being strong. I'd had a lifetime of it. I wanted Alain to hold me and soothe me, as though I were that ten-year-old child again. If I could cling to him, I could borrow his strength and quell the mounting terror inside me.

"Is that okay with you?" Alain asked.

"Sure," I replied automatically, although I had no idea what he was talking about. "Well, I didn't really hear what you said. I was concentrating on the kids," I explained.

"I was saying that I also have a Freenet account. Freenet is a free ISP that operates out of Carleton U. It's got lots of local newsgroups that people read all the time. I'm not sure which groups would be right, but we can log in there, and you can check them out."

Sure enough, there were several groups on the Freenet that sounded ideal. I posted notices on the feminism group, the humanism group, the social justice group, the info highway, Women's Place, Ottawa General, and Ottawa Events. *Some event,* I thought grimly.

I had a real sense of accomplishment after we had finished our Internet work. I even remembered to tell Alain about Julie and her panic problem. He showed me how I could do a Google search for panic disorder when I got home.

"Wow!" Alain said, as he stood up and stretched. "I need a smoke, and my back is killing me. Sometimes, I lift 100 pounds a day! It's a bitch."

"What you need is a good masseuse," I suggested.

"Are you offering me a backrub? 'Cause I could sure use one."

There was a God after all. Here was a once-in-a-lifetime opportunity to touch Alain's flesh in a non-threatening manner. I agreed without hesitation and hoped that I didn't appear too eager.

Alain stepped out on the balcony and blew smoke rings outside, so as not to pollute my airspace. I was hit by a cold blast of air and could smell the pungent odor of his menthol cigarettes. When I was sure that he wasn't watching me, I took his over-shirt from the chair and put it to my face, hoping to smell his perspiration—some manly kind of smell—but instead, it had a scent of mild cologne. It was an aftershave that I didn't recognize, and there was just a faint hint of smoke.

Clean, crisp Alain. I longed for him the way Nathaniel Kahn had longed for his father. It was a deep ache that reached into the crevice of my soul: a hole that felt as though it had been there all my life and was yearning to be filled.

When he returned, Alain took off his undershirt, and I marveled at the strong development of his hairless chest. I've never liked hairy men. Mark had a bona fide forest on his chest, and his back whereas Alain reminded me of my first love, Jimmy, who'd had a similar physique.

Jimmy and I had only gone out for nine months before I met Mark. Jimmy majored in philosophy. We spent endless hours discussing Nietzsche and Sartre, which seemed so sexy at the time. But Brainy Jimmy had a wandering eye, and I knew that he would never be faithful, so I chose good old trustworthy Mark.

I went into Alain's medicine cabinet in his bathroom, looking for a bottle of mineral oil. I found some Advil and took one. It had been an enervating day, and my temples were pounding.

Alain lay down on the small futon. I was practically sitting on top of him due to the space constraints. I poured a small amount of oil onto my hands to warm it up before I touched his hard, supple skin. As I made kneading motions on his strong back, I noticed a scar along his shoulder blade leading up to his neck.

"Oh," he laughed. "I was hit by a beer bottle one time in a bar. This guy thought I'd made a move on his girlfriend—I didn't!— so he threw a bottle at me, and I had no time to duck. But I got even. He needed five stitches in the face by the time I was finished with him." He moved his head to the right. "We were both pretty hammered at the time."

This was a novel side of Alain. I couldn't envision my sweet man/boy in a world of brawls and flying beer bottles. It worried me, and yet on some primitive level, this unexpected machismo turned me on. I knew what WAR would have said about that. They would have classified him as one step above Ryan in the battering department and given me a recommended reading list, starting with the book *Men Who Hate Women and the Women Who Love Them*.

It occurred to me that the couch must act as a pull-out bed at night. This was where Alain slept. I was literally in his bed. Images of Alain and Christine having sex together flooded my mind, and I tried to push them away.

I wondered if he had ever masturbated to the thought of me. He was so young, and Mark's sex drive was urgent at that age. Just about everything gave him a hard-on even though he wasn't particularly ardent with me. If Alain had never so much as stroked his swollen member and thought about me, there was no hope of him having any interest in me.

The bottom line with men was sex. It was the bottom line for many women, too, which was something that I was just beginning to learn now that I was reaching my sexual peak, and I was stuck with a partner who was about as appealing as leftover meatloaf.

There were really three people involved in a sexual relationship: the woman, the man, and his penis. No doubt about it. That penis was a third party, and much of the time, it was steering the ship.

Lisa used to tell me about the names that her lovers gave to their penises, such as One-Eyed Fred, Richard, and the Twins, Little Head and Big Head, or Pocket Rocket. Mark called his Mr. Johnson, and once when I was bathing one of my male patients, he warned me to be careful with Harry and the Hendersons. I'd never met a woman who had even considered naming her vagina. As sexist as it sounded, if I wanted to make progress with Big Alain, I would need to befriend Little Alain as well.

I had touched myself thinking about Alain many times. In a trance and sometimes in a frenzy, I reached for myself in the dark when the craving for him became so intense that I couldn't ignore it. During the few times that I'd had sex with Mark over the last few months, I would pretend that it was Alain sucking my nipples, Alain whispering in my ear, Alain pumping inside me.

I could have gone on forever rubbing his beautiful skin and listening to Alain's rhythmic breathing. However, the long hours were catching up to me, and the Advil had only put a dent in my head pain. Furthermore, I was due back at work tomorrow and so was he.

With reluctance, I told Alain that I was finished, and he rolled over and smiled at me. It took all my self-control not to lean down to kiss him. Delirium and desire must have been written all over my face since Alain looked startled, and he got up suddenly, talking about the need to call Christine.

When we said goodnight, I gave Alain a big hug. He returned my embrace tentatively, and I hoped I hadn't scared him off with my familiarity.

Alain reminded me that he had school tomorrow night—he was taking business courses at the university—so he wouldn't be able to join the search team until Friday. It was sweet of him to offer to give up so much of his free time. He said he'd call me the day after tomorrow.

When I got home, Dev was asleep, but Mark was waiting up for me. I filled him in on my emotionally draining day, and he told me that I had received several calls from the media. Two newspaper reporters and one radio producer wanted me to call them back in the morning.

Mark handed me the latest article by Elmore Stewart entitled "Missing Ottawa Woman's Car Found in Aylmer." Elmore was true to his word. He had written a concise description of events and had corrected the earlier portrayal of Lisa as an active drug addict. Stewart did imply that Lisa's judgment in men was lacking, but he stressed the fact that her disappearance strongly suggested foul play. He even spelled my name right, which always astonished me. I was impressed.

Mark told me not to worry about WAR's reaction. "Those women think everyone is guilty. They're just like Nancy Grace on *Court TV*. Of course, people are going to give Lisa flak about taking up with that moron, but it doesn't matter what anybody else says. This is no time to judge or blame her. And no one knows that she's dead! WAR doesn't have a crystal ball that can see into the future. They don't know that Lisa has been murdered or that Ryan is culpable in any way. What we do know is that the chances of finding her alive grow slimmer with every passing day."

Mark stammered, probably trying to think of something to say that would comfort me. "We just have to try our best to find her and, um, hope for a positive outcome."

My mind wandered as Mark told me that he'd spent half the day at the university dealing with Maya's "emergency," which consisted of allegations that she had plagiarized parts of her thesis. And he had taken Devon to hockey after dinner.

Devon played Bantam house league. He practiced one night a week and had a game one other night. His team was winding up for the championships, but they'd played poorly this year. According to Mark, tonight's session was no exception, and he didn't expect them to win the playoffs.

He talked about Devon while I lamented the fact that I couldn't return to Quebec to search for Lisa tomorrow. There was no way that Allison could replace me for three days in a row. I needed to work the last two days of my regular three-day shift unless I was able to find another nurse to replace me.

I was too tired to check my email or to look up panic disorder for Julie, but I promised myself that I would catch up during my lunch hour tomorrow. I also made a mental note to call Victoria's Secret to ask about the status of my order, although I couldn't envision taking my clothes off in front of twenty-four-year-old Alain.

In university, Lisa had a T-shirt that said, "So many men, so little time." She had such confidence about her appearance, even though the men she dated mistreated and disappointed her. Lisa had a perfect body and countless boyfriends, whereas I had only been with two men before I married Mark.

I was self-conscious about my age, my weight, the cellulite on my thighs, and the scar from my Caesarean section, not to mention my sagging breasts. I pictured my rival, Christine, with her perky little B-cup breasts, her short skirts, and heels. The least that I would have to do to have an affair with Alain would be to disguise my aging body in some decent underwear, to dim the lighting, and to pray that he needed contact lenses to see in the dark.

Mark said that he'd go up to Aylmer after lunch tomorrow. I yawned and announced that I was going to bed. Mark turned on *CBC Newsworld* and said that he'd be up later on. I was glad that he'd stopped trying to approach me sexually. Mark must have accepted what I'd said about the problems in our relationship since he had made no further overtures in my direction. I didn't know what he was thinking. Was he hoping that I was going through a phase? Did he also lack the energy to work on our relationship? Surely, Mark and I couldn't maintain this sexless arrangement forever.

It behooved me that I could obsess about Alain and Mark when Lisa had been missing for six days. My best friend could be dead in the Gatineau Hills. Instead of modeling lingerie from Victoria's Secret, I may be shopping for a black dress for a wake.

Tears slid down my face and onto my pillow. No! I refused to believe that. I would not go there! Neither would I blame Lisa for taking up with Ryan nor would I forsake her and conclude that Ryan had stashed her body in cottage country.

I began to pray fervently in a way that I hadn't prayed since my mother died. "Oh God," I sobbed. "Please make Lisa safe. Bring her back to me. If you don't care about me, have mercy on her parents. A parent should never have to bury a child. It's unnatural! I couldn't stand it."

No matter what age Devon was, whether he was fourteen or forty-four, I would always worry about him because he was my little boy. "I'll be a better mother to Devon," I pleaded. "I'll stay with Mark if that's what you want. Just bring her back!"

But images of the children on the Internet who had been missing for years taunted me. I thought of water-logged Laci Peterson and her unborn son, Conner, who was due to be delivered in less than one month. Had God cared about the Petersons? Had He answered the prayers of millions around the country who had begged Him to return Laci and Chandra Levy? Had He bothered to intervene in the lives of the starving masses in the Sudan, not to mention my affluent but tormented patients, Julie and Justin? How could I be such a fool to think that God cared about Lisa? I couldn't pray. All I could do was practice Lisa's advice and take the situation one day at a time.

CHAPTER TWELVE

Day two of the search was similar to day one except that more people turned out, thanks to the publicity from local newspapers, radio, and TV stations. Janie brought a contingent of women from Carleton University, who got along well with the members of WAR. Unfortunately, the feminists were not on the same wavelength as the Catholic searchers.

Jeannette, one of the Carleton students, had a bumper sticker on her car that read, "Volunteers do it for nothing." She parked right next to the Santoros, who didn't find the message particularly amusing. Good thing Diane hadn't parked next to them since her bumper sticker says, "God made me gay."

The police continued their exhaustive ground search along Aylmer Road and the Alexandre-Taché Boulevard. They had taken one of Lisa's nightgowns up to Rob Malveaux's house, but the bloodhounds hadn't picked up a scent.

Detective Desormeaux from the Missing Persons' Unit questioned me several times. I felt I was constantly repeating myself, but I knew that every piece of data was necessary. Perhaps I had forgotten to tell him something that I considered obscure but turned out to be crucial to the investigation. He introduced me to his colleague, Officer Shanley, and explained that Shanley would also be working on the case now. I was pleased to see the expanded personnel, but it wasn't bringing us any closer to finding Lisa.

CTV and CJOH news were interviewing people in the parking lot. I was hoping to avoid them, so they didn't photograph me with my bizarre hair, which I had hidden underneath a large kerchief, making me look like a chemotherapy survivor. But as luck would have it, I was ambushed by reporters from both stations. I tried valiantly to answer the same old questions without sounding tired or irritated, although sleep had eluded me for days. The reporters were especially keen to talk about Ryan, but I was guarded.

I made it clear that Ryan had not committed an offense. "On a daily basis, the Dalai Lama forgives the Chinese for the atrocities they continue to perpetrate on his people. Can't you disregard Ryan's past and focus on his behavior since he got sober?" I asked them, sounding foolish and naïve to myself.

I was angry at the people who were blaming Lisa, from the newscasters to the WAR members. Yes, she had taken up with a known batterer, but Lisa had every reason to believe that Ryan's history of domestic violence had been connected to his drug abuse. If he had reformed in one area, why wouldn't he have changed in the other?

That's what I said publicly. Privately, I also chastised Lisa for choosing Ryan. If she had married some nice, boring guy like Mark, none of this would have happened. But I couldn't say that to Lisa's family because I couldn't bear the thought of hurting them. And I could never tell WAR that I was upset with Lisa since it wasn't politically correct to hold her even partly responsible for her plight.

And I don't blame Lisa—not really. She and Ryan were both in the program together. She thought he changed. *Someone* had to give him a chance. *Someone* had to forgive him for his past. It's easy to be mad at Lisa and to say she brought this on herself, but if Ryan hurt her, all of the blame lands squarely at his feet.

Instead of even attempting to convey my conflicting

emotions, I ranted to reporters about how mean-spirited and unfair it was for the media to have lambasted Lisa for loving Ryan. I added that he was just a small part of the search, which was being conducted by the police, Lisa's family, WAR, the Carleton University Womyn's Centre, the congregation of the Campana's church, and Lisa's friends.

Despite my fear of making a public statement about Ryan and my preoccupation with my hair, I had the good grace to remember to thank all the goodhearted people from the community who had generously given of their time and the various organizations that had donated food, water, blankets, and first aid kits.

A small man of about five foot three, with bifocals and a conspicuous toupee, approached me and introduced himself as Elmore Stewart. He grabbed my hand tightly and smiled. I liked him right away and told him how much I appreciated his recent article about Lisa. We talked for several minutes, and then he asked if I'd seen Ryan. I shook my head.

Ryan had been a marathon runner like Lisa. His stamina was greater than that of all of the other searchers combined. He had been walking up and down the boulevard every day since she'd disappeared, stopping motorists and distributing flyers.

I left Stewart and went door to door again, heading west this time since I had gone east with the Santoros yesterday. I stayed with the women's contingent rather than the Catholic searchers because JC and Barb refused to alter their colorful vocabularies, and I didn't want to offend the Santoros any further.

Hours passed uneventfully, and we didn't seem to be making any headway. Janie was the first to burn out and left after two hours. There was no sign of Mark, who was probably engrossed in the problems of his doctoral students. I was annoyed that he wasn't making Lisa a higher priority.

As we returned to the parking lot, I saw Anna and Lorenzo. She had aged ten years overnight. Her large black eyes were bloodshot and glistened from too much crying. Lorenzo had a hard, stiff look on his face like a mask. Sandra wasn't with them, but Anna told me that she had taken over as the coordinator of the search, working in tandem with the police.

Sandra was now directing people, so they didn't cover the same terrain over again. She and her cousin Anthony were learning how to do briefings and debriefings: how to greet people in the morning and bring them up to date on the latest news and to collect information from them when they returned from their outing.

Soon Sandra would be setting up a central headquarters in the back of a real estate office in Hull, which had graciously offered space to the Campanas. Once that was established, all the searchers would be expected to check in at the office before going out on the hunt.

Hull was several kilometers away from the Hippodrome, which made the new office location inconvenient for the walkers and for people who took the bus, but Anna said there were about 200 volunteers circling the Hull and Aylmer area today, which gave us all great hope. One way or another, we were going to get to the bottom of this mystery. But after all this time, I wasn't sure I wanted to hear the answer anymore.

****

Friday morning, I returned to work unenthusiastically. As soon as I arrived at the hospital, Oliver Rathwell collided with me in the hall. He apologized and told me how bad he felt about

Lisa. He also said I looked like hell. I explained that I hadn't slept in three nights and had lost my appetite. Oliver offered to write a prescription for Ativan, which I accepted gratefully. He gave me a two-week supply. I hoped that would get me through the worst of the ordeal.

I resented being on the ward and thought how different it would be if Lisa had been a family member: a daughter, perhaps. Would Allison have given me time off then? I would have taken it anyway. The rights and feelings of friends weren't considered as important as those of blood relatives. I noticed how much sympathy the Campanas were receiving from the press and the community—and rightly so—but I felt envious. Lisa had been a part of me. When we'd been in university, we'd referred to each other as right and left lung. The thought of losing her was unthinkable.

People's reactions to Ryan were much more ambivalent. I doubted that he was being showered with much food and warm embraces except from his friends at AA. But the toll that this was taking on me, Lisa's friend, was certainly minimized, and I wanted to be out looking for her rather than dispensing Lipitor.

Nonetheless, I had to make the best of my time at Central Zoo. It felt as though I had been gone for a month rather than five days. So much had changed in my life since I had left these familiar halls, but the patients' lives had remained pretty much the same. Charlotte, the nurse on duty before me, had dictated detailed notes, describing the status of my patients.

Eleanor had gone home, which was a relief to all of us, and one of my knee replacement men had also been discharged. Julie was getting along better with her second psychiatrist yet she still had daily panic attacks, despite overcoming her fear of trying new medication.

Renee Blanc had Julie on twenty milligrams a day of Paxil, which can be quite effective for panic disorder, but it was making Julie agitated and light-headed. Spending the day sitting in a chair in her room was hindering her recovery from her broken ankle, eroding her general strength, and making her depressed.

She had been working with Don, the volunteer from the Anxiety Association, and liked him very much. They had been practicing behavior modification, and Julie had managed to take several steps out of the room into the hallway. Nonetheless, whenever she and Don left the safety of her hospital room, Julie felt so weak that she thought she might pass out.

Don had moved a large chair into the hall so Julie could sit there. She could manage that for five or ten minutes at a time, but it was torturous for her, and then she would have to drink a large bottle of juice or Red Bull to revive her lost strength. Everyone was frustrated with Julie's lack of progress, from physio to occupational therapy to her orthopedist.

Justin was doing a little better. He was benefiting by his work with the physical therapist and had less pain in the fingers in his right hand. With the aid of the OT, he had made tea and toast in the hospital kitchen and was pleased with himself. His spirits remained good. Justin would require one more week of intensive therapy on the unit. Then our home care worker would assess him to see if he'd be able to return home or if he'd need to go to a convalescent center.

Alfred, my 101-year-old, was recovering well from his pneumonia but wasn't strong enough to return to his retirement home. When I asked how he was feeling, Alfred told me that he felt much better when he was 100. Apparently, 101 was not what it was cracked up to be. I told him that he should have abused his body more when he was younger, which made him smile.

The diabetic, Erwin, had been caught eating a large bag of Nachos after visiting hours yesterday. How could family members think they were doing him a favor by bringing him poison like that? Of course, that was easy for me to say since no one had taken my Nachos away. Previously, it had taken all my willpower to resist my daily craving for a frothy latte or smooth chocolate milkshake. Only the thought of Alain had enabled me to forsake those foods, but I knew that whenever I wanted them, they'd be available to me. Erwin no longer had that option.

However, since Lisa had disappeared, I was having difficulty getting food down. The only foods that I wanted were soft and smooth like yogurt, ice cream, and vegetable soup. Solid food had become too hard to pass through my esophagus. I would take a bite of a sandwich, and it would get stuck in my throat. This was highly unusual for me, but I wasn't worried about it. Maybe the only perk from this horrific experience would be that I would lose five pounds.

Although I wanted to be with the search team, working forced me to concentrate on something other than Lisa or Alain. I checked in on Julie, who was much more relaxed about being in the hospital. The last time I'd seen her, she'd looked like a deer in the headlights. But we both knew that she wouldn't be able to make any real progress without something drastic happening. I still believed that her only salvation lay in drugs.

After I had completed my morning rounds and prepared the patients for physical and occupational therapy, I made several calls, trying to find someone to replace me over the weekend. No luck. I then snuck back to my computer and searched panic disorder. I came across several websites. One of them had a lively message board. I joined the group, using the password "Alain2004" and left a note asking what medications people were using.

During my lunch break, I listened to CFRA news and heard that almost 300 people were out looking for Lisa. I was moved to tears by the fact that hundreds of strangers were giving their free time to locate Lisa. *Right on, Ottawa! We're going to put you on the map right next to Utah,* I thought sadly.

After lunch, I logged on to the Anxiety Forum. I had received a note from someone with the handle "FearNoMore." FearNoMore claimed to have had complete success blocking his panic attacks by using the medication Clonazepam, known as Klonopin in the States. Discouraged, I wrote back saying that my patient had already tried this drug, and it had made her too drowsy. Moreover, psychiatrists were becoming increasingly reluctant to prescribe benzodiazepines because of their long-term problematic effects.

Finally, I retrieved my email. I'm not big on email and only check my account every third or fourth day. Since this week had been so chaotic, I hadn't collected my mail at all. It took a while to delete the spam and sort out the notes that required action from those that could be read and discarded.

My dad had written every day since Lisa had gone missing. Although he wasn't religious, he'd sent me a number of bulletins by the Mile Hi Church, which were meant to be inspirational. Each one had a different saying like, "Be the change that you want to see in the world" by Gandhi, or "Do not wait for extraordinary circumstances to do good; try to use ordinary situations" by Jean Paul Richter. I failed to see how those words of wisdom applied to my situation, but I knew that what Dad was trying to say was, "Hang in there!"

There were two notes from my sister, Denise. It would have been more considerate if she had called me. She must have thought I checked my mail daily like my son, who logged on every ten minutes.

That reminded me that Devon had his championship playoff tonight, so I scribbled out an email to him wishing him good luck. I wasn't able to attend the game, but Mark would be there. When it came to hockey, Devon cared more about Mark's presence than mine anyway, but I did enjoy going to his games when I was off duty.

As soon as I sent the note, I realized that Dev's game was next Friday night, not tonight. I definitely was not following his life. Tonight, I was supposed to pick him up at Jess's house. I took out a red pen and made an "X" on my hand to remind myself. I couldn't afford to forget about my son twice in one week.

There were four emails altogether from Denise, two of which were written before Lisa disappeared. One was a joke that she'd forwarded to me—I hate it when people fill up my box with junk—and another was a description of a mundane evening that she'd spent with her boyfriend, Corey. Twice, she'd used the term LOL, "laughing out loud."

Denise has never laughed out loud in her entire life, yet she is prone to using all kinds of Internet acronyms like ROFL ("rolling on the floor laughing,") and the pièce de résistance, LMAO ("laughing my ass off"). I would probably have a stroke if I ever saw Denise laughing her ass off since she was a somber investment banker, whose idea of a fun evening was to pour a large glass of Chardonnay and follow the rise and fall of the

Toronto Stock Exchange.

I shot off a brief note back to Denise, thanking her for her concern and telling her it would be easier to reach me by phone. It was a passive-aggressive hint that she could have been more emotionally supportive this week.

Since it was quiet on the floor, I stole ten minutes from my workday to visit the Victoria's Secret site to check the status of my order. It had been shipped and should arrive any day now. I felt a momentary twinge of guilt knowing that I was paying well over $200 for two pairs of panties and two bras that Mark would never see if I could help it. *Screw it,* I rationalized. I was having a bad week, to put it mildly.

Once I'd finished playing Internet hooky, I returned to patient care, and the day flew by. Jean-Claude was still out with the flu, which was unfortunate because he and I always had fun together, and I could have used his empathy on a day like today. On the other hand, he would have asked me probing questions that would have made me dwell more on Lisa's plight since he was my closest colleague. I had more of an officious relationship with the rest of the staff, and they were reluctant to pry into my personal life. It was just as well that Jean-Claude was ill. That way I could focus on Julie's agoraphobia and Erwin's blood sugar, which helped to get my mind off Lisa.

Just before my shift ended, I wrapped up my report for the new nurse and checked my email again. I had a note from cagedelrond@sympatico.ca. I nearly deleted it thinking it was junk, but I looked more closely and saw that it was from Alain! He had printed his signature in lowercase as "alain rivard." Mark would never do that. Mark Richards, Ph.D., was the first to let you know that he was a man of prestige.

Alain was in Quebec and had borrowed someone's laptop to fill me in on the latest news. The turnout had been impressive in the morning, but skies were overcast now, and it was threatening to rain.

Sandra was an effective director. She had sent Alain east, toward the Champlain Bridge. He was searching with some of the WAR members.

"A lady named Janie is walking with me, but she's slow and seems to get tired awfully fast," Alain wrote. Thank God it was Janie since she was pretty easygoing and had four brothers, all of whom had been supportive when she came out as an incest survivor. One of her brothers was about Alain's age. Maybe she could relate to him better than JC or Barb. I also made a mental note to ask if she'd had her thyroid tested lately. I'd been reading some interesting articles about the connection between fibromyalgia and undiagnosed or under-treated hypothyroidism. Poor Janie! I couldn't imagine what could be worse than being so exhausted every day, except being wildly infatuated with a younger man who found her about as appealing as his mother or being beaten senseless by your boyfriend in a jealous rage.

It was a real thrill to see Alain Rivard's name in my mailbox, although the email was short, and he had misspelled the word threatening, using two "t's." *Probably just a typo*, I thought and grinned at the little smiley face at the end of his note. He added a postscript saying he had uploaded Lisa's flyer onto four message boards, established five reciprocal links to other websites, and received emails from people who were interested in the case.

One claimed to have seen Lisa in West Virginia, buying a cartridge for her printer at a Kinko's store, and another said he saw her driving the car next to him in Green Bay, Wisconsin. A psychic claimed she'd had a vision where Lisa was in the woods with two dark men. Alain didn't place much faith in these sightings, but he felt compelled to pass them on to Officer Shanley.

Low and behold, there was another note from FearNoMore. He described his own situation in detail, saying he'd been taking Clonazepam at night for years because it made him sleepy during the daytime. His physician told him that the drug was short-acting and wouldn't block his panic during the day if he only took it at bedtime.

FearNoMore found that the opposite was true. Not only was his panic gone, but he also got an excellent night's sleep. If Julie had never tried Klonopin at bedtime, it might be something for her to consider.

I stopped in on Julie to see if she had tried the pill right before bed, and she shook her head. I asked if it had given her any other side effects besides drowsiness. Julie replied that she had tolerated the drug well except for the fatigue and indeed, she had chronic insomnia. Paxil, her current antidepressant, made her nervous and jittery. She would welcome a sleeping agent. *You and me both,* I thought, lamenting my own sleepless nights and looking forward to my Ativan.

"Benzo beauties," Lisa would have called Julie and me as both Ativan and Clonazepam are members of the benzodiazepine family, a class of drugs that can be highly addictive. But Julie had no history of substance abuse and had reacted poorly to the tricyclics and SSRIs. This was worth a shot.

I added the info about Clonazepam to my dictation for Gillian, who was coming on duty at 7 p.m. I also left a note for Dr. Blanc and printed out a copy of the email from FearNoMore for her. Usually, I don't forward people's emails since I don't want to violate their privacy, but FearNoMore had used an anonymous handle. I checked my voice mail one last time to find out if anyone had volunteered to do my shift on the weekend, to no avail.

However, I did have a message from Denise. Oy! Why had I hinted for her to call me? I had no desire to call her back.

Before I knew it, it was time to clock out. Weary, I walked down the long corridors, stopped in at the hospital pharmacy to fill my Ativan, and inhaled the fresh air in the parking lot. Alain was right. The sky was ominous, and small pellets of rain were beginning to fall.

I wanted to collapse, but there was still much to do with my short evening. I needed to pick Devon up at Jess's and to visit the Campanas. Lorenzo and Anna had always loved Devon. It would raise their spirits to see him. Judging by the weather and their fragile health, I assumed they would be home by now.

Meanwhile, I wanted to unwind. I felt bad about not calling Denise, but I was overwhelmed. I needed to forget about my troubled patients, my unrequited crush on Alain, and my relentless worry about Lisa. I switched on the Amy Tan book.

By the time that I'd pulled up in front of Jess Reyes's house, I'd almost finished disc one. His mother, Lucinda, answered the door. They lived in a crummy public housing area, which was situated in the middle of an upper-class neighborhood. The houses all looked alike with red brick exteriors and white carports. Most of the homes were joined together, and I could see the remnants of fires that had been set in sheds behind the houses.

A Christmas wreath was prominent on the house next door to

Jess's, and there was an ancient washing machine sitting at the top of the driveway. A pile of white plastic lawn chairs were stacked on the side of the walkway leading to the Reyes's front door. The neighborhood was quiet and solitary except for a handful of people who sat in the park, huddled under umbrellas, as they watched their children bicycle in the rain.

Lucinda looked tired, as usual. Her hair was platinum, which made her face look ghostly, and her blue eye shadow was much too bright. She was wearing skin-tight jeans, long dangling earrings, and high heels. I hardly ever wore heels anymore unless Mark and I went to a formal event.

"I'm so sorry about your friend, Lisa," Lucinda announced. "It must be a terrible worry to you, her being gone for so long and all."

"Yes, but we've launched a massive search for her," I said.

Lucinda was a stay-at-home mom because Jess's younger sister, Danielle, was only seven. Danielle was in school most of the day.

Maybe Lucinda could join the hunt. I hoped that she owned running shoes since I couldn't see her exploring the Gatineau in her two-inch heels.

"Would you be interested in helping us?" I asked.

She pursed her lips and put her hands behind her head. "I wouldn't mind going out for a day or two while Dani's in school. I can't imagine how Lisa's parents must be feeling."

I thanked Lucinda and gave her directions to the Hippodrome on Aylmer Road, along with Sandra's phone number at the new office in Hull.

Lucinda had lost her husband; she was no stranger to grief. That was why money was so tight. Her new husband, whom Jess hated so much, had been laid off from his job in sales. Lucinda needed to work full time, but she was reluctant to leave Dani.

We chatted about the pyromaniac who had been terrorizing the neighborhood. Lucinda said the police didn't have any leads on that. Then she ushered me into her small house where I could hear raucous music coming from upstairs. The book *Soccer for Dummies* was sitting on her coffee table. I admired her for taking the time to learn more about Jess's activities. I was clueless about sports. Lucinda pounded on the wall to get Jess's attention, and in no time at all, both boys materialized in the front hall.

Jess was taller than Devon and better looking with his long, wavy brown hair and confident stride. His father was Colombian, and Jess had inherited his swarthy South American looks. He wore a long pair of rosary beads, which would have looked effeminate on Devon but looked sophisticated on Jess.

Jess was overly polite to adults. My father had referred to him as an "Eddie Haskell." The reference had escaped me. My father explained that it described one of the stars of the old TV show *Leave It to Beaver; he* was a troublemaker and didn't like adults, but he was always solicitous and well-behaved in their presence.

Ordinarily, Devon looked exuberant when he was with Jess, which made me feel inadequate. He never looked that way at home. I was sorry that we'd only had one child. Perhaps Dev would have been happier if he'd had a brother. But today, both boys looked tired and listless.

Jess forced himself to grin at me, leaned up against the striped wallpaper in the hall, and said, "Hey, Mrs. Richards. That really sucks about your friend. It's good that everybody's out looking for her. The weather will be wicked tomorrow."

I wasn't sure if "wicked" was a good thing or a bad thing, but

I nodded and tried to appear affable. No doubt Jess was alluding to the likelihood of continued rain.

"Thanks very much, Jess. It's not often that someone disappears out of the blue like this. At least, it's not common in my life!"

"It's like the movies. People are always, like, getting shot or mugged or even poisoned on *CSI*. That show is sweet! You can never figure out who shanked who until the very end."

Jess looked up at me with his penetrating black eyes. "Oh! Sorry, Mrs. Richards. I'm not sayin' your friend got hurt or anything. Maybe she just took off to start a new life."

"Well, Jess, I don't think that Lisa would walk away from her responsibilities. Some women who disappear..." I stopped.

What was I going to say? Some women who disappear are victims of violence? The words got trapped at the back of my throat, and I couldn't finish my sentence.

"I get it. Hey, no worries. I'm sure you'll find her," Jess said, running his hand through his long curly hair. "And the dude here will be a big help," he joked, as he gave Devon a friendly push.

"Lay off, dog," Devon replied sharply, as he pushed Jess back with more force than the situation warranted. I shook my head but didn't want to nag Devon about his behavior.

I said goodnight to Jess and Lucinda, thanking her again for her kind offer to search for Lisa. Dev and I got back into the car. I told him I had to make a brief stop at the Campanas', but he said he'd prefer me to drop him at home. I urged him to reconsider, knowing how fond Anna and Lorenzo were of him, but his mood had turned black. He crossed his arms and looked out the window.

I asked about his day at school and what he did with Jess, but he was noncommittal. The only thing he sounded excited about was the upcoming playoff game. I hoped Devon wouldn't be too crushed when his team lost since it would be a miracle if they could break their losing streak now.

CHAPTER THIRTEEN

Sandra opened the door. I congratulated her on the marvelous job she was doing as coordinator of the search team. She smiled modestly and gave most of the credit to Anthony. She also mentioned how grateful she was to the various organizations that had donated food, tents, posters, ribbons, water, flashlights, and buttons.

Sandra was short—less than five feet tall—and was not a stunning beauty like Lisa. But she had strong features and bright white teeth, and she had Lisa's eyes and coloring. The family resemblance was so strong that looking at Sandra was spooky; it was as though a part of Lisa were right there in front of me.

Sandra had a good figure for someone who lived in a house full of pasta and cannolis. Normally bright-eyed, Sandra now had the same dark black circles that both her mother and I sported. It was clear that she had been crying for days.

"Tara! So glad to see you," Sandra said, as she gave me a big hug. In all the years I'd known her, I couldn't remember Sandra ever embracing me. There was affection in her touch but also desperation. I hugged her back tightly, hoping to convey optimism about finding Lisa.

"My parents, they're devastated," Sandra told me. "It's been almost a week, and they're totally freaking out."

What could I say? It seemed so false to console Sandra, and she wasn't confiding in me about her own feelings. She was talking about her parents. Typically, Sandra would be more concerned about the effect of Lisa's disappearance on her parents than herself. She would never have discussed her own emotions.

She was unlike Lisa in that respect: so private and reserved while Lisa was outgoing and candid.

It would be even harder to say the right thing to Anna and Lorenzo without sounding trite or patronizing. I felt a sudden sense of trepidation as I waited for them to greet us.

If Sandra looked bad, Mr. and Mrs. Campana looked like caricatures of their former selves. Anna's eyes were wild and unfocused, and her hair was disheveled. Lorenzo hadn't shaved in days and ambled with his shoulders hunched over. They were both exhausted from the vigorous searching in the Gatineau, combined with the chronic worry about Lisa's whereabouts.

I hadn't had anything to eat since the roast beef sandwich that I'd bought in the cafeteria around 2 p.m. I'd eaten half of it and thrown the rest away. So I was delighted when Anna served scrumptious looking plates of chicken parmesan. I couldn't imagine when she would've had the time or energy to cook, but perhaps doing so had taken her mind off her daughter. I scraped most of the cheese off mine while she wasn't looking, because I was still feeling nauseated, and was also picturing myself looking fab in the new pink push-up bra, which would be arriving any day now.

I brought the Campanas up to date on my meeting with WAR, my work with Alain, and my conversations with Laura Anne.

The Campanas had been deluged with calls from the media, which was a mixed blessing. They resented being photographed and harassed by TV cameras and microphones, which were thrust into their faces during their time of unimaginable horror. On the other hand, it was essential to court the press. We depended on publicity to sustain our volunteer base and to receive critical feedback from the community.

In between passing plates of eggplant, bowls of Caesar salad, and refilling glasses of Cabernet Sauvignon, we talked about Ryan. I was surprised to learn that the Campanas had hired a private detective. They did suspect Ryan but had no proof of his involvement. They were not returning his phone calls and were thinking about changing their phone number. I cautioned them about doing anything rash in case Ryan was an innocent victim like themselves, but they seemed adamant.

"I never liked him," Anna declared.

"We never liked him, Tara," Lorenzo echoed, as he devoured a large piece of garlic bread.

"All those boys Lisa had to choose from, and she chose a bum who beats up women." Anna's eyes began to water. She blew her nose. "Such a beautiful girl but such bad judgment with men! From the time she was a teenager..." Anna's voice drifted off.

"Lisa really changed, Mrs. Campana. I mean, Anna," I stammered. "Yes, she was attracted to bad boys when she was drinking, but that wasn't what drew her to Ryan. On the contrary, the traits she admired in Ryan were his tenacity and commitment to the program. Ryan worked hard to get sober. He even went through a counseling program on anger management for batterers."

"Anger management?" Lorenzo asked, raising his eyebrows. "I could teach him a thing or two about anger management. I could rearrange his face so that no girl ever looks twice at him again!"

"Calm down, Papa! You'll have another heart attack if you keep up this way," Sandra cautioned, patting her father on the back.

"What made you change your mind about Ryan?" I asked.

"We don't have all the details yet, Tara, but I will tell you this.

Ryan has approached the bank manager, requesting access to Lisa's private account. He says he can't afford to live in the house on his salary. She's been gone for seven days! What makes him think she's not coming back or that he has any right to live in her house if he can't pay the bills?"

Lorenzo looked directly at me, wagging his index finger. "Not a word of this to anyone, Tara. Nothing we say here leaves this table."

"Yes, sir!" I replied.

This was a complicated development. Lisa and Ryan hadn't lived together long enough for Ryan to be entitled to money in her account. But were his motives malevolent or benign? Realistically speaking, Ryan couldn't afford to pay the bills that Lisa had been paying. What was he supposed to do? Abandon the house? Wasn't it just as much his house as Lisa's? What if he were only trying to keep the house going until she returned? To the Campanas, petitioning for Lisa's money was proof of Ryan's underhandedness, yet to me, it simply added one more brick to the wall of confusion.

We made small talk. The Campanas looked so beat that I urged them to take a day off to rest and to see their family doctor. They vetoed my suggestion.

I noticed it was almost 9:30 p.m. I was dying to pop my sleeping pill and crawl under my favorite duvet. I stood up, announcing that I had to leave. The whole family walked me to the door.

On the way home, Laura Anne called to inform me that Ryan would be speaking at an AA meeting on Monday night. She asked if I could be there. I said that I thought only alcoholics could attend meetings.

"No," she explained, "there are two different types of meetings. AA has closed meetings that are reserved for alcoholics or people who suspect they have a problem with alcohol. But they also have open speaker meetings. Someone gets up to talk, and kind of tells his or her story of recovery. Anyone can go to an open meeting."

Laura Anne put me on hold for a minute while she took another call. "I'm back!" she declared. "Anyway, this'll be the first time Ryan has spoken publicly at a meeting. He's not considered an official suspect, but everyone is watching him, and he knows it. So it's going to be really hard on him. He'll need a lot of support. Can you come?"

"Yeah, I think so." Lisa had always wanted me to go with her to a meeting, but I'd never gotten around to it. Never made her addiction a priority in my life. I sighed, hoping I would have an opportunity to make that up to her. I wouldn't get off from work until seven o'clock, but Laura Anne said the meeting started at eight. Great! Another ball-busting day, but I wouldn't miss hearing Ryan speak for the world. Would talking be hard on him? Maybe but hopefully, it would be illuminating for the rest of us.

I pushed the buttons on the radio. The Steve Miller band was singing, "Time keeps on slipping, slipping into the future." I had a sense of motion. The car was moving forward, and with every traffic light I passed, I was moving farther away from Lisa and our routine evenings at the ByTowne Theatre. The rest of us were going ahead, and Lisa had been left behind. I wanted to go back, not just to last Thursday night, but to my university days, so I could live my life all over again.

I wanted to be sixteen or twenty-six again, making decisions based on what I knew now. So many lost opportunities. How had

I managed to completely screw up my life? I'd done everything wrong except that I hadn't become a street prostitute or a serial murderer. Too late for the former—who would want me? But there was still time for the latter.

My frantic fear over losing Lisa, combined with my angst about getting old, had suddenly made my life seem overwhelming and hopeless.

Laura Anne warned me that she had drawn the Moon card from her Tarot deck, indicating emotional instability and feelings which were by nature volatile, nebulous, and uncertain. Meanwhile, I was so lost in thought that I popped my CD out of the deck! I slammed on the brakes, pulled the car over to the side of the road, and stopped my conversation with Laura Anne in mid-sentence. Once again, I had lost my place with Amy Tan. I was never going to finish that goddamn book.

"My book on CD!" I shouted to myself. "That's what I listen to in the car to relax!"

"Chill out, Tara," my sane self repeated. "Jesus, if you've been using this to relax, it's totally not working."

"What's wrong, Tara?" Laura Anne yelled, still hanging on the other end of the phone, which had fallen to the floor in the shuffle.

Taking a deep breath, I bent down and picked up the phone. "Nothing," I mumbled, angry about my inability to complete the book and my road rage meltdown. I could have easily hit the car in front of me. My frustration tolerance was at an all-time low, which was no excuse. I was so ashamed of myself that I felt like crying. I was coming unglued.

Lisa was missing. My relationship with Mark was over. Devon hated me. I was bored stiff at work and couldn't find a replacement, so I wouldn't be able to continue participating in the search.

Last, but not least, my hair was a catastrophe. I looked like Marilyn Manson with my new streaks. I should return to see Chan Juan but couldn't face her again. I would have to find another hairdresser or shave my head. Maybe I would get a chic, short cut for the summer. The thought lifted my spirits.

I had lost two or three pounds in the last week, partly by watching my diet, but mainly because the sight of food made me ill. My newfound relationship with Alain had also made me more conscious of my food intake.

Alain was the only ray of sunshine in my life. How I looked forward to seeing him tomorrow night. Just thinking of his laugh and sweet baby face gave me the strength to get through the rest of the night and to face Mark, which I had dreaded since our fight.

****

Mark was sitting in the family room with his feet up on the table, drinking a beer and watching *The Comedy Network*. He had been out looking for Lisa, but unlike Alain, Mark hadn't sent me any emails about his adventures. He flicked the TV off when I walked in, and I could hear loud music playing upstairs where Dev was supposed to be doing his English assignment.

Mark was keen to tell me about his day. I poured myself a Molson Ex and sat down on the couch next to him. Between my excessive drinking and nightly tranquilizers, I would soon qualify for a space at one of the closed AA meetings.

"Turnout was good, Tar. You would've been pleased to have seen how many people showed up. But it was useless. Ryan and I passed out flyers to drivers. Lots of people stopped, and we asked if they'd passed by last Friday. No one saw her."

Mark crossed his legs, scratched his head, and leaned toward me. "I don't know what to make of Ryan."

"Why?"

"He contradicts himself. When you first talked to him, he seemed so composed, but today he was ranting about his grief. Said he hadn't slept all week and that he felt guilty, like at the one moment Lisa needed him, he wasn't there."

"What's wrong with that? Maybe he was numb when he talked to me on the phone Sunday, and his feelings are just starting to surface."

"I know," Mark replied. "Obviously, people handle stress differently. Remember that couple in Australia who were accused of killing their baby when it'd been captured by a dingo? The police suspected those parents because they thought they weren't reacting appropriately. I'm not judging Ryan for his affect. He just sounded scripted, as though he'd read a book on psychology or had been in a grief chat room.

"Ryan was using words like 'post-traumatic stress' and 'bereavement,' and he was parroting a lot of stuff that you and Anna have been saying about insomnia.

"He looks fine! He doesn't look like he's lost sleep, and he's been shaving, unlike Lorenzo, who looks like he's one step away from intensive care. I just felt wary about Ryan today. Your little Castration Circle didn't seem too pleased with him either."

Apparently, JC, Barb, Sheila, and Diane had gone out of their way to disassociate themselves from Ryan. The police and volunteers had covered five or six kilometers in every direction on Aylmer Road and Taché Boulevard. They continued interviewing people in stores, bars, houses, and restaurants, but they hadn't turned up one solid lead.

"There was some talk of dragging the river, but that would only be done as a last resort," Mark added.

What could anyone expect to find in a river except a body? I felt a cold chill down my spine and thought that I might lose the chicken parmesan, which was churning away in my stomach. I drained my beer and got up for another, wondering if I had finished the Gaviscon or if I'd have to take another Gravol before bed. Combining the Gravol with the Ativan might knock me out for the evening.

I felt agitated and irritable and tried to picture what life must be like for Julie Appleton. Had it really been less than a week since I'd met Julie and bragged about what a calm person I was compared to her? Everything had changed at the drop of a dime. I had a sense of free-floating anxiety all the time now.

I was startled when the phone rang or if someone came up behind me. I worried about Devon if he was ten minutes late coming home. I picked on him for the smallest detail. Sleep was impossible, and I had violent nightmares.

I was too exhausted to tell Mark about Ryan trying to access Lisa's money. I must have looked ghoulish because Mark stared at me sympathetically for the first time since our argument. He reached out to touch my cheek and asked if I was all right. I burst into tears and put my arms around him. He held me while I sobbed.

"We'll never find her," I said. "I've watched shows about missing people. The first forty-eight hours are crucial. After that, they've lost the trail."

"That's just TV, honey. All kinds of people are found weeks or even months after their disappearance."

"Yeah! They're found dead!" I cried. Mark didn't respond.

Either he couldn't think of anything to say, or he didn't want to give me false hope.

After a long silence, Mark said, "We don't know that yet. Let's just deal with today. Don't project." We sat there for a while with our arms around each other, and it felt comforting to be back on friendly terms with Mark.

But I didn't want to mislead him. Nothing had changed. The closeness I felt to him was more like a brotherly feeling. I had no intention of going upstairs to make love to him.

Finally, I whispered, "I'm sorry about us." He stroked my hair and told me not to worry. I was giving him the wrong message, but I couldn't clarify it. Couldn't say, "Our marriage is over" because I couldn't bear the thought of hurting him or him being angry at me now when I needed him.

It was selfish, but I couldn't deal with any more conflict in my life until I found out what happened to Lisa. I was already starting to think in terms of the passive tense—something had happened to Lisa— rather than thinking of finding Lisa.

The idea of carrying on without Lisa filled me with such anguish that I simply blocked the thought from my mind. Maybe it was a good thing that I wasn't involved in the search on a daily basis in case I went berserk and started beating on one of the police officers. I didn't think I could cope with anyone finding a body, or worse, a bodily part.

Mark went upstairs to prepare his lessons for Monday. I cleaned the kitchen, made coffee for the next day, and threw in a wash. Then I took the dog outside so that he could relieve himself. Afterward, Monday rolled onto his back on the floor, clearly wanting me to rub his belly, and he put his paws over his ears.

Monday and I checked in on Devon. He was finishing *South Park*, a show that I disapproved of, but my vote didn't count for much in terms of Devon's viewing habits.

"What's going on, Dev?" I asked.

"Kyle and Cartman got some older Trekkie geeks to take them time traveling so they can, like, go back to Grade Three. They hate their teacher in Grade Four. Their old teacher, Mr. Garrison, he got all bent out of shape 'cause he can't deal with the fact that he's gay. Hello? We've always known that Garrison was gay! Anyways, he's hiding in a cave. Don't talk now, Mum! I have to see this part."

I waited impatiently, stifling my yawns. *South Park* had a gay character? Maybe it had some socially redeeming value after all. I stared at a picture on the family room wall that was taken a few years ago at a picnic.

Devon was about nine and was wearing an oversized, black bathing suit. He looked skinny and sunburned and had a big smile on his prepubescent face. I missed the happy boy in the photo and cursed the fact that the only joy I'd seen on Devon's face had been two weeks ago with Jess and now, watching an idiotic cartoon.

Just as the show ended, the phone rang, and it was Devon's friend, Tabatha. I smiled weakly and told him I wanted to see his essay on *To Kill a Mockingbird*.

"It's not done!" I heard Dev say, as I went upstairs to read. It seemed futile to reprimand my son yet again for his failure to deliver. I should have taken the time to have had a heart-to-heart with him, but I had lost my patience. Maybe being fourteen was equivalent to the terrible twos. Perhaps fifteen would be a better year.

CHAPTER FOURTEEN

Back at work, I was pleased to discover that Julie had been able to tolerate 2 mg of Clonazepam before bed. She hadn't felt any positive effects from it yet but, on the other hand, it hadn't given her palpitations and anxiety like the antidepressants. I was tempted to write back to FearNoMore but thought it wise to wait a few days.

Instead, I checked my email and was delighted to discover a new note from Alain, confirming our plans for this evening. He was still receiving tips on his website but nothing that sounded "promising," which he had spelled with two "m's." I guessed that I wouldn't be asking Alain to tutor Devon with his English homework if Alain and I eloped and got married.

I dropped Denise a short note, explaining that I had been working twelve hours a day and had been busy all night with meetings related to Lisa's disappearance. I said I would call her soon and tried to get my mind back on patient care.

Justin was making excellent progress with both physical and occupational therapy. He was prohibited from moving his fingers for two more weeks, so Catherine and Greg were making arrangements for Justin to be transferred to a local convalescent home.

Jean-Claude had recovered from his flu and offered to accompany me to the hospital chapel during our lunch break. He was such a sweetheart, and I envied his religious faith. I had none, but as the old saying goes, "There are no atheists in a foxhole." I didn't see how prayer could hurt although I hadn't had much success the other night. But I was feeling stronger today after my deep and dreamless sleep, courtesy of Molson and the manufacturers of Ativan. I desperately wanted to share Jean-Claude's conviction that we were not alone in this struggle: that a Higher Power cared about our distress and would help lead Lisa back home, even though my rational mind told me that it wasn't so.

Mark called to say that the search was losing volunteers. They'd already covered six to ten kilometers of territory, and the ground was damp and mushy from last night's downpour. He reminded me that we had dinner plans with his parents and his brother, Peter, Tuesday night. I couldn't think of any way to get out of it. Reluctantly, I agreed and informed Mark that I would be returning to Alain's tonight to resume our Internet work. Alain was actually giving up his Saturday night to help me.

The day flew by, and when I arrived at Alain's apartment, he greeted me with the unexpected news that Christine had broken up with him. I was shocked. Alain and Christine had been going out for years, since they were in high school. She meant everything to him.

"What happened?"

"She wanted a firm commitment. She wants kids, and I'm not ready for that. Kids drive me a little crazy, if you wanna know the truth. Anyways, she says, 'Let's take a break.' And I says, 'A break?' We've been together since we were sixteen! I've never thought about anyone else." He looked crestfallen, and I felt sorry for him.

However, I was also excited. Alain was a free man! I could make a move on him without worrying about his relationship. Of course, I wasn't free until I left Mark. And there was the minor problem of our age difference, but I was sure that Alain liked me.

Why else would he spend all this time with me and be so wonderful?

We sat down at his computer and leafed through the dozens of emails regarding Lisa from webmasters. Some of them offered leads, which we forwarded to Detective Desormeaux, although as Alain had said, they didn't look particularly "prommising." We posted Lisa's picture on message boards across North America and chatted with other distraught surfers who were looking for loved ones.

It was already late when I arrived at Alain's, so we only spent an hour online. By then we were both wrecked. Despite my good night's sleep, the physical and emotional strain of the last week had taken its toll on me. Alain took a cigarette break, and we descended on the IKEA couch, drinking more Labatt. Soon I could take Lisa's place in the program. I really needed to cool it with my drinking.

"So who are you voting for in the upcoming election?" I asked Alain.

"I don't know," he said cautiously. I sensed that Alain had strong opinions about politics but was afraid to voice them too vociferously in case we disagreed. I decided to break the ice so he would know where I was coming from.

"Well, for the first time in my adult life, I'm considering not voting. One scandal after another with the Chrétien Cabinet makes it difficult to have any faith in them, and Paul Martin is an arrogant son of a bitch. On the other hand, I'm reluctant to vote NDP."

The NDP was the New Democratic Party, which was to the left of the liberals. The NDP had traditionally supported the rights of labor, women, and minorities, as well as lobbied for environmental protection and against free-trade. The Liberal party was much like the Democratic Party in the U.S. Quebec had a party of its own called the Bloc Québecois, whose sole purpose was to advocate for the separation of the province from the country.

Under the leadership of dynamic Stephen Harper, the Alliance Party recently merged with the former Progressive Conservatives. The original Conservatives maintained a greater concern for social welfare than the Republican Party. Both believed in smaller government, but the former wanted to maintain Canada's universal health care system and our network of social programs. The religious beliefs of the Alliance were similar to those of the right-wing Christian Coalition in the U.S. Alliance supported the war in Iraq and a more amicable trading partnership with the States.

Mark and I had been voting NDP for years, and he still supported them. However, I felt that their message was out of touch with the new millennium. All across North America, we had seen a shift toward moderate rather than left-wing policies over the last decade. Bill Clinton was a moderate Democrat and was fiscally conservative in many respects, such as his emphasis on balancing the federal budget.

The U.S. seemed to be split right down the middle in terms of support for liberals and conservatives. However, today's liberals—with the exception of Hillary Clinton or John Kerry—were more centrist than their predecessors. The same was true in Canada. Although Jean Chrétien was finance minister in the Trudeau administration, his policies had been far more fiscally conservative than Trudeau's.

The NDP had a small resurgence of popularity over the last

few years, but they still had so little support that they had difficulty maintaining party status in Parliament. Voting for them was a throwaway vote. It was a protest statement that I was willing to make when I was younger, but I wasn't going to stand on principle any longer.

The liberals and conservatives were running neck and neck in Ontario. If I voted NDP, that would be one less vote for the Liberal party. It would be like a left-wing advocate in the States voting for Ralph Nader and inadvertently helping George W. in the process.

"The liberals are a disaster on a federal level, but I do like my Member of Parliament. Voting for the NDP would be as effective as taking my ballot and throwing it down the sewer."

"The NDP? Oh, my God, Tara! You're a lefty?" Alain threw back his head and laughed.

"What are you?"

"The less government, the better!" Alain said. "Look at the way these guys piss our money away. They're killing us with the GST tax, which I might add, came in with the NDP government."

"But what about Iraq? Harper supports the war!"

"I have no problem with the American position on Iraq. Saddam was a maniac. The Americans sacrificed their lives to free that country. Canada should've sent troops. We're so lame, always relying on the Americans to protect us."

"Right," I replied. "The Americans have almost 140,000 troops in Iraq and 20,000 in Afghanistan. They invaded Iraq without any evidence of weapons of mass destruction and took unilateral action although the whole world urged them not to. Almost 10,000 Iraqis and Afghanis have been killed, along with 700 Americans, not including the thousands more who have been wounded or scarred for life. While Bush focuses on Iraq, he's ignoring Afghanistan, the new opium capital of the world!

"Bin Laden and the terrorists came from *Afghanistan*. They're not directing enough postwar reconstruction effort into rebuilding that country. If they hadn't invaded Iraq, they could've had all those troops in Afghanistan or Pakistan looking for Bin Laden. Bush wants you to think there's a connection between Iraq and al-Qaeda, but there isn't!" My face was turning purple, and I was perched angrily on the edge of the futon.

"They didn't take unilateral action! What do you consider England, Japan, Italy, or Poland? Who cares about WMD? Saddam was evil. It's as simple as that. He gassed his own people. What more do you need, eh?" Alain scowled.

"Whatever!" he added, lighting another cigarette and forgetting to step out on the patio for my benefit. The strong, minty odor of menthol filled the room. Alain asked if I wanted another beer. I declined.

I had never suspected that my irresistible Alain might be one of those right-wing freaks that Lisa and I had mocked and feared: what the Kinks called the "Young Conservatives." Didn't he believe in abortion and same-sex marriage? Didn't he care that the waiting list for public housing in this town was five to eight years long? Ottawa had a thirty-five-week waiting list for an MRI, and almost 11,000 patients were waiting for appointments.

I was no great fan of the liberals, but I loathed the Conservatives, especially since they had joined forces with the fundamentalist religious sects. If I wanted to keep my evening with Alain on a friendly tone, it was clear that we should steer away from politics.

Although I should have gotten up to depart, I couldn't bear to leave my little Republican, so I brought the conversation back to Christine. Alain became angry and animated as he talked about her. He couldn't believe that she would just walk out on him. I asked if there could be someone else, and he shook his head. I had a perverse interest in Christine, wanting to know all the details about her, yet feeling insanely jealous at the same time.

Even more confusing was the depth of my affection for Alain. I didn't want him ever to be hurt by anyone at any time. I knew how much he loved Christine and how he was suffering. Just as he wanted to soothe my pain over Lisa, I wanted to make his anguish disappear. If that involved Christine taking him back, so be it. I couldn't have Alain looking so unhappy. I sighed. I would certainly make a poor seductress if I kept worrying about his broken heart.

We were both feeling depressed when I forced myself up from the couch and thanked him for his help.

"Hey, no problem!" he said.

We hugged goodbye, and his sorrow over Christine made me feel that I had permission to hold him for a longer period of time. I inhaled his fresh, foreign aftershave and felt the stubbles of hair along his cheek. I wanted to climb into his futon bed, pretend that he was a comrade from the progressive left, and hold him all night.

As I was walking toward my car, I took off my jacket because the weather had turned humid. A scruffy looking pair of men walked past me. One had an unruly beard, and the other had a leer on his face.

"Nice tits!" The second guy grinned at me.

"Up yours," I replied automatically. They both laughed. I walked faster to get away from them and put my jacket back on.

I was annoyed, offended, and repulsed, but I'm ashamed to admit that I felt vaguely flattered and pleased to have been noticed.

WAR would consider me to be a lost cause, but I couldn't help but ask myself how many more years of sexual harassment I had left before I became completely invisible. Sheila and Diane often joked that one of the few benefits of being close to sixty was that they didn't have to deal with men whistling, calling them lewd names, and attempting to grope them on the street.

Once, I heard Germaine Greer on a talk show, saying that she'd lost her sex drive after menopause, and she felt relieved not to be at the mercy of her hormones and desire anymore. Although my ardor for Alain had become painful, I definitely did not want to be "liberated" from it.

****

Sunday, I returned to work, delirious as always that this was the last day of my work week. I planned to sleep until noon tomorrow to regain my equilibrium. Then I would fax flyers of Lisa to different women's groups across the country, respond to emails from the missing persons' websites, post on forums, and discuss additional strategies with WAR. I could return to Aylmer to search with the rest of the group on Tuesday morning, but the search had begun to feel futile.

Most of the territory had been covered, and the team was becoming demoralized. Not a single clue had been found, although it was hard to say if that was good or bad. If the group had discovered one of Lisa's running shoes, or a piece of her jewelry, wouldn't that suggest that she was dead?

As long as we didn't have a body, we could hold on to hope for her return. That likelihood seemed more remote as time went on. Consequently, I kept a clear image in my mind of Elizabeth Smart, who was only fourteen when she had been kidnapped at gunpoint. To everyone's amazement, she was located nine months later by the police.

Unfortunately, there were no similarities between Lisa's case and that of Elizabeth Smart, who had been abducted by a fundamentalist Mormon in search of a new "wife." Lisa was an adult without any enemies. I couldn't imagine why anyone would want to kidnap Lisa and tried not to think about her as I went about my workday.

I was having a hard time concentrating on nursing until unexpectedly, two incredible things occurred. First, Julie was feeling some positive effects from the Clonazepam. She was able to walk thirty or forty feet down the hallway without a panic attack, but the real revelation was that she had almost fainted in the lunchroom and Erwin, the diabetic, was the only person who had thought to take her blood sugar with his own glucose meter; it was at forty-five milligrams, a clear indication that she had reactive hypoglycemia. The dietitian had put her on a diet high in protein, with moderate complex carbohydrates, lots of good fats like olive oil and avocado, and no sugar, caffeine, white flour, or junk food. And she was eating six small meals a day now.

Julie felt like a new person already; her mood and energy swings had stopped, and her anxiety level had gone way down. Over time, she could expect to feel even better as the diet and pills became more effective. She was so excited that she couldn't stop talking. Julie recited all of the medications that she had tried unsuccessfully over the years.

"It's just like Janis Joplin said," I quipped. "All you need is one good man. In your case, you were only one good anti-anxiety agent away from functioning!"

"I can never thank you enough," Julie replied, as she fondled a little Teddy bear that said, "I miss you." Her friends must have been up to visit because her room was full of pink carnations, crossword puzzles, and a jar of sugar-free peanut butter with rye crackers.

"Nonsense," I said. "The medication and diet will only do half the job, you know. The rest is up to you."

"Yeah, but at least it gives me a fighting chance. I didn't have a hope before the Clonazepam and the hypoglycemia diagnoses. It never made any difference how much effort I put into overcoming the panic. I tried to ignore it, and I tried to accept it. I spent years trying to work through it, and it was a total waste of time! Now, I can start over." She smiled broadly, and I noticed what a pretty girl she was now that she was able to bathe regularly and the color had returned to her face.

"Also, I'm really indebted to Don. He's been a lifesaver, and he's going to help me when I go home, too." Her face flushed. Oh my, it looked as though this could be a potentially romantic match. Things had worked out very well for Julie.

Julie was not the only one who would have a new beginning. When I went to visit Justin, he was exuberant. His daughter, Donna, was pacing back and forth in his room. Justin was so nervous that his hand shook as he gave me a letter. He held the letter out to his left with his good hand. The letter was several feet away from me since Justin couldn't see exactly where I was.

Before I had time to read it, Donna explained that Justin had been chosen to participate in an experimental trial for retinal implant surgery. An ophthalmologist in the States had teamed up with his engineer brother to create a silicon retinal microchip.

It had only been implanted in ten people so far. Thus, Justin would be a test case. All were blind when the surgery had been performed, and every one of them could now see some sort of shapes, contrast, or figures.

"Did you see him on *Dateline*?" Donna asked, brimming with excitement. "They did two shows on the implant, and the brothers were also in *Time* magazine and *Fortune*. It's a miracle! Making the blind see. It's like science fiction!"

"It's more like the second coming of Christ," Justin declared.

"Well, look at the cochlear implant. We never thought that the deaf would hear again. Doctors have restored vision before with corneal transplants and the removal of cataracts, but they've never been able to halt retinal degeneration because the retina is attached to the back of the brain. When you recover from the surgery, I expect you to come back and visit. But when you can see more clearly, you're not allowed to comment on my weight!" I teased Justin.

"When I come back here, I will photograph the ward, so I can immortalize the faces of those who have been so kind to me." Justin was such a beautiful man. I sincerely hoped that the surgery would give him back a small part of his vision. I gave his daughter my email address, fully conscious of the fact that I was adding one more patient to my hectic life after hours.

I helped Justin and Donna to organize their effects. The occupational therapist escorted the Drakes to their car and sent them on their way to one of the local retirement homes. Justin would stay there for another two weeks before he could return to his own apartment. He would have to wait months for the retinal surgery.

The social worker and I packed up Julie's possessions, and

Don took her home. For the first time in a decade, Julie felt capable of attending outpatient psychiatry sessions. She expressed her undying gratitude to me when we said goodbye, which I dismissed. It was dumb luck that I had managed to discover a way for her to effectively utilize a medication that she had already tried without success. And Erwin had been smarter than our whole medical team put together because he never ruled out a physical cause to her anxiety.

I felt bereft after Julie and Justin left. One thing that differentiated rehab nursing from regular nursing was that we spent significantly more time with our patients. After seeing patients regularly for four to six weeks, I often became attached to them, no matter how burned out I was feeling. Fortunately, both patients had left on very positive notes. I wished I could say the same for my own life, which seemed to be disintegrating.

When my thirty-six hours were over, I was eager to go home and crawl into bed with my Ativan. Just before I began to listen to Amy Tan in the car, Mark called to say he'd found Devon and Jess smoking pot in Devon's room.

Mark and I had completely different disciplinary styles. He was relaxed and permissive, believing that kids learned from their own mistakes. I thought that kids needed structure, rules, and clear guidelines about what the consequences were for breaking those rules.

Mark was not overjoyed about Devon's indiscretion. However, he had smoked more than his own share of weed in his youth and was an advocate for the legalization of marijuana. I had also gotten high in university with Lisa, but that seemed like ancient history to me now.

I was opposed to decriminalization, not to mention

legalization; drugs were dangerous. Look what they had done to Lisa's life! So, as usual, Mark and I did not present a united front to Devon. I could tell from our conversation on the phone that Mark didn't consider the issue to be a big deal. I did! Devon was only a freshman. What if he and Jess had been caught smoking in school?

When I dragged my weary butt into the family room, Mark was watching *Star Trek: the Next Generation*. He pretended to enjoy the Enterprise's moral dilemmas, but I suspected that he just wanted to see Deanna Troi in her sexy jumpsuit. I was tempted to remind Mark that *Star Trek* was not a Canadian production, but things were already tense between us.

Judging from the pulsating bass sounds coming from upstairs, I gathered that Devon was in his room. It was hard to know how to punish a kid nowadays. I could hardly send him to his room. A kid's bedroom was a verifiable treasure house of expensive toys and gadgets. Between the computer and the entertainment center—not to mention the phone—it was impossible for a teenager to get bored in his room. I may have to force Devon outside or to devise a long list of chores for him to do. Clean up the yard, empty the compost, sweep the basement.

I asked Mark to help me prepare supper, so we could talk about Dev before he came downstairs. Mark was a hopeless cook. He burned everything, including the pots. Sometimes I thought it was a deliberate ploy because he much preferred to eat than to cook. I gave Mark some vegetables to chop because I figured that he couldn't botch that task, and I offered to sauté the fresh trout he'd bought at the fish store.

"So, how are we going to handle this?" I asked, as he passed me the garlic.

"It's normal behavior, Tara. I don't know why you're getting so bent out of shape. He bought two joints! Does that sound like someone with a serious drug problem? He's probably never gotten high before."

"And he never will again, as long as I have any say in the matter."

"That's unrealistic. You can't prevent him from making his own mistakes. Anyway, I'd rather see him getting stoned than drinking beer," Mark replied.

"He's fourteen! He shouldn't be doing either one. He could've been suspended if he and Jess had been caught at school. How can you make light of this?"

"Oh, those juvenile records are usually expunged. The kids are given some community service work and counseling if it's a first offense. No one hears about their indiscretion later on. And he didn't smoke up at school. He was too smart for that," Mark said, as he peeled the zucchini.

"Plus, you're missing the larger picture. Devon's scared about what happened to Lisa. In many ways, he was closer to her than he is to either one of us. Lisa never told him what to do. She didn't reprimand or criticize him. She was like a 'cool aunt,' and he's disturbed about her going missing, so he's acting out. He needs our support right now. We'll only make things worse by coming down hard on him."

Much to my chagrin, I knew that Mark was right. Devon's behavior had been prompted by Lisa's disappearance. I had been so preoccupied with my own feelings of loss, and with the search party, that I had neglected Devon all week; I never thought about his feelings. Perhaps he wanted to escape from the constant worry and anxiety about what could have happened to her. Or maybe he was trying to get our attention since everyone's mind had been solidly focused on Lisa for the last week.

I decided to surprise my son by taking the news in my stride. As upset as I had been earlier, I would force myself not to let Devon know that. As Bill Clinton said, I would try to "feel his pain," and I would forget about whether or not he had inhaled.

I buzzed Devon on his pager to let him know that dinner was ready. He entered the kitchen with his head down to avoid looking at me. He looked pale, and I was afraid he might have one of his asthma attacks.

Dev sat down at the table and turned his nose up at the sight of the trout. "Ugh, fish," he said with disgust.

"What would you prefer? A New York sirloin?"

"No, meat is gross. Tabatha is becoming a vegetarian."

She'll have to watch her folic acid and B12 intake, I thought to myself but bit my tongue before I could say it out loud.

"Seriously, what would you like to eat if we weren't having fish?"

"But we are having fish."

"Just answer the question."

"No contest. Pizza!"

"Done deal," I replied and handed him the phone. I recited the number for Pizza Pizza and told him to order what he wanted. I would wrap up the trout, and we could have it for lunch tomorrow. Devon was shocked, not only that I hadn't mentioned his pot smoking but also that I seemed to be rewarding him for it.

"Dev, we can talk about the drugs later. I'm sorry I haven't been there for you this week. I know Lisa was your godmother and you're scared now that she's missing. I am, too, sweetie. Lisa is all I thought about all week," I said, omitting any reference to my other obsessions with Alain and my hair.

"Lisa was awesome," Devon said. "She gave me the *Eminem Show* on CD and told me not to tell you. I think she even, like, owned her own copy. And she listened to 50 Cent and managed to pronounce his name right, unlike you guys! All you ever do is rag on me about my music and my tattoo. Lisa told me she listened to lottsa bands her parents hated like the Clash, Billy Idol, and Joan Jett. She remembered what it was like to be young. You could talk to her the way you could talk to other kids, maybe, because she didn't have her own kids or because she'd been an addict. I don't know, but she was like that." He started to cry.

Devon folded his arms across his chest when I went to hug him. Mark wolfed down his trout and vegetables and announced that he was going up to his room to grade papers. He gave me the thumbs-up sign when Devon wasn't looking to let me know that he appreciated the way I was handling the situation.

I suddenly realized that both Devon and I were talking about Lisa in the past tense. There was a long silence. I sat there rapping my fingers on the table while Devon downed a king-size glass of Pepsi. I stifled the impulse to warn him against drinking caffeine at this hour.

The doorbell rang, and Dev went to get the double cheese pizza. He was grinning when he brought the food into the room. It was the kind of smile that I had only seen him wearing when he was with Jess or watching *South Park*.

Devon dug in heartily to his pizza while I forced myself to eat small morsels. Although the pie smelled delicious, when it entered my mouth, it tasted thick and doughy.

"Um! This is awesome! I'm so glad you didn't make me eat

that fish." He wiped the back of his mouth with his hand.

"Mum, I'll go with you to one of those WAR meetings if you want?" Devon said to my astonishment, his voice rising at the end of his sentence. "There's only one condition. You have to watch *8 Mile* with me."

"*8 Mile*? Isn't that the movie based on the book by Stephen King?"

"Nah, you're thinking about *The Green Mile*," Devon replied. "*8 Mile* is the story of a rapper in Detroit. It's based on the life of Eminem, whose real name is Marshall Mathers. Eminem even stars in it," he said with increasing enthusiasm.

"I think it'll give you a better idea of where he's coming from. You know, you're always talking about these girls who've been, like, abused and what horrible lives they've had. You even feel bad about boys who were taken advantage of by priests or their hockey coaches. So why don't you have any sympathy for Marshall? His mother was abusive. She was mean to him, and she did drugs! Also, she, like, gave him something called Munchkins syndrome," Devon added uncertainly.

"Munchausen syndrome?" I asked, trying to picture the tough guy with the tattoos and bad attitude as a small child with a manipulative and controlling mother.

"Yeah, that sounds right. She made him feel sick when he was totally healthy. And, Mum, I know you would respect the way Em felt about his little brother, Nathan. He, like, didn't wanna leave him alone in the house with his mother when he finally split from Detroit. He's also really keen about his daughter, Hailie Jade. He talks about her all the time in his songs and on TV."

"But didn't Eminem write a song about his wife, threatening to cut her up into small pieces and put her in the trunk of the car?"

I asked, pushing the cold pizza around on my plate with my salad fork.

"Sure, but they were fighting at the time. She'd been cheating on him, so he went ballistic. His mother was a bitch, and his wife betrayed him, so he started to hate women. How different is that from the women in your WAR group who were treated bad and ended up hating men?

"I've seen some of the books in your study. That Andrea Dworkin? Oh, my God, does that lady have a problem! I just skimmed some of her stuff, but she, like, talks about all men like they're rapists! Is that what they teach you at WAR? Is that what you want me to hear in a lecture by one of those girls who's been raped—that men are perverts and I'm gonna be like that when I grow up?"

I tried to explain that Dworkin's work was a metaphor, that she didn't really believe all intercourse was rape, but she had written the book at a time when women had fewer choices than they do today; getting married was inevitable for most women and rife with power imbalances. Thus, the lack of choice and decision-making power affected their ability to give consent to sex, Dworkin argued. The concept of rape within marriage didn't exist in those days—people thought it was impossible to rape a wife or a prostitute because one had agreed to unlimited sex when she said, "I do," and the other sold her body, and therefore forfeited the legal ability to ever truly say no. Devon didn't buy it completely, but he understood her and WAR's philosophy a little better after our talk.

His breathing was still rapid, and I asked if he was up to watching the movie. He had looked so asthmatic earlier that I was worried about him, but he said he felt much better, and he was "stoked" about viewing the show with me.

After supper, I changed into my jogging pants and a T-shirt. I carried a cup of espresso into the family room, trying to disguise my yawns from Devon. I was close to collapsing but would have to make myself watch this film with my son. I hoped it wasn't boring or hopelessly obscene. Devon fiddled with the brightness contrast on the DVD player while I plumped up some soft pillows to sink into on the couch. I kicked off my Nikes and tucked both my feet under my rear end, as I thought about what Devon had said.

Marshall Mathers had been hurt and deceived by the women in his life. How did his situation differ from that of a woman who had been verbally and emotionally abused by her father and went on to marry a man who cheated on her? I had always heard that Eminem was a misogynist, but in order for me to continue seeing him that way, I'd have to admit that some of the women in my WAR group, and many of the authors on my bookshelf, were misanthropes.

Actually, "misanthrope" wasn't the right term because it meant someone who hated people. "Misogynist" meant a hater of women, but what was the word that denoted a man hater? "Misandry" was probably the correct term, but I hardly ever heard anyone use it.

On the other hand, just because his mother hurt and emotionally abused him didn't give Marshall the right to become a bully and a woman hater. We all sympathize with the victim, particularly a child who's been physically or sexually abused, but the empathy stops when a person becomes a victimizer himself. Calling women "ho's" and thinking of them as nothing more than pieces of meat is indefensible. I may understand *why* he does it, but I still can't excuse it.

Dev fast forwarded through the previews, bounced down onto the other end of the couch, and rubbed his palms together. He was excited about watching *8 Mile*, although he'd probably seen it twenty times already. I refrained from asking how he had managed to buy a movie that was rated R. I was going to be more like Lisa and less of a pain in the ass to my poor son. That would take a lot of work on my part.

To my amazement, Slim Shady was cute. The story was a semi-biographical account of his life growing up in Detroit. Kim Basinger did an excellent job of portraying Marshall's calculated, clinging, and demanding alcoholic mother. The young man's life was bleak, replete with poverty, abuse, and dead-end jobs.

Marshall's only saving grace was his phenomenal rhyming ability, which enabled him to compete in club contests where he was scorned as a white rapper. He met a pretty blonde, and for a while, it seemed as though her love might release him from the chains of his trailer park life. But she moved quickly on to another guy. Devon assured me that in real life, Marshall's wife was much worse to him than the girlfriend in the movie.

"Kim really hurt him bad. She totally screwed him over," Devon said, as he paused the movie and got up for a glass of water. He was thirsty after all that pizza. I stopped worrying about Eminem's misogyny and began to ruminate about my crush on Alain. What would Devon think of me if he knew? Soon enough, I would have to tell Mark that our marriage was over.

How would Devon cope with the news? Our relationship was so fragile. This was the first time in months he and I had done anything alone together that he seemed to remotely enjoy.

Devon microwaved some popcorn after the movie. I had a

couple of handfuls but could hardly swallow the dry kernels. We discussed the movie, laughing together for the first time in years. I couldn't believe it when I looked at the clock, and it was after 11:00 p.m.

Devon had school tomorrow. Mark was already in bed. He had come downstairs for a snack just as we were finishing the movie and we had "Sshed" him right out of the room.

"Well, kiddo, we'd better call it a night," I suggested.

"It's a night!" Devon said and grinned. Then, without any provocation on my part, he hugged me.

My eyes were moist, and I wanted to beg Devon's forgiveness for not being there for him during his time of need, but I was afraid that he'd recoil if I got sentimental. I did manage to give him a big kiss on the cheek as he pulled away, and I said, "Baby, I'm sorry I wasn't paying attention to your feelings. We're all scared about Aunt Lisa. Every day we pray she'll be returned to us."

I don't know why I used the term "pray." Maybe I didn't want my atheism to rub off on Devon. He was old enough to make his own choices about religion, and although he didn't talk about it much, I suspected that he still believed in God.

We walked upstairs together, and Dev gave me an impish smile before he entered his room.

"Wow, wait until I tell Jess that you watched *8 Mile* with me! He'll freak out," he said.

"Hey," I said, as an afterthought. "I don't want you becoming a pothead! Don't you dare think that I've forgotten about you and Jess getting high. I just didn't want to make that the central issue tonight when the real problem is that you're upset about Lisa. No more joints in your room! For God's sake, you have asthma!"

"It's a deal," Devon said sheepishly and closed his door.

I was thrilled that Dev and I had bonded—over Eminem, no less—and I went to bed feeling better than I had since all this trouble with Lisa had begun. I knew that it would hurt Devon terribly if I left his father and that pained me.

But now Dev and I had a foundation of a relationship again. As long as he knew that he could count on me, I was sure he'd be able to handle a separation. What Dev could never cope with would be infidelity on my part. That would make me just like Kim, Eminem's wife: the "ho."

I still viewed the term "ho" as derogatory and gender-specific, but Devon had taught me something about gender politics tonight. Or had it been Slim Shady who had shed a different light on my perspective on the battle between the sexes? Fortunately, Dev also saw WAR more clearly after our talk; they would never be "Mum's crazy women's group" again, and he understood how crucial they were in the search for Lisa.

CHAPTER FIFTEEN

It was a cold, dreary Monday with heavy rains. The number of searchers had dwindled, but the police maintained their presence on the boulevard. The volunteers were probably glad to have a break because they had looked high and low and had not found a single trace of Lisa.

The Quebec Police had issued a statement saying that Ryan Whitman was not an official suspect. JC told me that was just a formality. It was a way for the police to protect themselves since they didn't have any hard-core evidence against Ryan. But I took it as a negative sign. The Aylmer cops had spent the entire week searching for Lisa, and Detective McCarthy continued to assist. Would they write her off now or close the file?

I did my workout at the Y, spending an hour on the treadmill instead of attending a class. From there, I went to Loeb. Alain wasn't on duty, which made grocery shopping much more relaxing. I didn't have to worry about my appearance, although I did wear my Saab baseball cap to disguise my pitiful highlighting job.

I purchased Midol and orange flavored Metamucil, which I would never have bought if Alain had been working. I would have preferred to have been constipated for a month rather than to have Alain see me buying geriatric products. Another young guy took care of my meat order, and I never looked twice at him. He barely looked older than Devon.

It was approaching lunchtime. I didn't know if it would be rude to land down on the Campanas, so I decided to head off to the hairdresser's again. Luckily, no appointment was necessary at my shop, and Chan Juan had Mondays off. I waited about twenty minutes and was assigned to Cameron, a petite, talkative girl with beautiful hair. It was brown with blonde highlights and had been cut in short layers, which framed her heart-shaped face. This was exactly the sleek and sophisticated look I was hoping for.

"My cut would be perfect on you," Cameron nodded. "It's simple. No maintenance. That's great for people like you who're always working out."

Normally, I'd rather be trying on bathing suits than presenting my damaged mane at the hairdresser's, but today I felt unusually confident. Cameron was bubbly, and her hair was magnificent. I sat there calmly while Cameron clipped away at the ruins of my hair.

Pieces of frizz and over-processed ends fell like leaves from a tree. I closed my eyes and imagined myself looking like Brittany Murphy, who played Eminem's girlfriend in *8 Mile*, as Cameron described the trouble she was having with her new Hyundai. When I opened my eyes, I was horrified. I looked like a shaved rabbit. Sinead O'Connor had more hair than me!

I bought a large cappuccino with whipped cream from the coffee shop next door to cheer myself up. I drank half of it in the car as I drove to the Campanas, carefully balancing the drink between my legs, since the coffee holder was full of coins.

I checked what was left of my hair in the mirror before I walked up the laneway to the Campana's house. Maybe no one would notice my new look.

"Tara, what have you done to your hair?" Lorenzo asked. "You look like a little bird."

"Time for a change," I said, trying to sound nonchalant, although I felt like putting a paper bag over my head. But the

Campanas had no time to analyze my compulsion to change my hair faster than most people changed their underwear. They were eager to apprise me of their most recent conversation with Pierre Lafarge, the private investigator.

"Come in, come in," Lorenzo said, as he placed his large reassuring arm on my shoulder. "We have some news! Tell her, Anna." He shut the door.

"Ryan cannot possibly be the father of Lisa's baby. He had a vasectomy!" Anna said.

"Vasectomy? That's ridiculous. Lisa's been trying to get pregnant all year," I said.

"We know! He's been lying to her. Lafarge says Ryan never wanted children. He made sure of that years ago."

"But a vasectomy is reversible," I declared. "He could have changed his mind. How did Lafarge discover that anyway? It's private medical information. I can't imagine Lisa's family doctor disclosing that to him."

"He has his ways, Tara," Lorenzo said, lowering his voice, as though he were discussing classified defense documents. "Lafarge also tells us that Ryan sold Lisa's computer."

"Didn't the police confiscate Lisa's computer? I would've thought that they'd review her emails."

"Yes, yes. They checked her emails at work, looking for a suicide note, and any correspondence with a stranger or new person in her life. But they couldn't read the email at home because her computer had the worms, Tara," Lorenzo explained. "Could Ryan have given her computer the worms?"

"I don't know much about viruses, but I think they're really easy to get. Devon complains that whenever he posts to a newsgroup, he gets a ton of mail, supposedly from Microsoft. But the messages are fakes, and if you click on them, you can get a Trojan worm." I tried to sound hip and well-informed, but I didn't even know if a Trojan was a worm or if it was another kind of virus.

"Spam! Worms!" Lorenzo waved his hands in the air. "What if there was something important on her home computer that Ryan didn't want people to find?"

"That's possible. Devon has had viruses that have been repaired. Even if the machine was irreparably damaged, Ryan should've kept it. Lisa will kill him when she finds out that her PC is gone," I said, afraid that Lisa would never have the opportunity to be mad about a missing appliance.

"But that's the point, Tara. Don't you see? Ryan doesn't expect her to return," Lorenzo said.

Two damning pieces of evidence against Mr. Whitman, but they weren't conclusive. The Campanas wouldn't tell me how Lafarge had discovered that Ryan had a vasectomy. Maybe his source was wrong, but if the information were correct, it would give Ryan a motive for murder.

Undoubtedly, Lisa would be distraught about the loss of her computer. But what if the machine had gotten a simple virus and Ryan hadn't known how to fix it? Perhaps it had been easier for him to unload the machine for cash. He would have trouble paying the bills shortly and had already tried to access Lisa's money.

The vasectomy was another story. I asked the Campanas if they had told this to McCarthy and Desormeaux. They said yes.

"What are the police going to do about it?" I asked.

"They told us to be patient, Tara," Lorenzo responded. "It is in God's hands now." He looked at me with his haggard, droopy eyes.

My heart broke for the suffering that Lisa's family was enduring. They were so much stronger than I. God was not working quickly enough for me. I was running out of patience. I was eager to see how Ryan was going to present himself at the AA meeting and why he chose this time to speak out publicly.

Laura Anne picked me up at 7:30 p.m. to take me to the meeting. She drove an old Ford minivan with broken hubcaps. I hoisted myself up onto the seat next to her. Laura Anne was worried about Lisa because she had drawn the Knight of Swords from her Tarot deck. Knights indicated swift and sudden change, and the Knight of Swords was especially reckless.

"I hope that Ryan doesn't feel uncomfortable tonight," Laura Anne remarked, as she checked her gas gauge, noting that she had less than one-quarter of a tank.

"He's not accustomed to talking at meetings, and he's not that articulate. We must envision him as strong and confident. That will help to balance his chakras and keep him in perfect harmony."

I wasn't particularly concerned with Ryan's mental health or his comfort level, but I did hope that he would say something revealing. I considered mentioning Devon's pot smoking to Laura Anne but hesitated because I didn't want her to pathologize his experimentation.

The rain had stopped, and the thick evening air was warm and humid. The meeting was held in the auditorium of an old red brick school. Several people were smoking outside and greeted Laura Anne by name.

"Hi, Joe," Laura Anne said effusively to a dark young man dressed from head to toe in black denim. "Haven't seen you in ages," she exclaimed, as she kissed him on the cheek.

"I've been a good boy. Following my program," Joe replied and winked at me.

"No one was implying that you weren't, " Laura Anne retorted. "He practically runs this group," she said proudly, for my benefit.

"Keeps me out of trouble. God knows, trouble used to be my middle name," Joe said.

I stepped back a bit to get out of the way of the smoke and landed on the foot of an older man. He was hefty and wore a green flannel shirt that looked too heavy for this weather.

"How's it going, Norman?" Laura Anne asked the beefy looking man, who was leaning against the wall.

"Can't complain," he replied, tossing the end of his cigarette away with his yellow-stained fingers. "Well, I could, but no one would listen," he joked, but his strained expression didn't match the levity of his words. I wished that I had my blood-pressure cuff. This man with his red face, broken capillaries, and chunky physique was a perfect candidate for a heart attack.

About thirty or forty people were perched on gray folding chairs. At the front of the room, there was a stage draped with tattered blue curtains. Plaques lined the walls with sayings like, "Easy Does It," "One Day at a Time," and "Live and Let Live." There were several wall hangings of a spiritual and philosophical nature. One quoted Pete Seeger, paraphrasing from the book of Ecclesiastes: "To everything...there is a season...and a time for every purpose under Heaven."

Norman sat down at a desk in the front of the room, next to a large woman in her thirties. Some of the men were bald or had receding hairlines. The women were cloaked in rayon and polyester. They didn't look much like the fashion plates at Le

Skratch, but they did resemble most of the regular folks I saw shopping at Loeb.

"Are all meetings like this?" I asked Laura Anne, refraining from commenting on how normal everyone looked, in case she found that to be insulting. What had I expected? People with two heads?

"Oh, no! There are as many different types of meetings as there are people. There are beginners' meetings, gay meetings, all women's meetings, meetings for young people, and closed private meetings for executive, Parliament Hill types who could never take the risk of coming to a meeting like this. Remember—this is an open meeting. That means anyone from the general public can attend. Look at those kids over there." Laura Anne pointed at two adorable prepubescent girls. "Addiction starts early but not that young! They're probably here for their dad."

Before I could ask why a father would bring his children to an AA meeting, Laura Anne escorted me to the coffee machine. We poured ourselves two large cups of decaf. She was greeted warmly by two women that she knew. I was beginning to feel at home in this cozy, informal environment when I saw Ryan looming behind Laura Anne's acquaintances. I felt such trepidation at the sight of him now—confusion, ambivalence, anger that he had lied about the vasectomy, and fear that he may have harmed Lisa if he knew that the child wasn't his.

Ryan was wearing a plain white T-shirt and faded blue jeans. He needed a haircut, and his long locks were falling into his hazel eyes. He looked muscular and gave off a virile scent. Although Alain was gorgeous, his manner was neither boastful nor threatening, and Mark's was positively placid. Ryan emanated machismo and testosterone. He had always unnerved me, but now he seemed downright frightening. He was Stanley Kowalski, but although I was scared, I was far from the fragile Blanche DuBois.

"Hey, Tara. Great of you to come hear me talk. You dunno what that means to me. I'm kinda nervous about getting up there," Ryan said, looking directly into my eyes without blinking. I couldn't picture Ryan being nervous about flying a plane into Baghdad, let alone standing up in front of a few dozen people. "But I gotta get the word out about Lisa. These people are my friends, and I really need their help. Plus, it's good for me to vent. I shouldn't keep these feelings bottled up inside. It could jeopardize my sobriety."

"Look at the time," Laura Anne said. We had less than five minutes before the meeting began. Laura Anne led me to a folding chair right next to the young girls. One appeared to be about twelve years old. She had gold hair and wore brown horn-rimmed glasses. She seemed to be extremely wound up.

"Is it your anniversary tonight?" the girl asked me. I shook my head. "It's my father's anniversary. He's celebrating ten years, and I have to get up and give him his pin." She took a large gulp of air, and I saw that she had a missing tooth. "I don't think I can do it."

"You'll be just fine," I reassured her. "Lots of people feel uneasy speaking in public for the first time. It's common, but it'll pass, and you'll be great. "

"I hope so," the girl replied. "The last time I got up there, uh, I cried." She blushed and crossed her right leg over the left, making circular motions with her foot. Her little sister was sprawled on the floor, preoccupied with Marilyn Monroe playing cards and her game of solitaire. She seemed oblivious to the meeting, which was about to start. I patted the young girl's thigh reassuringly and turned my attention to the front of the room.

Laura Anne had explained that a series of people would be talking. First, we would hear from the Chairperson and the Vice Chair, who would give introductory comments. Then someone from the floor would get up and read the twelve steps. The main speaker had thirty to forty minutes to talk. After that, the group would celebrate sobriety anniversaries. I hoped that my anxious little friend could survive the next hour without wetting her pants.

The Chairwoman wiped her brow and pushed her waist length, light brown hair behind her ear. She rapped a gavel on the large desk and brought the meeting to order.

"Welcome to the Open Speaker meeting of Alcoholics Anonymous. We have a busy agenda ahead of us. The Chairperson is supposed to qualify, so I guess I'll do that." She looked around the room, gathering her thoughts.

"My name is Michelle, and I'm a grateful alcoholic."

"Hi, Michelle," the crowd roared back.

"I was raised in Kingston, which has three main institutions: the mental hospital, the penitentiary, and the university. By the time I was twenty-two, I'd already been in two out of three, and it doesn't take a rocket scientist to figure out that didn't include the university!" The group laughed.

"I've heard lots of speakers talk about their miserable childhoods and how that drove them to drink. I wish I could blame it on that, but I was, uh, happy as a child. I wasn't mistreated, but I did feel inadequate and unsure of myself till I discovered Vodka Tonics. Suddenly, I had so much confidence. I felt witty and attractive. Brilliant, even! Funny how so many of us alcoholics are brilliant." Another long laugh from the audience. They seemed like a jovial bunch.

"Anyways, I was so clever that I started sneaking bottles of vodka up to my room in Grade Ten. By the time I was old enough to drive, I was, um, drinking and drugging all night. I was just a partyer. That's what I told myself. All my friends drank as much as me, but that's because I only hung out with alcoholics. One night my boyfriend and me had dinner at Howard Johnson's. We met there, and I brought my car.

"Anyways, he noticed I was pretty wasted, so he tried to take my keys away. He didn't succeed and I...drove right into a Ford Taurus with a family in it. There was, uh, a mum and a dad, um, and a little boy." Michelle stopped speaking and gazed up at the ceiling. The room had become uncomfortably silent.

"Well, the kid broke his neck and was paralyzed. Because it was my first offense and I agreed to go into treatment, I only did eighteen months at the Prison for Women. That was before it closed down in 2000. Now they don't have maximum security prisons for women in Ontario. There are regional centers like Grand Valley in Kitchener, and they put us in little houses where we could cook and everything. Anyways, they told me at P4W that alcoholism is such a deadly disease that it kills people who don't even have it."

Michelle guzzled about half of her bottle of water. "I haven't had a drink since that night seven years ago. But I've developed a slight problem with food—like you haven't noticed!—so I just started Overeaters Anonymous. One thing at a time, eh? I'm just grateful to be sober. I guess that qualifies me to be here. Thank you."

Everyone clapped. If I hadn't been a rehab nurse, I would have been shocked by her story. But I saw so much carnage every day that nothing surprised me. I felt sorry for Michelle yet angry at her for her irresponsibility. Somewhere there was a family who grieved for their little boy's lost potential, thanks to this woman's hedonism.

Of course, it wasn't rational to refer to her behavior as hedonistic and to call it a disease at the same time, and I did believe that alcoholism was a disease. Yet unlike other illnesses, there was an element of choice in addiction; people didn't choose to develop Hodgkin's disease, but they did decide to pick up their first drink or to snort that first line of cocaine.

Some would argue that it wasn't free will at all that separated the social drinker from the alcoholic, but rather something more insidious like a genetic predisposition. Was it fair of me to blame this woman for harming a child if her biological makeup had made her alcoholic?

Lisa had never done anything reprehensible when she was drinking. She had never hurt anyone except herself, but she could have. She always had the potential to cause harm when she was intoxicated. How would I have felt if this were Lisa's story?

It was complicated. I wondered how the preteen next to me was processing the tale. She crossed and uncrossed her legs, swinging the foot of her right leg round and round in circles. She wasn't even listening to the speaker. Her concern about her own upcoming performance was too intense.

Norman thanked Michelle and began to read the twelve traditions of AA. After he finished, a pockmarked man with a long black ponytail got up to read the twelve steps. He introduced himself as "Karl, a grateful alcoholic." The meeting had hardly begun, and I'd already heard the word grateful three times. It was starting to gnaw at me like nails on a blackboard. Where was Lisa? How was I supposed to feel grateful about that?

I was getting restless. The young girl's nervousness was contagious, and I was anxious to hear Ryan talk. After suffering through the repetitious steps and traditions, I was pleased to see Ryan get up and walk over to the desk. He stood tall and straight and shook Michelle's hand firmly.

Ryan was so much better looking than the rest of the men in the room. Good looks were powerful. They influenced our impressions of others. I'd read a psychology study once where mock jurors were given pictures of people who had committed crimes and people who were innocent. The experimenters described the innocent people as guilty and vice versa and then measured the effect of physical appearance on the jury. Sadly, the better-looking people were perceived to be less culpable.

There was a trial in Manhattan back in the 1980s where a handsome young man was accused of murdering a young coed by the name of Jennifer Levin. Robert Chambers was convicted of the charge but acquired a whole slew of groupies, who attended the courtroom regularly to support him. They also wrote to him and visited him in jail. What if they had been on the jury? Even one could have hung that jury.

There was also Gillian Guess, the crazy Canadian juror who developed a crush on the male defendant, but thinking of her reminded me of my absurd infatuation with Alain. How could I judge her? One thing I could say about AA was that it had prevented me from thinking about Alain all night. Maybe I should join myself.

Ryan sat down and picked up the microphone. It made a screeching noise. "I don't think I'll need this," Ryan said, as he put the mike aside.

"Hi everyone. I'm Ryan W., and I'm cross-addicted."

"Hi, Ryan!"

Just don't say that you're grateful, I thought grimly, as I pictured Ryan hocking Lisa's computer. I glanced at my little friend's sister, who was absorbed in her game of solitaire on the floor. How I wished that I could be that oblivious eight-year-old, sitting cross-legged and matching up 9s and 10s with her Jacks. Her worst fear was that she couldn't get all of her Aces out, whereas the adults in the room were holding onto their sanity for dear life. Thankfully, the girl's father was celebrating ten years tonight, so she and her sister were largely products of sobriety.

"Sorry. No jail or mental hospitals in my story."

Right. Just deceit and possible murder.

"I was a blackout drinker from the get-go. That means the first time I took a drink, I got drunk and couldn't remember what happened. My pop was an alcoholic and used to beat my ma. I'd lie awake at night, listening to them fight. When I was a kid, I couldn't do nothing about it, but as I got older, he started to hit me 'cause I tried to protect her. I begged her to leave him, but she always had excuses—no money, no way to raise my brother and me. I thought that was legit at the time, but now I see she was codependent on him."

Ryan stopped to drink his coffee. I envisioned Ryan as a little boy feeling helpless, frightened, and enraged. What kind of a man would he have become if he hadn't grown up in an abusive household?

"So, I started to rebel against my old man by doing bad in school. Later, I got arrested for stealing cars. I had a real temper when I was drinking. Pop took me to meetings because he was in the program by then, but all I could hear were things that hadn't happened to me yet. One guy lost his job—hadn't happened to me. Another guy lost his wife—hadn't happened to me. People like Michelle had accidents and ended up hurting people— hadn't happened to me!

"Pop told me to ignore stuff people said at meetings that didn't apply to me. If I couldn't relate, I was supposed to leave it there and only take things I could identify with. But I couldn't do that. I couldn't think right." He paused and cleared his throat. "And of course, it was only a matter of time," Ryan continued, his voice shaking, "before I went to prison for 18 months for beating my wife."

Ryan looked at the audience. His piercing eyes rested on me. "Man, I don't why I'm going on about the past. My partner Lisa went missing last Thursday. I been crazy with worry, and I been looking for her everywhere in Hull, Aylmer, and the Gatineau. Some of you been helping me out. Thanks. I can't tell you how thankful Lisa and I are to have your support. It's only 'cause of you that I haven't picked up a drink or started using again, although I been tempted!" He grinned, and the crowd laughed weakly. The time for humor had passed.

"Yeah, it's been really rough on me. The police suspect me 'cause I was arrested for hitting my first girlfriend, but she dropped the charges. I was all coked up at the time. Anyway, I can't sleep anymore. The stress of having the cops breathing down my neck and the lack of closure are killing me."

To my astonishment, Ryan started to cry and had to stop to blow his nose. It seemed rehearsed—a big tough guy like Ryan. I had never seen him cry, and he hadn't been emotional with me at all on the phone or in person in Aylmer.

"I been crying in the supermarket, too, 'cause whenever I walk in there, I think of Lisa since we used to shop together. It's embarrassing, but I don't give a damn what other people think. The only thing that's important is to find Lisa or the person who took her. That'll give us resolution."

What had Mark said? That Ryan's behavior and his words had seemed scripted and that he was using psychological jargon. "Closure" and "resolution" were not words that belonged in Ryan's vocabulary; "closure" was something that Ryan probably did to the door of his truck, and "resolution" would apply to the quality of the picture on his home entertainment system.

"I dunno what else to say here, so I'm just gonna wrap it up, and ask all of yous to keep looking for Lisa and praying for her sobriety. I can't live without that girl, and I know you can help me find her. Thank you," Ryan said, as he stood up and shook hands with Michelle.

"Oh, I forgot to mention, I couldn't have done none of this without the help of my sponsor, Norman. Thanks, man." Ryan nodded in Norman's direction, but Norman looked uncomfortable, and his face was flushed. I guess it wasn't easy to sponsor Ryan Whitman.

It was odd that Ryan had mentioned Lisa's sobriety when it seemed so obvious that foul play was involved. How much drinking could she have done without her wallet? And why would he say that he had to find the person who took Lisa if she had left voluntarily? There was ambiguity in his speech and insincerity as well. It all seemed disingenuous.

I felt a strong sense of anger and disappointment after Ryan had finished talking. I don't know what I had expected him to say, but I was hoping for some clue, mannerism, gesture, or inflection in his voice that would help me to determine his guilt or innocence. There had been nothing except my intuitive sense that he had been dishonest.

Michelle thanked Ryan and spoke briefly about his ordeal and how much the group missed Lisa. She asked for a moment of silence to pray for Lisa. Now I was in danger of crying. Fortunately, the moment was brief, and Michelle's cohort, Larry P., declared that there were no dues or fees, but "we are self-supporting by our own contributions." I fumbled through my purse, looking for a five, and tossed the bill into the basket.

My sidekick was becoming increasingly wired as we approached the end of the meeting. I thought she might knock her little sister in the head by the way she was spinning her foot around on her leg. Finally, the preadolescent was called to the front of the stage for her big performance. Her braces gleamed as she gave a wide grin and started speaking faster than the speed of light.

"Well, I'm feeling pretty nervous being up here 'cause the last time I gave my dad his award, I started to cry. But I was only four then! I'm not planning to cry this time. Dad, I'm so proud of you for not drinking for, like, my whole life and when I listen to people talk here about how they messed up their lives, I'm just so glad you didn't do that to us. Thanks, Dad!" She finished abruptly. Everyone clapped, and her father stood up to receive his well-earned pin.

When the meeting ended, I turned to the little girl and congratulated her on her big feat.

"You were terrific! I knew you would be," I said warmly.

She beamed, nodded, and ran off to find her dad. Maybe there was hope. Perhaps this sober father would break the cycle of abuse and neglect, and his children wouldn't suffer as Ryan had.

CHAPTER SIXTEEN

Speaking of parents, I felt obliged to go to the Tuesday evening function at Mark's parents' house; they lived in an elegant older home in the Glebe. Unlike my easygoing dad, Mark's father, Jeffrey, was about as mellow as Rush Limbaugh. At the age of seventy-two, Jeffrey was painfully thin, walked with a stoop, and his bald head shone like a bowling ball. He was a big fan of Dr. Laura Schlessinger's.

The last time I had the pleasure of talking to Jeffrey, he had expounded on the selfishness of mothers in the workforce and the critical need for them to stay at home with their children like Dr. Laura did. Of course, stay-at-home Laura somehow managed to pursue her high-powered career, to write books, and to conduct her infamous radio show from home after the birth of her son; she didn't exactly practice what she preached.

Moreover, Laura missed the point that many women had to work for economic reasons. And for all her talk about ethics and the importance of family, she was outrageously rude to the people who called into her show. I couldn't stand Dr. Laura, but Jeffrey worshiped her.

I would make a concerted effort not to get embroiled in another fruitless dispute tonight. I was still reeling from my debate with Alain the other evening and from the depressing realization that Alain probably shared many of Jeffrey's political views. Mark's brother, Peter, was worse than Jeff and Alain combined.

At least Mark's mother, Madeleine, was reasonable but for all the wrong reasons. She was a shy, gentle woman, who rarely disagreed with her husband. I had no idea what her views were on any topic. She may not have shared all her husband's positions, but she valued peace, harmony, and pleasing other people above everything else.

Peter was about my age, which made him six years younger than Mark. He worked in commercial real estate and had been married to Evelyn for seven years. Evelyn was a buyer for Holt Renfrew. Both she and Peter were conscious of status and clothes, whereas Mark boasted about not having bought a suit in ten years or finding great bargains at discount stores like Winners. They had a young son, Hugh, a small blonde boy with freckles that covered his nose and sparkling green eyes.

Hugh loved to cause mischief. The last time we had a family supper, Hugh put sugar in the salt shaker and laughed hilariously at the expression on our faces when we bit into lamb chops that tasted sickeningly sweet. Hugh was only six and was definitely my favorite member of the clan.

Jeffrey led Mark, Devon, and me into the living room where we greeted Peter and his family. My shoes clicked on the hardwood floor, and I sat down gingerly next to Evelyn on Madeleine's gold embroidered couch. Evelyn wanted to hear all the details about Lisa, so I filled her in on our progress in Aylmer. Like Lucinda, Evelyn offered to join the hunt. Her support touched me, and I wondered why it hadn't occurred to me to ask her earlier.

Predictably, Peter began to criticize Lisa, saying she should never have taken up with Ryan. I was so tired of hearing people blame Lisa for her choice in men. Even the Campanas and I had begun to suspect Ryan of being involved in her disappearance, but what good did it do now to berate Lisa for her actions? Ryan was an alcoholic like herself, and Lisa had believed in him.

We had cocktails while Hugh raced around the room, causing a commotion. He was carrying a small book called *The Shrinking of Treehorn*, which he described as a story about a boy who was shrinking, but his parents and teachers didn't seem to notice.

"Play with your Lego, darling," Evelyn said to her son. "He just loves to build racers and rescue rigs with his Make & Create: Maximum Wheels," she explained, as Hugh ran his red fire engine along Madeleine's flawless mahogany table. His long shoelaces were untied, and it looked as though he could trip at any moment.

Devon was standing in the corner of the living room, pretending to examine an old family photo.

"Dev, can you take Hugh outside to play until we're ready to eat?" I asked.

"Can we play Quidditch?" Hugh retorted, referring to the sport for young wizards like Harry Potter. "I want the Nimbus 2000!"

"Don't be such a dork," Devon said with affection, putting his arm around Hugh to direct him outside. "The 2000 is way out of date! You need the Lightning Bolt 3000 Purple Flying Broomstick."

Evelyn frowned at Devon and told him in French that Hugh had only been allowed to see parts of the first Harry Potter movie, since the sequels were too violent for a child his age.

"The international wizard gaming federation is considering banning the Lightning Bolts, honey, because they give riders an unfair advantage," Evelyn told her son. Hugh looked crushed.

"Hey, I can show you some pretty mean Taekwon-Do kicks," Devon said to Hugh, whose spirits picked up. Hugh began practicing his own side kicks and nearly knocked over Madeleine's Dresden doll collection.

Mark and Peter started talking about the Senators, and I began to daydream about Alain, wondering what he was doing on a Tuesday night without Christine. Was he out getting drunk? I tried to picture Alain's parents and his relatives. Did he also feel trapped at family gatherings?

I remembered a line from one of Al Franken's books where he declared that the next time he went home to visit his family, he was going to stay in a motel. I also wished that I was playing Quidditch with the boys, or that I could wear an invisibility cloak that would allow me to sneak out of this boring, stuffy family affair and spy on Alain and his friends.

Madeleine announced that the food was ready. We proceeded to the dining room. As usual, Madeleine had put on quite a spread: there was a huge roast chicken with mashed potatoes, carrots, peas, and dark brown gravy. Little crescent rolls had been carefully placed in a special wicker basket on the white tablecloth, and fresh greens with tomatoes, cucumbers, radishes, and onions were in a large glass bowl.

Jeffrey poured the Bin 65 Chardonnay and said grace before we began to eat. "For what we're about to receive, may the Lord make us truly grateful. Amen."

"Butterbeer!" Hugh said, as he guzzled his apple juice. I envied his enthusiasm for the meal. Despite the fabulous looking dinner, my appetite had not returned. I took miniscule bites of my chicken, and tried to hide the potato and peas underneath a large piece of skin from the bird.

"The china is lovely. Is it Limoges?" Evelyn asked Madeleine. I wouldn't know Limoges from ceramic. As far as I was concerned, Limoges could be the holy site in France where sick people bathed in the water in order to be cured.

Peter was talking about hunting season. He loved to hunt black bears although he knew how much this disturbed Mark and me. Just to get us riled up, Peter went into excruciating detail about how delicious black bear stew was.

"I can make black bear marinade, black bear barbecue, or black bear meatballs," he bragged.

"Great!" I replied. "You can open your own kiosk."

"Hunting bear is very productive right now," Peter exclaimed with his mouth full, ignoring my comment, "because food sources are in short supply. They're so hungry that they'll eat at baiting sites on a regular basis. April is ideal for bear hunting because they have much nicer coats early on in the season. By the time September rolls around, they often have spots on their skin."

"God forbid," I said, tapping my empty wine glass lightly, and looking expectantly at Mark's father in the hope that he would refill it.

"Well, they don't make the same kind of trophies when their skin isn't sleek," Peter said indignantly.

I failed to see the challenge in hunting a huge, slow-moving mammal, which weighed up to 400 pounds. The very sight of Peter's "trophies" hanging in his family room made me want to join PETA.

Peter turned away from me and began to speak to Mark in French, presumably so that Hugh wouldn't understand. Apparently, Peter had left his rifle at our cottage because he didn't want Hugh to discover it at their place. Normally unflappable, Mark was upset to hear that the gun was at our cabin and told Peter to get it the hell out of there before we opened the cottage in May.

The conversation resumed in English, and Jeffrey and Peter engaged in their usual diatribe about the advantages of a minimalist government. They agreed that there was no need for Social Insurance because people should be saving for their own retirement.

Tonight's special topic was the problem of immigrants or as Peter liked to call them, "those people with towels on their heads." Peter said that he didn't mind the younger ones coming into Canada since they could work, but the older ones should be prevented from immigrating because they were living off his tax dollars.

I bit the inside of my cheek so hard that I almost drew blood. Mark argued that it was a fallacy that many of the immigrants were unskilled; that applied largely to the refugees. Despite my own strong views on the topic, I was determined to keep quiet, only making small talk with Evelyn about the food.

Jeffrey and Peter moved on to talk about aboriginals. Mark said that they were killing themselves in large numbers, and Peter said, "Not fast enough," and he laughed. I didn't know how Mark stood his family. They were so ignorant.

My mind wandered back to thoughts of Ryan and his presentation at AA. Had Pierre Lafarge's information been accurate, and if so, who had squealed on Ryan? Maybe it was his sponsor, Norman, who had looked so squeamish during the meeting. Ryan was a puzzle. I needed to watch what he did, not what he said. That would be the only way to handle him: to trust him about as much as I trusted George Bush.

****

Thank God for the Americans with their workaholism and

their six-day postal delivery service. My Victoria's Secret lingerie arrived in the mail early Wednesday morning. I had lost five pounds in the last week because solid food kept getting stuck in my throat. I felt weak, had dizzy spells, and was living on soup and protein shakes, but my thunder thighs were shrinking. I imagined myself looking like Jennifer Aniston in my sexy push-up bra and panties, but when I tried them on, I still looked like a large maternal pear. I was just a smaller pear than I had been the week before.

I wasn't sure when I was going to be able to return to work. I was a nervous wreck and couldn't stop thinking about Lisa. When I left the pharmacy this afternoon, my car refused to start. I sat there for ten minutes, trying to turn the engine over, to no avail. Finally, I called the Canadian Automobile Association and fumed with rage that it took them more than forty-five minutes to arrive. The driver took one look at my gearshift and said, "Lady, sometimes it works better when the car's in park."

I was so humiliated. I had left the gear shift in drive! I was disintegrating and didn't want to make any mistakes at work that might seriously harm my patients.

I sat outside Alain's apartment, preparing myself to see him again. During the last three weeks, I had colored my hair reddish-brown, added psychedelic highlights, and cut it ridiculously short. I knocked on his door, thinking I should be wearing a name tag so he would recognize me.

Polite boy that he was, Alain never said a word about my appearance. I told him about the Campana's private detective, and we discussed Ryan's vasectomy.

"What will the police do now?" I asked.

"What can they do? They're probably waiting for a body,"

Alain said. "I mean, look at what we've got here. No body, no weapon, no confession. Who's to say she's not up in Thunder Bay?"

He popped a piece of Juicy Fruit gum in his mouth, explaining that he was trying to quit smoking. His head looked a little too large for his body tonight, and he was still wearing the same shirt. Laundry challenged?

"Thunder Bay?" I shouted. "She would never have taken off on her own without her car or her purse. Get real, Alain!" I snapped. His mention of the term "body" had thrown me.

Alain noticed how upset I was and suggested that we forgo our Internet work. He grabbed a beer and a bottle of Sambuca and poured me a shot. I sat at the opposite edge of the couch, feeling mad at him until the liquor started to take over. Then I felt like weeping. Images of Lisa and her fetus lying in a coffin, floated through my head.

I looked over at the phone. It seemed so long ago that I had called Alain's house when he was at work, just to hear the sound of his voice on the answering machine. Could it really have been just ten days ago that Lisa and I were at the movies, and I'd wanted to confess my stalking behavior to her?

Now Lisa was gone, and ironically, as a result, Alain and I had a relationship. We were alone in his apartment, and he had officially separated from Christine. My weight loss made me feel younger, and I almost looked svelte in my tight red pullover and jeweled jeans. I had pumped about a pound of mousse, jell, and hair spray into my pixie haircut, which had given it more volume. Knowing that I was sporting lingerie from Victoria's Secret made me feel like a wild woman.

Alain was yakking, but I couldn't hear what he was saying. I was watching the little space between his front teeth and the pinkness of his tongue. I moved closer to him to take another shot of the liqueur. His dark bushy eyebrows gave him an ethnic look like Hans Matheson, who played Yuri in the remake of *Dr. Zhivago*. How I wanted to reach out and stroke that beautiful face. He kept on talking, but all I could think was, *I want to fuck this boy.*

Me, using the "f" word to refer to sex! Of course, I used the word in my everyday vocabulary, although not as often as Lisa did, but when it came to sex, I rarely thought that way. It had always been Lisa who would whistle when a hottie would pass by and whisper to me, "He can screw me anytime." I was never so crude or bold.

If I were attracted to someone, I'd say something like, "He's a major babe," or "I wouldn't kick him out of bed." But when I looked at Alain, "fuck" was the only word that came to mind: the *only* term that could convey the depth and intensity of my passion except for the word "love." Because surely, I was in love with Alain.

How pathetic. He was just a boy, and nothing could ever work out between the two of us. I was fully cognizant of that. But I wanted to make love to him more than anything in the world. To see his perfect naked form, to feel his warm, throbbing tongue licking mine, and to feel his hard, twenty-four-year-old dick inside me. I wanted Alain to comfort and console me with his body in a way that Mark could no longer do—to hold me and love me, so that the searing pain of Lisa's absence would melt away.

It was now or never. I had to make a pass at Alain. It was clear from his behavior that he was never going to make any overtures in my direction. After all, I was a married woman, and he was a principled guy. I took a deep breath and tried to tune in to the conversation that Alain thought that he was having with me.

"So her dog ate my slippers. And then it ate my best shoes. Chewed them to pieces! Now I have to buy new shoes. That'll cost at least $150! I only buy shoes every four years," Alain said. He was talking about Christine again and the disagreements they used to have about her dog. I needed to make him forget about Christine. His testosterone levels must be taking quite a beating if he hadn't had sex since they broke up. I inched closer to him on the sofa.

Then I made my move. I placed my hand on his left knee and gradually began moving it up his leg. I was too afraid to look at him to see his reaction. Quickly, before I lost my courage, I moved toward him and began to kiss him on the mouth. His lips were soft and warm, and I could feel my mind sliding into an opiate-like haze. I put my other hand on the back of his neck and could feel the roughness of his crisp black hair. I was hoping that he wouldn't touch my hair in case he got razor burns.

Delirious now with desire, I opened my mouth to insert my tongue into Alain's waiting orifice when I felt him frantically pushing me away.

He looked startled and confused. "No, Tara! What're you doing?" He wiped his mouth.

"I think that's obvious," I replied.

"Oh, my God! You've got the wrong idea. I'm not interested in you that way. You're married, and I'm in love with Christine. Not to mention you being twice my age. You're too old for me!"

Old. Twice as old as him. The words echoed in my head. He didn't want me because I was ancient, matronly, fossilized. No amount of weight loss, mousse, or teenage jeans would make me look like anything other than Devon's mother to Alain. I had completely misread the situation and felt like a fool. I also hated him for rejecting me. I stood up abruptly while he motioned for me to stay.

"Tara, don't be mad. I value your friendship. Every week, I look forward to you coming into the store. Do you know how many people actually spend time talking to the butcher? Hardly any! How many customers do you think even know my name? But you're different. You always ask about me. You care about me and see me as someone other than the meat man. I'm a person to you."

He stared at me, imploring me to understand. "Hey, you're upset over Lisa. It doesn't look good for her anymore, and when we do find her, I'm not sure she'll be alive. You need to prepare yourself for that."

"Don't tell me what I need!" I reached for my car keys.

"Don't go! Just because I don't want to sleep with you doesn't change anything between us. We're still friends, and you need me to find Lisa."

"Everything has changed, Alain, because now you know how I really feel about you. It was never a friendship for me. I've always wanted you, and now I find out that you have no interest in me. No, how could you?" I screamed. "I'm too old!"

I slammed the door and walked out of his apartment, leaving Alain with a bewildered expression on his face. I was devastated, ashamed, humiliated, and frustrated out of my mind.

Old! There wasn't a word in the English language that he could have used that would have hurt me more than that one. Here I was in the midst of my midlife crisis, overwhelmed by the dread and loathing of turning forty, and Alain had confirmed my worst fear. I was indeed unlovable and undesirable. I was in a state of rage when I got back into the car. I couldn't go home. Couldn't face Devon in this condition. I wanted to buy a six-pack of beer, so I could smash the bottles on a deserted railroad track. Perhaps I could take up smoking again, but my real craving was for chocolate chip mint ice cream. Maybe it would actually go down because it was a semi-liquid.

I was close to Loeb but refused to go into the store, even though Alain was safely at home. I'd stop at the Super Loblaws instead. I went directly to the frozen food section and chose a large carton of Häagen-Dazs. I was seduced by the bakery aisle where I gazed longingly at an Entenmann's apple crumb cake, but I didn't think I could stomach it.

I considered going up to Lisa's cottage and spending the night there since I had the key. But I would have felt like a trespasser, and the ghost of Lisa would have haunted me. It was too spooky for me to stay at her cottage alone, and there was always the possibility that Ryan might go up there. I could check into a hotel, but I would feel conspicuous walking in with my huge container of Häagen-Dazs—a clear sign of a woman in distress.

Then it occurred to me that I could go to my cottage. We hadn't opened it for the season yet, and I'd need some basics such as milk, coffee, and cereal. But at least I could be alone there, and it would take less than an hour to drive up to McGregor Lake.

Maybe I'd drive out to Kingston to see my dad and Marie tomorrow if I were feeling less crazy by then. It had been a long time since my dad, and I had sat down and had a heart-to-heart talk. I missed him. I added the extra breakfast ingredients to my grocery cart and returned to the car.

Just as I was about to leave the parking lot, my cell rang. It was Alain. Screw him. I wasn't taking his call. However, I needed to pull myself together in order to call Devon. I hoped that Dev was still at Jess's house.

Lucinda answered the phone, and I've never been so happy to hear her nasal voice. I told Lucinda I had the stomach flu: said I was almost up at the lake and didn't feel well enough to drive home. That was a lie. I was nowhere near the cottage, but she wouldn't be able to trace me. She agreed to keep Devon for a day or two and to check in on Monday to feed the dog in the morning.

Lucinda was solicitous about my health. I felt bad about fabricating a story, but I was having a breakdown and needed to be by myself for several hours.

Being a mother meant that I rarely got time alone. Most of the time, I was okay with that. He was my son, and I adored him, no matter what kind of phases he went through. But I needed to be by myself tonight, and I was grateful that Lucinda was taking Devon in. The boys were watching a DVD, so she didn't put Dev on the line. I was relieved that I didn't have to lie to him to his face.

Likewise, I was lucky that Mark was at a conference in Toronto. I got his voice mail at the hotel and Allison's answering machine when I called her at home. I gave them both the same line about having the flu and told Allison I wouldn't be able to work tomorrow.

All the way up to McGregor Lake on Highway 50, I thought about Alain. The words "too old" ricocheted through my head. That little Alliance Party prick! I never liked that Pearl Jam song anyway. The Cavaliers did a much better job on "Last Kiss."

Why had he looked so content after my backrub? Why had he

sacrificed so much of his free time for me? Was I just a charity case? Had he ever had any attraction to me? I wanted to kill him, and the image of domestic violence brought my thoughts back to Lisa and Ryan.

Traffic was steady, but I enjoyed the distraction. A man cut me off as I was going over the Alexandra Bridge. I honked and took great pleasure in giving him the finger as I sped off under the underpass on Maisonneuve Boulevard.

The radio was playing, but the music was too mellow for my liking. I ejected Amy Tan from my CD player and threw the disc out the window. I felt liberated! I hated everyone and everything, and that book on CD had driven me crazy. LuLing's relationship with Precious Auntie would remain a mystery.

Searching through the glove compartment, I reviewed the CDs in the car: Sam Roberts, Avril Lavigne, and Matchbox Twenty. Not one was angry enough for me. Then I noticed a new disc underneath my regulars with a little note attached to it. It was the soundtrack to *8 Mile*! Devon had attached a post-it note saying, "Just try it, Mum. You never know."

What the hell? I thought to myself, as I slipped the CD into the player. Surely, Slim Shady would have enough rage for the two of us. I thought of Lisa giving Devon the CD. Had she really owned a copy of her own but was too embarrassed to tell me about it? Lisa always took so many more risks in life than I had. On the one hand, I envied that about her, but on the other hand, I wondered if it had killed her.

It was dark by the time I arrived at our cottage, which looked like a big log cabin from the outside with a large screened-in porch. During the day, the sun streamed into the living room and dining room since they faced south. We had a vaulted ceiling in the family room, and a majestic stone fireplace with old snowshoes mounted on the walls. Our little black-and-white TV only received three channels, but we entertained ourselves with the games, puzzles, and decks of cards in our oversized bookcase.

I brought in the food and flipped the switch that turned on the pump for the toilet. It was on a septic system. We kept the electricity on low all year and drained the pipes in the winter, so I just turned the heat up and opened up some windows for ventilation. It smelled damp and moldy, but that would pass soon enough. The cottage was my second home, and I was happy to be alone in my Hobbit Hole.

I plopped down on the faded, flowered sofa with its broken springs, put Eminem back on the portable radio/CD player, and perused the music collection that I'd kept from my younger years: Nirvana, Hole, and Alanis Morissette. This was going to be some night.

I tried to throw my purse on the table, but I missed, and it landed with a thud on the floor. The contents spilled out onto the rug. I swore under my breath and bent over to pick them up when I discovered Devon's joints. Eureka! What better way to escape and to take my mind off both Alain and Lisa than to get high?

I hadn't smoked dope in ages. Mark got stoned once or twice a year with his basketball friends, but I had stopped completely once I got pregnant. I had fond memories of my pot smoking days. Despite my high score on the Addiction Research Foundation's alcoholism quiz, I didn't have an addictive personality like Lisa. I had found it relatively easy to quit smoking cigarettes, was a moderate drinker, and only toked up occasionally in my university days.

Lisa and I used to get high in our dorm room. She would sit on the floor in her white bathrobe, her long brown hair still wet from her shower. Lisa would sing along to Culture Club or Duran Duran in perfect pitch. She had a beautiful soprano voice.

I felt close to her when we smoked pot together. It was as though we were conjoined twins. We could even finish each other's sentences. Everything either seemed profound or hilarious when we were high, and food tasted like the nectar of the gods.

Tears rolled down my cheek. Those carefree days were gone forever. My youth, my marriage, and my best friend had all evaporated. Yet somehow, I sensed Lisa's presence in the cottage. She was talking to me through Eminem and the marijuana, something that I never had in my possession. It was as though she was taunting me to go ahead and "Just Do It."

After all, my sobriety wasn't at stake. I didn't have a problem with drugs. I could indulge once and never want it again. I needed something to ease the heartbreak of Alain's rejection and to calm my mind down well enough so I could think clearly about what to do about Ryan.

But how would I light it? I rummaged through the drawers in the den but could only find empty packs of matches. I would have to bring matches the next time I came up here in case I needed to light a candle during a power outage. I lit the joint on the gas stove. Fortunately, I didn't have to worry about burning my hair since I had none. I took several deep tokes, coughing loudly because my lungs were unaccustomed to smoke.

I felt like I had entered a time machine but wasn't sure if I had gone back in time or forward. Who would have believed that Devon's mum would have tried unsuccessfully to seduce a twenty-four-year-old, to have run away from home overnight, and to have ended up smoking pot and listening to rap music?

Was I trying to imitate Lisa? Her life would not have been so pitiful. The twenty-something guy would never have turned her down. The music wouldn't have seemed juvenile to her and Lisa definitely would not have stashed one quart of ice cream in the refrigerator. The only thing that seemed characteristic of me on this bleak evening was the fact that I had a truckload of ice cream waiting for me in the fridge.

Lisa. My Lisa, as Lorenzo would say. I sobbed uncontrollably. The pot was hitting me, and I felt my face getting wet. I could hear myself groaning, but I was removed from it. I was in pain yet I was detached at the same time. I started talking out loud to Lisa and asking her what to do. She was the only one I could have told about my failed seduction. I felt so humiliated—washed up, over the hill, unwanted. Poor judgment on my part. Incredible stupidity to have thought for a minute that the beautiful boy could have wanted me.

I couldn't tell anyone about his rejection except Lisa. If she'd been around, I wouldn't be getting stoned by myself and listening to teenage music. I would have put in an emergency call to Lisa. She'd have met me at Denny's where we both would have splurged on wicked desserts. Yes, for me, she would have broken her diet! She would have listed five other men who were attracted to me to make me feel better.

Lisa would have referred to Alain as a pool-hustling grocery boy who hadn't finished university. She would have called him "Busboy" since he didn't own a car and "Airhead" because there were no signs of fiction—or even a bookshelf—in his apartment. We would have laughed ourselves silly about the words that he had misspelled in his notes.

Lisa would have taken Alain's email address and subscribed him to dozens of male clothing catalogs so that he would think twice about wearing the same shirt five days out of seven.

There was no one else for me to confide in. JC had little understanding about women whose relationships didn't work out since she and her partner got along really well. She was a pragmatist and had no patience or interest in analyzing problems between couples.

Sheila and Diane would have sympathized, but then gone on at length about what bastards men were. It would all be Alain's fault. He'd be the villain in WAR's mind whereas Lisa would have simply emphasized the fact that Alain was all wrong for me. She would never have said anything malicious about him because, of course, Alain hadn't done anything wrong.

Alain had become my greatest confidant since I'd lost Lisa and now, I had destroyed our friendship. I was overcome with self-loathing. The pot was going to my head. My crying had stopped, and I gave up trying to talk to Lisa since the music was too loud for me to hear myself speak. I had a warm glow in my stomach, and my limbs felt heavy and leaden. I wanted to get up for the ice cream but wasn't sure that I could send a signal from my brain to my legs to get them to move. I stared at the blank TV screen. Eminem was still playing in the background.

"Opportunity knocks once in a lifetime." "You only have one shot." "You can do anything you want to, man." *How encouraging! Eminem is a motivational speaker*, I thought to myself and giggled.

With great effort, I managed to stand up. The room swayed. I staggered over to the radio and took Devon's CD out of the player, which was stationed on top of a table with an old lamp that used to be a well pump. Devon had painted the lamp red and plastered a picture of the dominion of Canada on the lid. We were a patriotic bunch.

Enough of Marshall Mathers, although I must admit that he had served my mood well. I put on Courtney Love and Hole, and went directly to the song "I Think That I Would Die."

Holding on to the wall, I made my way slowly into the kitchen where I knocked over a bottle of Dasani water that I had brought in from the car. It spilled all over the floor on to the old linoleum, which was buckling. I felt idiotic, like a kid who couldn't hold her liquor. At the same time, I was grateful for the buzz, which had succeeded in deadening my feelings of shame and dejection.

"Screw him. Who needs him?" I said out loud angrily, as I grabbed the container of ice cream and a large spoon. I poured myself a glass of Coke and sat down at the kitchen table amid the sugar fest.

The ice cream was cold and deliciously sweet. I let every spoonful linger on my tongue, savoring the taste. The pot must have helped my esophagus because the food slid down effortlessly. No wonder people with chronic nausea, like patients on chemotherapy, smoked up. Mark was right after all. I made a mental note to join an advocacy group to fight for the legalization of marijuana for medicinal purposes.

I wished that I had bought a crumb cake since I was starving. I was high, high, high and the pain of Alain was somewhere far away, as though it belonged to another person. The despair and worry about Lisa had been dulled, but I felt angry and mixed up.

Courtney was screaming, "I want my baby. Where is the baby?" I vaguely remembered Courtney's baby being taken away by family services when she and Kurt Cobain were having drug problems. Not much had changed there! I had always seen

Courtney as a wild child, with whom I had nothing in common, but now we shared grief. We had both lost a loved one and wanted them back.

Round and round in my mind, I tried to envision various scenarios to explain what could have happened to Lisa. I pushed the food away and felt pleasantly full. I unbuttoned my jeans. Ah, yes, if Alain could only see me now; I looked like such a sexpot. A demented chocoholic was more like it. I drained the rest of my Coke and shuffled off into the den to look for paper and a pencil.

I turned Courtney off, and a deafening silence fell upon the room. It was so quiet that I almost felt afraid, but attributed the bad vibe to the ordinary paranoia that accompanied smoking pot after a fifteen-year hiatus. I felt better when I heard the hummingbirds in the distance.

I placed the yellow legal pad on my lap and began to formulate a new plan of action. I could worm my way into Ryan's life and turn his house upside down, looking for clues. Or I could seduce Ryan under the pretense of offering him comfort in Lisa's absence. Last, I could get him drunk and make him lose his sobriety. Certainly, he would say or do something incriminating if he started drinking again.

My rational mind was leaving me. No doubt the police had already conducted a thorough search of his house. The thought of touching Ryan made me cringe, and I couldn't imagine why he would agree to get drunk with me. We weren't exactly best friends.

I needed answers. It took years for the Scarborough rapist and serial murderer, Paul Bernardo, to be apprehended and Ardeth Wood's killer was still out there. I'd go crazy if I never found out what happened to Lisa. The Campanas and I would be trapped in purgatory like the Levys and the Zhangs before their daughters had been discovered. The lives of those families revolved around the constant torment of waiting, wanting, and not knowing if their loved ones were dead or alive.

I couldn't wait two months, six months, or a year to find Lisa. I would end up in the Royal Ottawa mental hospital. There had to be another way.

Who said that pot made people mellow? It didn't give them enough energy to swat a mosquito, but they could still lie in a drug-induced haze and plot a wicked revenge. I thought about Kurt putting the gun inside his mouth.

Bingo! The rifle that Mark's brother, Peter, had left at the cottage. It took me almost an hour to find it in Mark's tool shed. Peter wouldn't be shooting any more, black bears with this gun. But I couldn't find the ammunition and vaguely recalled Peter saying something about keeping it with him in his car.

Great! A gun without bullets. How very Canadian of me. But Ryan wouldn't know that there weren't any bullets in the gun. I could threaten him with it and force him to tell me where Lisa was. That was all I wanted to know. I had lost my faith in finding her alive and whatever confidence I'd had initially in Detective McCarthy had vanished. But I would locate her body. I would drug Ryan with my Ativan, tie him up with some of my scarves, put the gun to his head and shout, "Don't think for a minute that I won't use this, motherfucker," just like Thelma and Louise.

Ryan would break down. Explain to me that they had fought. He had lost control. "It was all a horrible accident," he would sob, and then he would tell me where he'd buried Lisa.

My head was pounding from the pot, and I felt nauseated. The lie about the stomach flu was becoming a reality. Gorging myself on the ice cream had made me ill because I hadn't eaten much of anything all week. There was also a shadow on the wall that looked remarkably like Lisa, and I felt as though she were there with me.

I tried not to think about the meat man because that was depressing. No time to ruminate about Alain now. I needed to crash. I could devise a more detailed plan for Ryan in the morning.

Since I hadn't planned to come up to the cottage, I didn't have a nightgown, a toothbrush, or even a change of clothes. Luckily, there was an old flannel shirt of Mark's in the bedroom that was large enough for me to sleep in.

After I found Lisa, I would request a separation. Hopefully, Mark and I would remain on friendly terms. Devon would adjust—about one-third of all marriages in my age group ended in divorce. Statistics weren't very reassuring, but unfortunately, divorce was routine, and Devon would survive.

I still felt the glow from the night that Devon and I watched *8 Mile*. I felt closer to him than I had in years. And it was so cute of him to have slipped the Eminem soundtrack into my car with his little post-it note. He was still keeping something from me. I sensed that, but after all, he was a teenage boy. What could I expect? He wasn't going to confide his deepest darkest feelings to his mother.

And I didn't like him hanging out with Jess. There was something phony and reckless about that boy, but I was glad that Devon had a close friend. Just thinking about best friends made me want to scream. Where was Lisa? I did not see a happy ending to her story. I gargled with plain water in the bathroom, trying to remove the taste of chocolate chip mint from my mouth. No use.

I dreaded going to bed without brushing my teeth. The mattress on the king-size bed felt rock hard compared to the Sealy Posturepedic mattress that we used at home.

Fortunately, the pot was strong enough to knock most thoughts of my son and my best friend out of my mind for the better part of the night, saving me from my usual struggle with nocturnal demons.

As I pulled out of the driveway late the next morning, sipping my third cup of coffee which I had poured into a thermos for the car, I noticed how shabby the property looked during the daylight. The windows were rotting, and the white clapboard was sorely in need of paint. Our lake was rife with weeds, slime, and algae. Several of the large oak trees had been damaged in the Ice Storm of 1998. Dead branches were suspended in midair, reminding me of The Scarecrow in *The Wizard of Oz*.

We should make some renovations this year. Mark had resisted getting a generator and a speedboat, and we had both vowed not to bring our laptops or work up to the cabin. We had agreed never to upgrade to satellite TV like some of our neighbors, but just because we didn't want to make the cottage high-tech didn't mean that we should allow it to fall apart. But how much remodeling do couples do when they're in the midst of a separation?

Traffic on Highway 50 was much lighter going home. My head throbbed, and my stomach lurched, as though I had just gotten off the Tilt-A-Whirl. I had taken two Advil before leaving McGregor Lake, but they had barely put a dent in my pot hangover.

I decided to call Ryan and ask if I could see him for dinner. I would tell him I'd received a confidential call about Lisa's whereabouts that I could only discuss in person. When we were alone, I'd slip some Ativan into Ryan's drink. Two or three of those ought to knock out even a strong man. Then I'd tie him up and threaten him with the gun. If I were persuasive enough, he might crack.

First, I called Lucinda to check in on Devon. The boys were at the mall, but Lucinda reassured me that she had been in to feed Monday and had brought the dog back to her house. I complained that I still felt unwell, which was now true, and I would need to spend another day at the lake. I thanked her profusely for her help and asked if it would be all right if I picked Devon up tomorrow afternoon.

Lucinda said, "Sure," and told me to drink red clover tea to clean the toxins from my system. I proceeded to give Mark the same story.

"Where are you? Lucinda said you were sick. You never get sick!" Mark said accusingly.

"Must've been something I ate," I mumbled.

"You spent the night at the cottage? Why'd you go all the way up there?"

"Oh, I left something up there that I needed," I said, wanting to get him off the line. I've never been a good liar. When I was young, I used to stammer even when I told a white lie. "Pinocchio," my father called me fondly. "I just don't feel up to speed. I'm going to buy some Gravol and chicken soup and go back to the cottage."

"Want me to come get you tomorrow? I fly in around four. Can easily run over to get Devon and Monday and be up at the cottage by seven or eight."

"Don't be silly. I'll be fine by tomorrow. I'll just relax with a good book and sleep it off tonight. I'll call you early in the morning before I leave."

"Who's Steve?" Mark asked.

I could hear static and muffled sounds, which indicated that my battery was about to die.

"Steve?" I said, echoing Mark. "I'll call you tomorrow morning before I LEAVE."

"I can give you a shout again later on tonight, if you want," Mark offered.

"No, honey, I'll be fine. Really. I haven't even asked about your conference." I hoped that he'd be brief for the sake of my phone.

"One guy was pretty interesting. Talked about art in the age of terrorism."

"Fascinating. Well, I should go now. You don't have to call me back, but it'd be nice if you called Dev later on. You've got Lucinda's number?"

"It's programmed into my phone. Okay then, Tar, take care of that tummy of yours, and we'll see you tomorrow." He hung up without saying that he loved me, our usual salutation.

Finally, I placed the call that I dreaded most. My battery was fading fast, and I didn't feel like stopping at a pay phone. Ryan answered on the first ring, as though he'd been sitting next to the receiver. I tried to sound normal and asked if there was any news about Lisa. He said no. I said that I'd enjoyed listening to him speak the other night, which seemed to perk him up.

"Ryan, we haven't really sat down to talk since this whole thing happened. You must be lonely without Lisa. I know I am. My phone is about to die, so I can't talk long, but how would you feel about me bringing supper over to your house later this aft? We could catch up. Just name the dish," I said.

"God, Tara, that would be great! I haven't seen many of Lisa's friends since she went missing, and her family's cut me off. Hmm. I really miss Lisa's lasagna. She learned the recipe from her mum, who's a fantastic cook."

Lasagna. It would take me a week to make lasagna; however, I could easily pick one up at M&Ms. But I had no intention of bringing the frozen lasagna over to Ryan's and talking to him for fifty minutes while it cooked. And I didn't have salad ingredients.

There was no way I was going into Loeb today even though Alain didn't work on Wednesdays. I didn't want to see his ugly face and have that nasty reminder of his painful rejection. I was furious with him, but along with the anger and pain was the clear recognition that last night had been entirely my fault. I had used poor judgment, put him in an awkward position, and jeopardized our friendship.

Sweet Alain had sacrificed so much of his time to help me look for Lisa, and how did I repay him? I tried to jump him the minute he had reservations about commitment in his relationship. He was probably hurting after Christine left him and could have used my maternal sympathy. Instead, I tried to attack him. And he hadn't wanted any part of it!

Old, too old. Tara, I don't want you. You're too old! No. Although I had an intellectual realization that my behavior had been inappropriate, emotionally I was still shattered. It would take time for me to lick my wounds before I was able to befriend Alain again.

There were salad ingredients at home. Maybe I'd go there after I got the lasagna. I could pop it in the oven and snooze while it cooked. I was exhausted and had to go to the house anyway to get the Ativan.

It was 2:30 p.m. "I'll see you around five o'clock," I shouted. Ryan tried to answer, but my phone had already conked out. I threw the phone on the car seat and concentrated on my driving.

It was refreshing to be on the highway rather than stopping for every red light in town. Ottawa was so crowded now. Traffic on Merivale and Baseline Road was bumper-to-bumper with the road rage freaks in high gear.

My dad often reminded me that there were almost no cars on the road on Baseline back in 1972 when he and Marie bought the house in Country Place. Sounded like science fiction to me.

"Nothing but cows and empty fields in Barrhaven and Kanata," my father had bragged. Now the only green spaces left were the large acres of land that had been bought up by the government.

The food at M&Ms was delicious. I ordered two lasagnas and a box of Chicken Kiev for dinner tomorrow night. Devon loved that along with Caesar salad. Mark would question how my stomach had bounced back so quickly. I would attribute it to a twenty-four-hour bug.

It was strange to be sneaking around in my own house like a burglar. I worried that Mark and Devon would smell the lasagna and know that I had been there. I would explain it to them tomorrow night when this ordeal was over. I was convinced that Lisa was dead, but I would find her body if it killed me.

A big black SUV was on my tail going south on Woodroffe, so I was glad to turn off at Knoxdale. Some of the houses in Craig Henry were quite nice, but they were interspersed with low rental apartments, attached homes, and townhouses. The area had wide boulevards, which were overgrown with grass, weeds, and dandelions.

Lisa and Ryan lived in a modest townhouse with a garish red door and red shutters. Half of the house was composed of old, dark brick, and the other half was made of yellow clapboard, which clashed with the shutters.

As I pulled up to the visitors' parking lot, I noticed an older couple sitting outside on their lawn chairs. It was too cold to be outside, but the sun was shining, and we Canadians were antsy for fresh air after being confined all winter. How was I going to get the gun past the neighbors? Instead of looking cool and collected like Thelma, I would look maniacal like Granny on *The Beverly Hillbillies*. Moreover, I'd read too many stories where guns were used against the owner, especially if she was inexperienced like me.

It was a ridiculous idea. I thought of Officer Shanley and shuddered. He would be furious at me for taking the law into my own hands, not to mention risking my life if something went wrong. I needed a new plan. Somehow, I had to manipulate Ryan psychologically, not physically. Walking briskly past Ryan's neighbors, I held my head high in the air. I tried to look confident and authoritative so that they wouldn't notice me. If something went wrong, the neighbors could be potential witnesses.

The lasagna was hot, and I shifted it from one hand to the other, so as not to burn myself. It was hard to juggle the pasta with the bottle of grape juice that I held in my other hand.

I rang the bell several times, but there was no answer. I began to worry that I'd lose my nerve. My head was still spinning from last night's adventure. How long did it take those Advil to kick in? My hand started to shake. If he didn't come soon, I'd be the one who needed the Ativan!

Finally, Ryan opened the door. He was talking on his portable phone and motioned for me to come in. Loud country music was playing in the background.

"I told you, they'll just have to wait. I can't be three places at the same time! So we'll take the loss. Whadda ya expect from me, man? That's bullshit! Look, I gotta call you later."

"My partner, Alex," Ryan explained to me after he hung up the phone. "He's going ballistic because we were supposed to be raking some guy's lawn and putting down fertilizer. The guy keeps calling us. Christ, doesn't he read the paper? Plus, Alex already called him, like, a million times on Monday. The guy doesn't care about us—just his frigging property."

I hoped that Ryan didn't see the tremor in my hands when he reached for the lasagna.

"Wow, Tara, it was really thoughtful of you to make this. I didn't know if you were even talking to me outside of AA. Lots of people aren't!" He laughed as he walked toward the kitchen.

Dirty dishes were piled in the sink. There wasn't an inch of free space on the small kitchen table, which was cluttered with newspapers, unpaid bills, rotting flowers, and a bowl of half-eaten cereal. I couldn't see the garbage disposal, but it smelled as though no one had emptied the trash in days.

"Well," I said, trying to sound upbeat, "Neil Young knew what he was talking about. A man needs a maid." I perused the disaster which was once known as the kitchen.

"Can't deal with it. You should see the rest of the house, eh? The bed's unmade. Laundry's piling up in the back hall. Kitty litter everywhere, and I don't know where the cat is. Stupid animals—cats. I never wanted one but Lisa..." Ryan hesitated.

"It's all right." I forced myself to put a reassuring hand on his shoulder. The son of a bitch. Had he graduated from the Lee

Strasberg School of acting? He looked so wounded: childlike even, with that forlorn look in his eyes. He was trying to make me feel sorry for him when the only victim in the situation was Lisa.

I shuddered to think how she would react if she could see her kitchen, which looked as though it'd been overturned by a gang of bikers.

"You'll feel better after you eat something. You need your strength."

I was adopting my nurse role. Treat him like a patient. Make him think that I cared about his insomnia, if in fact, he was lying awake at night like the rest of us. Maybe he was. Maybe he was imagining what it would be like to spend the rest of his days in the Kingston Penitentiary.

Y105 was blaring a love song that was grating on my nerves. I asked Ryan to turn the radio down, opened the microwave, and found two containers of Chinese food inside, in paper containers. That was what smelled so bad. Neighbors had been delivering food in droves to the Campanas, but I bet no one besides the folks at AA had thought to nourish Ryan. Had everyone else suspected him from the start just as WAR and the Campanas had done? Why was I the only idiot who had given him the benefit of the doubt for so long? No more.

It was a good thing I'd brought a salad because I wouldn't have touched the food in his refrigerator with a ten-foot pole. It looked like fertile grounds for salmonella poisoning. I didn't want to use the glasses either, which looked stained and discolored, but I noticed a small package of plastic cups, in the back of one of the cupboards. I took them out and poured us both a glass of grape juice. I removed the disgusting sweet and sour chicken balls from the microwave and placed the lasagna inside, trying not to dwell on the appalling sanitary conditions.

"Cheers! Next best thing to a dry red wine." I handed Ryan a glass.

"I could sure use the wine!"

He led me into the family room. Upholstery was coming out of the side of the worn, brown leather couch, and grimy fingerprints were visible on the large glass sliding doors leading out to the patio. There were cat hairs all over the hardwood floor.

"Have a seat," Ryan indicated with his right hand.

My house was so much more luxurious than Lisa's. It wasn't fair. She had worked just as hard as me, but she'd had bad luck. She had to take several months off from work to go through rehab and had a number of low-paying jobs before she settled in at Straight and Narrow. And she lived with a man who was marginally employed. How much of my own financial status was vicarious? Where would I be without Mark? Living in a two-bedroom condo where there would be nowhere to escape from Devon's music.

It only took five minutes to nuke the meal, but I couldn't rush Ryan to the table. Supposedly, I had made the trip out of concern for his well-being. I had abandoned the ludicrous idea of drugging him and had decided instead to appeal to his greedy nature.

Ryan was yakking about his moronic customers, expecting him to show up for work in the midst of the crisis.

"So I says to them, have you ever lost your partner? Did your woman just walk outta the house one night and disappear? Would you have been able to get back to work the next day? I'm gonna finish that job, if you can only be patient. Have a heart, for

God's sake." He reached into his pocket and pulled out a crumpled package of Export A.

Only twenty-one percent of all Canadians over the age of fifteen smoke, but I know them all. Ryan's pack was almost empty. He tapped his fingers on the small pine table next to the couch.

"Shit. Meant to stop for a pack on my way home this morning. Guess I'll get some after you leave."

Not likely, baby, I thought to myself, as I drained the remainder of my juice.

"Mmm. That tasted great, and I'm really thirsty." That was an understatement. Between my hangover and the Advil, my mouth was as dry as Ryan's unwatered flowers. I also felt a migraine coming on, courtesy of Devon's pot, and I was trembling. Ryan scared me.

"It must be hard for you to keep up the house financially," I said, never letting on that I knew that Ryan had tried to get into Lisa's bank account.

"Yeah, it's a bitch. It costs almost $1,400 a month for rent alone, not to mention food, hydro, and cable." Ryan downed his juice with one gulp, which left a slightly purple stain above his lip. "I can't afford that on my salary."

What salary? I thought. "Of course not," I said out loud, trying to sound empathetic. "You know, Ryan, things aren't looking good for Lisa. She's been gone almost two weeks. Statistically speaking, the chances of her returning are almost nil."

That was untrue, but Ryan didn't know that. "But without a body—" Tears rolled down my face, and I didn't have to fake that. I cleared my throat. "Without a body, there's no way to settle Lisa's estate. I'm sure she'd want you to have everything. You were her partner!" I was deliberately talking about Lisa in the past tense.

Ryan's eyes sparkled, and he leaned forward. I had his attention. He licked his lips.

"I never thought about it that way."

"Oh, yeah. Both Lisa and I prepared our Wills last year, and she left everything to you because her parents' business is thriving."

Lying was becoming easier for me as I went on. Why would I have prepared a Will at the age of thirty-nine? I was old, but I didn't expect to pop off anytime soon. Of course, Mark and I had talked about dying, but we hadn't gotten around to doing anything about it yet. But Ryan didn't question my story, and I continued to emphasize the importance of finding Lisa's remains.

I felt anxious and light-headed at the thought of Lisa's body and tried not to think about what Ryan could do to me if he suspected that I was setting him up. I took several deep breaths. To my great surprise, Ryan then said that there was one more place in Quebec that we hadn't checked yet. He asked if I'd like to go up there after supper. I agreed.

Back in the kitchen, I tossed the salad, removed the bubbling lasagna from the microwave, and searched for two halfway clean plates that weren't breeding any new life forms. The silverware looked suspiciously greasy, so I ran it under hot soapy water. I wanted to get this meal over with as soon as possible. I was feeling overwhelmingly drowsy, and my head was pounding. I prayed that I could stay awake long enough to get through the evening.

Several minutes later, I was as composed as Martha Stewart in her prime, serving my scrumptious dinner on the dining room table that Ryan had cleared. I kept up a running conversation while we ate since I needed Ryan to believe that he was with an earnest friend, who was trying to help him through this traumatic event.

"Basil and sausage. Almost as good as Anna's," Ryan said.

The lasagna smelled tempting, but my stomach was queasy from last night. I ate small mouthfuls of the spicy dish. The cheese was gooey, and I feared that I might lose a molar chewing it over and over again. I thought of all the times that Lisa had forfeited bread, potatoes, and dessert. If she had known that she would never make forty, would she have eaten more bagels and pecan pie? Was all that sacrifice worth having a perfect figure?

I wouldn't know. I'd never lasted on a diet for more than a week. That's probably why Alain hadn't wanted to sleep with me—that and my rabbit haircut.

After dinner, Ryan offered to drive up to the Gatineau. I wanted to take my car so as not to be alone with him. However, I felt too exhausted to drive and didn't want Ryan to think that I didn't trust him.

We got into his truck, and I looked around for the nosy neighbors, who were nowhere to be seen. The truck had a manual transmission, and I couldn't drive a stick shift. Ryan turned on the radio, and the sweet sound of Emmylou Harris made me unbearably sleepy.

I struggled to stay awake, to no avail. I had forgotten to nap when I was at home earlier during the day. Don't let anyone tell you that you can't have a monstrous hangover from marijuana. My wild night, and the hectic pace that I had been keeping all week, had finally caught up with me. I could feel myself drifting off despite my fear of being alone with Ryan.

When I woke up, I was sitting in the driveway of my own cottage. I was confused. Why had he brought me here?

It was early evening. The sky was as blue as Marge Simpson's hair with big white clouds that looked like whipping cream. I was alone in the truck. I got out, yawned, and tried to regain my balance.

"Ryan! Ryan!" I called. I heard his voice in the backyard.

He motioned for me to follow him into the woods behind my house. I asked what on earth we were doing there. Ryan said he had a hunch: that someone may have brought Lisa here in an effort to frame me.

"Think of Malveaux. That guy despises you! And he thinks Mark is a real snob. What if he had a fight with Lisa Friday night and hit her the way he used to? What better place to get rid of her than your cottage? Who would ever think of it?"

"Nobody," *including me*, I said, exasperated with this turn of events. But as we walked through the dense, muddy terrain way behind the cottage, we came to a small clearing, and I gasped with shock.

Lisa was lying in a fetal position. She was wearing her tight pink sweater and the Guess jeans she'd had on at the ByTowne. Her gold cross glistened, as if to mock me, and there were brown marks around her neck. Ryan must have killed her the night she left me at the theatre when she told him about the baby. And now I was alone with him up in the country. I had to keep my cool and pretend that Ryan's conspiracy theory about Malveaux was on target.

The horror that I felt at the repulsive odor of rotting flesh was only surpassed by the sickening sight of maggots, caterpillars, and carpet beetles parading down Lisa's body.

I started to heave.

"Lisa!" I heard myself moaning, and the words sounded distant and disembodied. I collapsed onto the wet soil, shaking and weeping uncontrollably. It was true. She was dead, and nothing would ever be the same again.

Sounds of Ryan sobbing behind me made my blood boil. Crocodile tears. That bastard! I would make sure he paid for this if it was the last thing I did with my life.

SIX MONTHS LATER

The cemetery was peaceful. It was well-tended with birch and maple trees that looked magnificent in October with their red, yellow, and light green leaves. Lisa's stone was made of pink granite with the words "In loving memory" inscribed at the bottom. Her parents planted geraniums and silver leaf plants and watered them every day. Soon, the ground would freeze over, and the flowers would die.

Lisa had a beautiful Catholic service. More than 300 people attended the ceremony. It was standing room only in the small elegant church on Kent Street. The priest mentioned the old cliché about God's work being like a quilt that we saw backward. Only the person who created the tapestry knew the way that it was meant to look. We could only see a small part of the underside.

Those of us who had not crossed over beyond the veil didn't know what the finished product looked like or why there were flaws in the design. Death existed simply because our bodies were mortal. The Lord had created a room for each of us in His house, and Lisa was now in that room.

I didn't derive any comfort from the priest's sermon. The day after the funeral and large reception at the Campana's house, WAR had its own memorial service for Lisa. JC spoke about male violence and December the 6th, the day a disgruntled man killed fourteen female engineering students in Montreal in 1989 because he thought that they were feminists. She read the names of every woman that had been murdered by a male with whom she'd had a relationship and whose name was on the Women's Monument at Minto Park.

Members of WAR passed out white ribbons. Women marched outside carrying signs that said, "God Is Coming and She Is Pissed."

It was a chaotic scene with dozens of TV crews and reporters. A young anchorwoman hijacked me, pretending to care about my loss, but all she really wanted was for me to cry on camera. I wasn't consoled by either service and was relieved when they were over, but I felt heartsick leaving Lisa at the funeral parlor.

The makeup artist had managed to restore her face, but it had a waxy, surreal look to it. I wanted to drag Lisa out of the casket and gently place her in the back seat of my car. I wanted to tell her every detail about what had happened during the last two weeks. I wanted to hear her voice one last time.

The newspapers continued to blame Lisa for her involvement with Ryan and to subtly imply that her death could have been avoided if she hadn't been one of those "smart women who made foolish choices."

Only Elmore Stewart defended Lisa's actions as those of a truly spiritual person. She had been loving and forgiving. She had given Ryan, the felon, a second chance. How could she have known that her choice would have resulted in such dire consequences?

My own feelings lay somewhere in between. On the one hand, Lisa was a big person to have accepted Ryan, flaws and all. On the other hand, out of all the men that she could have had, Lisa knowingly embraced a man with a battering history. Obviously, this was a catastrophic mistake.

Today is Lisa's birthday. She would have been forty. After all my bitching about the turn of the decade, when my birthday finally arrived, all I could feel was grateful to be alive. Ryan could have strangled me up at my cottage, although that's not how he murdered Lisa. She died of a skull fracture. Ryan must have pushed her down a staircase, but no forensic evidence was ever found in their home or at her cottage.

The soil on the bottom of Ryan's boots did match the soil outside my cottage, but he had been wearing those boots the night we went up there together. Nonetheless, he was arrested and charged with first-degree murder. His trial hasn't come up yet, but I'm sure that he'll be found guilty. Meanwhile, he's safely ensconced in the Ottawa-Carleton Detention Centre where the conditions are about as hospitable as a rat-infested cave. He was never officially charged with killing Lisa's unborn baby.

Ontario doesn't consider the murder of a fetus to be a crime, unlike California, which changed its law in 1970 to decree the killing of a fetus of at least seven weeks gestation to be murder. Ontario's stand was a relief to WAR since they didn't want to deal with the messy issue of fetal rights, but it was painful to the Campanas. As Catholics, they were outraged that their unborn grandchild had no legal rights, and their dual loss had not been recognized. Not only had they lost Lisa, but they had also been robbed of the child that they referred to as "Little Lorenzo."

I stood at her grave wondering what could have prompted a guy like Ryan to lose his sanity like that, after all those years in AA. I guess he never changed; he was the same man who beat his first girlfriend, tried to steal Lisa's money, and led me directly to the body. He lied to Lisa about wanting children and withheld information about his vasectomy from the police. He always knew that he wasn't the father of Lisa's baby.

I hoped that Ryan would be given the maximum sentence. The requirements for establishing guilt beyond a reasonable doubt are just too stringent. What can we do in cases without DNA? How many times will we have a full confession, a murder weapon, or a videotape of the crime? Juries have to make tough decisions with inadequate information. They'll make the right decision with Ryan. When I think of the torment the Campanas are enduring, I pray that Ryan will pay a stiff price.

Lisa's parents are shattered. Anna cries all the time, and Lorenzo seems lost and disoriented. Sandra has been a great help to her mother, and the church has been incredible. The Campanas would never have survived the last few months without their faith and the ongoing support of their fellow parishioners.

I feel helpless to comfort Lisa's parents. I would give anything to relieve their suffering, but my hands are tied. All I can do is listen and be there to affirm that they have a right to their rage, sorrow, and anguish.

So I'm forty now. It's not such a big deal. Devon bought me the Amy Tan book in hardcover for my birthday. He made me a special copy of his essay on *To Kill a Mockingbird* and had it placed in a spiral binder at Business Depot.

I even laughed at the mug that JC got me. It said, "How many forty-year-olds do you need to screw in a light bulb? None! Forty-year-olds don't get screwed."

It's inevitable. We either get old or we die, and I've accepted that now. Forty isn't really that old except to someone like Alain.

I hated Alain for weeks after he turned down my proposition. Whenever I thought about him, I felt the sharp sting of rejection. In order to quell my desire for Alain, I began to envision him with an unsightly birthmark that covered half his body or a virulent case of herpes. I stopped shopping at his grocery store and did my best to avoid him.

Then one night, I was surfing the Net and went to the website that Alain had created for Lisa. I was stunned to see that he had turned the site into a tribute to her. He had posted pictures of Lisa from high school, which he must have gotten from her parents. I was so moved by Alain's kindness that I called him up and apologized for my behavior. He said, "No worries, Tara," and we've been friends ever since.

We aren't close friends, mind you, because I couldn't stand to spend much time with Alain—I'm still attracted to him—but we keep in touch occasionally on email. Devon invited Alain and Christine to the "surprise" party that he threw for my birthday, which I knew about weeks in advance. Alain wore the same shirt that he'd been wearing when we were working together on the Internet. He looked so young.

In a flash, I realized that it would never have worked out between Alain and me. I would have wanted to go to the National Arts Centre to see Jann Arden or to Carleton University to hear Pamela Wallin speak, and Alain would have preferred to shoot pool or sit at home with a six-pack of beer watching *The Sopranos*. I was glad that he had gotten back together with Christine because they were meant for one another.

My son is the only man in my life now. It was a hard adjustment to make when I first left Mark, but we've been separated for more than four months, and I've gotten used to it. I don't dislike Mark; I just don't love him anymore. He has accepted the separation fairly well, and for the most part, we're amicable.

After I found Lisa's body, I couldn't concentrate. I couldn't read, and my memory was like a sieve, so I took a leave of absence from my job and started to see a grief counselor, who's helped me a lot. Ironically, after all my smug criticism of the program, I chose a counselor with a twelve-step perspective because Laura Anne recommended her. And I must say, much of what my counselor says makes sense. Actually, I think if I could master the Serenity Prayer—knowing what I can and can't change and being able to accept the latter— along with the Golden Rule, I'd be fairly together. I'd also be pretty much God damn perfect like the Buddha; I'm not going to get there in this lifetime, but I'm still trying.

In the beginning, I felt numb and frozen, like someone had sliced my arm off with a chain saw. All I could think about was the phantom limb, but it didn't feel real to me. After several weeks had passed, I began to feel guilty that Lisa had been unable to confide in me about her pregnancy, and I couldn't shake the belief that if I had known, I could have helped her. If I hadn't been such a judgmental bitch and a lousy friend, maybe she would have told me that Ryan had become abusive, and I could have persuaded her to leave. If only…

I also couldn't stop thinking about what I'd said to her at Nate's when I was teasing her about her Atkins diet: "It's your funeral." Silly, sarcastic words on my part, but how could I have known that I would never see her again?

I kept expecting Lisa to reappear. My phone would ring, and I'd snap at the caller because she wasn't Lisa. I'd be shopping at the Rideau Centre mall, and I'd see someone who looked exactly like Lisa from behind. I would have to force myself not to run up to the poor, unsuspecting stranger and cling to her. I had a chronic craving for Lisa that was similar to what I'd felt as a child after I lost my mother. The loneliness was overwhelming. Lisa was dead, Mark and I were separated, and I no longer had my obsession with Alain.

Marianne, my counselor, told me to take one minute at a time or one deep breath after another. It sounded trite, but it did help when the pain washed over me like a blanket, and I felt that I was being smothered. Marianne believed that the hole in my head that I had filled with Alain was the unresolved grief that I had for my mother, much like the longing that Nathaniel Kahn had for his father.

I didn't entirely agree. My mother's death had left me with an insatiable void, but I was never in love with Mark. I ached for my mother *and* for romantic passion. Even if Alain was inappropriate, I had loved him. After I had experienced that passionate, albeit unrequited, love, it was impossible for me to stay with Mark.

Marianne advised me not to make any important decisions for the next year, but I'm already investigating a two-year program at Algonquin College in Early Childhood Education. I don't like working with sick people. I'd much rather spend time with kids like Hugh, although I recognize that they may end up being a lot more like Dudley Dursley, Harry Potter's obnoxious cousin.

Devon is adjusting to my breakup with Mark. Mark wanted to take Dev to the Sens' games, but the players refused to sign off on their contract, so there's a hockey lockout this year.

Dev spends his time playing sports or hanging out with Jess. I don't like Jess, but I don't get to choose my son's friends. Occasionally, Devon and I watch videos together after dinner. I've expanded my horizons to include action movies like *Men in Black* and *The Matrix Reloaded*. Jess doesn't like Tolkien, so Dev and I also view the *Lord of the Rings* together.

Devon never watches *Finding Nemo* anymore. When I asked him about that, he said that it was a "lame, dumb ass" movie with a stupid ending when Dory rescued Nemo. I think Dev really expected us to find Lisa. He was more shocked than anyone when we found her body; he actually trembled and seemed terrified. He didn't speak for days. I thought I might have to send him to see a therapist, but he vetoed the notion and seemed to snap out of it a bit. It saddened me to see Devon lose his innocence at such a young age, but I had no control over the matter. Sometimes I think he's still smoking pot despite his asthma because his eyes are so red, and he seems preoccupied with something. He spaces out a lot, which Marianne tells me is normal for a teenager particularly after trauma. Maybe when he gets older, he'll trust me more and open up a bit. Right now, I'm working on letting him just be who he is and where he is.

Often, I feel ashamed for not having enjoyed every moment that I had with Lisa when she was alive. I have remorse for all the things that I didn't say or do and for all the ways in which I hurt or disappointed her. Marianne says I mustn't hold on to the guilt because it wasn't my fault. We all hurt each other. No one is perfect. We're all works in progress, and there was no way that I could have known that my time with Lisa was limited.

On the other hand, it's ironic because somewhere along the line when I lost Lisa, I began to find myself. I realized that just as Lisa had taken too many risks in life, I had taken too few. I had always played it safe, which was why I stayed in my stale marriage and stressful job. I've tried to become less critical of my son and myself and to accept the fact that I've entered early middle age; I have decades to go before I become officially old, and even then, age is more a state of mind than an actual number.

I don't lie about my age anymore, but I don't let the number define me either. I am more than just some birth-date on my driver's license.

I've come to terms with the fact that WAR and I don't agree on everything. When I was twenty-five, I thought I was right about everything, and everyone needed to be on the same page as me. I didn't want friends who were Conservatives or opposed to abortion. I was intolerant; I saw everything in terms of black-and-white thinking. Now I see infinite shades of gray. The same is true with WAR. We don't always agree, but their work is phenomenal, and I love each and every one of them. They've helped me get through Lisa's death more than anyone except Marianne and my family.

I've stopped tampering with my hair, pursuing younger men, and wishing that I were fifteen pounds thinner. Thank God I don't have to pretend to like Pearl Jam anymore! I now listen happily to my soft rock without having to pretend to be any cooler than I am.

There's one song by Boyzone that I play repeatedly. I'm like that woman in England, whose neighbor sued her for putting Whitney Houston's "I Will Always Love You" on instant replay. I've heard that damn Boyzone song so many times that I know it by heart:

> *No matter what they call us,*
> *However they attack,*
> *No matter where they take us,*
> *We'll find our own way back.*

****

I know that about myself now. Regardless of what happens to me in life, I will always be able to cope with it. Losing Lisa has made me a better person. It's made me stronger and able to cope with adversity more effectively. And it's helped me to come to terms with the aging process.

But I would give all that up in a flash just to see Lisa's face one last time. Even if she were ranting about AA, or munching on that inedible keto combination of meat and oily vegetables, I would never mock her again. I miss her so much. It breaks my heart. I'm never going to get over her death. I'm just going to learn to live with it over time.

I have to say goodbye to Lisa now because Devon is at the other side of the cemetery, paying his respects to my mom, the grandmother he never knew. He has difficulty visiting Lisa's grave. At first, I thought it would be therapeutic for him to come here more often, but no. He always starts shaking; sometimes he even hyperventilates there, so I don't push it anymore. Graves are not for everyone. Dev would be back any minute, so I took one last hard look at the ground that housed my beautiful friend.

"Happy Birthday, Lise," I whispered, as I patted the top of her pink tombstone and put a box of Russell Stover chocolates down next to the red and white flowers. "Little Lorenzo would have been lucky to have had you as his mother," I said, as I wiped my tears away and turned to join my son.

***

Devon was quiet on the drive home as he always was when we left the cemetery. I dropped him at Jess's and went home to process the events of the day. Forty years old. Our milestone. Lisa and I had talked endlessly about what it would be like to enter our middle years, but only one of us had made it.

I was tired when I got home and emotionally depleted. I made a protein shake because I didn't feel like eating and sat down to read *Vanity Fair* magazine. After a while, I felt restless and decided that I would clean the house, starting with Devon's room. It had been ages since I had been in there.

New life forms were probably fomenting. I emptied the dryer before I went upstairs and started folding socks and T-shirts as I stood in his cluttered space. One by one, I put things away and took some of the hangers out of his closet. I was so exhausted that I knocked a small box over. It had been sitting in the very back of his closet underneath several pairs of well-worn jeans. The box popped open, and I saw a plain black Nokia cell phone.

I began to sweat. My hands were so wet, I wasn't sure if I could even pick the phone up, but sure enough, I just barely grasped it and flipped the phone over. There was a small pink heart on the back with the initials LC—Lisa Campana. How many times had I seen the back of that phone in her well-manicured hand? And more importantly, what the hell was it doing in my son's closet?

Beads of perspiration continued to drip down my face, and I wiped them away with my arm. I had a charger, so I could rev that phone up and call Dev on it to demand some answers. But I couldn't wait long enough for the charger to kick in. I needed to do something instantly although I felt frozen. I made myself get up from the floor and walk into the master bedroom. Like a zombie, I dialed Jess's number from the landline and spoke to Devon. "You need to come home now," I said. "I found her phone. *Now,*" I repeated, sounding robotic, and then I hung up.

I sat in my bedroom for an eternity, feeling like a cracked egg. Thoughts that I should call Mark raced through my head, but I didn't want to involve him yet nor did I want to call Officer McCarthy or Shanley until I talked to Devon. Surely, there would be a reasonable explanation. Maybe Lisa had left the phone here one day, and Devon hadn't wanted to hurt me with the memory, so he had hidden it in the closet to keep as a memento. Maybe the dog got hold of it...but I was being crazy. The only dogs that could leap to the top of closets were on *Family Guy*. And I had a clear recollection of Lisa opening her phone to check her voice mail the night we left Nate's.

Devon was taking his sweet time coming home. When he arrived, with his head down and his hands in his pocket, the sun had set, and I was sitting alone in the dark in my bedroom, cradling Lisa's phone. I looked up at him helplessly and mumbled, "Tell the truth. I don't care what it is, but I have to know."

He opened and closed his mouth several times and swallowed. His eyes were red and swollen as he sank down to his knees and said, "We didn't mean for it to happen, Mum. I never would've hurt her. You know that!"

We. We hurt her. The words rang in my head. Who were we? I couldn't speak. I just took him in my arms and shook him. Once he started talking, there was no stopping him. He had been holding this in for months.

"We were in the Market Friday night, not far from where you were at the theatre the night before. Jess was buying some X...Ecstasy...when we saw Lisa. She was walking down George Street, and she recognized Jess's dealer. I rarely do drugs, Mum, I swear—just some pot sometimes, but Jess likes meth and X. We ran into a parking garage, and Lisa followed us into the stairwell. She started to give us shit, screaming at Dane, the drug guy, telling him how irresponsible he was.

"It started out fine. She was just going to give us a lecture about the danger of drugs, blah, blah, blah. I wasn't scared. I knew you'd be mad, but Dad would have been okay, and we'd get past it. But Jess was upset. He said his stepfather would beat the crap out of him if he found out. He always hit him in places where the bruises wouldn't show.

"Lisa tried calling you, so Jess grabbed the phone out of her hands. But he's tall. He's stronger than he knows, and she resisted. Why did she resist him so much? It never would've happened if she hadn't fought like that. And Jess was so mad! I've never seen him that angry except before he set the fires, which he said calmed him down."

The fires. It was no coincidence that the fires had taken place in Jess's neighborhood, but he had never been caught for that.

"Dane tried to take the phone from Lisa, too, and she scratched his face because the two of them must've been hurting her. I know Jess didn't mean to, but he goes crazy when people touch him. His stepfather is an animal. And Dane was pissed at Lisa. He's tried AA a hundred times and just can't get it. He hated her righteousness and the fact that she had gotten sober there and he hadn't." Devon gasped for breath, cheeks bright red.

I couldn't speak. I wanted him to shut up, but I couldn't say so. *This is not happening,* I kept repeating to myself. *This is not real.*

Devon continued. "Lisa started shouting, and Jess was afraid someone in the garage would hear. He pushed her hard and gave the phone to me. I put it in my pocket, and then, before I knew it, Lisa fell backward—it was wet, remember? It snowed the night before, and there were patches of, like, black ice even inside the building. She must've hit her head when she fell down the stairs. I tried talking to her, but she couldn't answer. We freaked, and Dane and Jess put her in..."

"No! Stop!" I finally screamed. "I don't want to hear this! Ryan killed her. You were at home watching *Nemo*."

"That was the night before. I was at home then. Man, I wish I had stayed home on Friday night. You have no idea! I didn't want this to happen. I haven't been able to live with myself since that night."

"You left the Market. Then what?" I shouted.

"I suggested the cottage," he sobbed. "I thought if we left her there, she might revive, come around. Maybe she would forget what happened because she had such a bad hit to her head. She was still breathing, Mum! I begged Dane to drop her at the emergency room. But he was afraid because he had priors. He has a record. He can't be busted. He would be in deep…"

"You took her to *our* cottage? Left her there outside on the frozen lawn?"

This was not my son. Not this callous boy. Not the stranger sitting in front of me who was still lying to me and to himself. Didn't know she could die alone outside in the cold by falling asleep after sustaining a head injury? Refused to take his own godmother to the emergency room? Where had I gone wrong to have raised such a heartless, stupid boy?

"I wanted to take her inside. I had the key. But we couldn't lift her. She was too heavy for Jess and me. Dane stayed in the car. Her body had gone all stiff and hard, and we were going to ask Dane for help when Jess and me heard sounds like a car close to the property. We needed to get out fast. We just dumped her."

"But her car. Her car was found on D'Amour Road with her purse and keys inside."

"Jess and I drove it there."

"You don't know how to drive," I said.

"Yeah, I do, Mum! Dad taught me last summer at the cottage."
Devon rolled his eyes at me. He continued. "Anyways, me and
Jess wore gloves. It was winter. It took forever to drive back and
forth there twice. It was a long night—the longest night of my
life. I'm sorry, Mum! I know you must hate me. I understand if
you have to call the cops. I've been expecting you to figure this
out every day since it happened. I'm ready. I'll turn myself in."

He gulped. "Mum, Lisa had a bruise on her face."

"Of course she did. Your moronic criminal friend pushed her
down a staircase!" I yelled. "A pregnant woman," I added.

"No, no. I mean, she had a bruise on her face before she fell.
A big reddish-purple mark that looked fresh. I asked her about
it, but she wouldn't say nothing."

A bruise. Maybe Lisa had told Ryan about the pregnancy, and
he had reacted badly. But I had no time to worry about him. I
needed to direct all my attention to my son. My son, who was
neither scholarly like his father nor dependable like his
mother…apparently, my son was a hardhearted delinquent who
associated with arsonists. But whatever he had done was
ultimately my fault, just as what he would become was my
responsibility. After all, he was only fifteen now, fourteen at the
time of the incident. And there was no way that I was going to
ruin his life by sending him to the Ottawa Detention Centre
instead of Ryan.

Ryan! Chills went down my spine. Ryan had been innocent
all along, and everyone had been quick to accuse and incarcerate
him. That's probably why the police missed any forensic
evidence in Lisa's car that may have belonged to Jess and Devon.
If Ryan hadn't hurt Lisa, how could I let him take the fall? Who
would be the unscrupulous one then? He had lied about the

vasectomy, was lazy about working, and he was much too eager to get his hands-on Lisa's money, but he was not a murderer. Yet he would be convicted when the trial came up; I was sure of it.

I had a momentary twinge of guilt, but then I remembered the bruise, and I thought of WAR—"once a wife beater, always a wife beater," JC would say. Ryan was a bastard. Why should I care about him? It was too late to save Ryan, whether he had killed Lisa or not. He was a bad person, unlike my son who was still unformed. Maybe there was hope for Devon, but he could not reinvent himself without my help.

How had Ryan known that Lisa's body was at my cottage? Dumb luck? Why didn't Lisa go to work or call in on Friday morning? Did she fight with Ryan about the pregnancy when she got home on Thursday night, and that's why she had a bruise on her face? I understood now that crime solving was complex; sometimes we don't get all the answers. Instead, we have to focus on the probabilities of what most likely occurred.

I needed a drink. Water, or better yet, scotch straight up. My throat was parched. I stood up on wobbly legs and tottered downstairs, one step at a time. Devon followed. I drank ice cold water so quickly that it dribbled down my chin, but I felt fortified. Some small semblance of energy and sanity was returning. I turned to my son and informed him in a cold, steady voice that he was to pack a bag and take only essential items. He looked resigned but almost hopeful. He thought I was going to do the right thing and take him to the police station. Nothing was further from my mind.

I packed my own bag and threw together some food for the dog along with his favorite snuggly bed. Monday was excited when we got in the car. He loved car trips. I rolled the window down a bit so he could poke his little head out, and I envied his ignorant bliss.

Since I wasn't working, there was no one to call to say that I wouldn't be in tomorrow. I texted Mark and said Dev and I were taking a short vacation in the Bahamas. We had found a cheap flight deal on Expedia. He texted back saying, "Fabulous. You deserve it. Take lots of pics."

I wouldn't be taking any pictures where I was going. And what's worse was that as I backed out of my driveway in Nepean for the last time, I didn't know the road or the route or the plan. But I had a new grit and determination. All those months of counseling had not been wasted on me. I had a mission—to save my son—and although it felt at that moment that I didn't have the strength to do it, I knew I would find it.

I thought of my mother and how painful it would be to leave her and a lifetime of memories in this house behind. I thought about how Mark would be out of his mind with worry and then eventually grow to despise me for kidnapping his son. I thought about Ryan and how unethical and revolting it was for me to let him take the rap for Devon's panicked reaction and stupidity.

But all I cared about was that my son had made a terrible error in judgment, and he was not going to spend the rest of his life paying for it. I would make sure of that. Nothing could bring Lisa back, but Devon would have a future, even if it was in Kamloops, British Columbia, and he would finally be able to change his name to Paul.

The failure had been mine. Essentially, I had killed Lisa by parental neglect. I had allowed my teenager to become a shallow, selfish, insensitive human being. Her blood was on my hands. And I could only avenge her death by redeeming my lost boy.

AUTHOR'S TITLES

Be Your Own Editor

- Author: Sigrid Macdonald
- Paperback: 162 pages
- Language: English
- ISBN-13: 978-1451596120

Shipping Weight: 8 ounces (View shipping rates and policies)

Are you uncertain when to use affect or effect? Loath or loathe? Compliment or complement? Do you struggle with character development, establishing realistic dialogue and composing articles, proposals or manuscripts? *Be Your Own Editor* by Sigrid Macdonald offers a crash course in grammar basics, starting with punctuation and proper use of the dreaded apostrophe. It suggests ways to identify frequently misused words; to devise strong characters and background settings in fiction; and to structure nonfiction. Nowadays, we're all writers - we write blogs, essays and business proposals. Professional authors write short stories, newspaper articles and manuscripts. If your writing is good, but you question your grammar and organizational skills, this informative, reader-friendly manual is for you.

Getting Hip

- Author: Sigrid Macdonald
- Paperback: 160 pages
- Published October 28, 2004
- ISBN: 978-1418478377

GETTING HIP is a personal account of one woman's recovery from a total hip replacement. From the painful arthritic deterioration of her joint, to making the difficult decision to have surgery at the relatively young age of 47, Sigrid Macdonald takes us with her on her postoperative journey. She discusses how to prepare for hip surgery and the potential complications of the operation. A detailed description of her rehabilitation is provided, along with interviews with 10 people from all over the world, whose recovery time from hip surgery varied considerably. This reader friendly book is written with wit, candor, and empathy for the prospective hip patient. It offers useful tips for acquiring essential services and coping physically and psychologically with hip surgery, as well as important information about how to treat a new hip in order for it to last as long as possible. *GETTING HIP* provides the most up-to-date information on different implants, such as the ceramic hip, which received FDA approval in February of 2003, the metal on metal prosthesis, hip resurfacing and exciting advances in cartilage regeneration and stem cell transplantation. It also provides an extensive bibliography and Internet references.

www.ingramcontent.com/pod-product-compliance
Lightning Source LLC
Chambersburg PA
CBHW061600100726
47898CB00002B/449